Carbs &
Cadavers

Books by Ellery Adams

The Secret, Book & Scone Society

The Secret, Book & Scone Society

The Book Retreat Mysteries

Murder in the Mystery Suite
Murder in the Paperback Parlor
Murder in the Secret Garden
Murder in the Locked Library

The Charmed Pie Shoppe Mysteries

Pies and Prejudice
Peach Pies and Alibis
Pecan Pies and Homicides
Lemon Pies and Little White Lies
Breach of Crust

The Books by the Bay Mysteries

A Killer Plot
A Deadly Cliché
The Last Word
Written in Stone
Poisoned Prose
Lethal Letters
Writing All Wrongs
Killer Characters

More Books by Ellery Adams

Supper Club Mysteries

Carbs & Cadavers
Fit to Die
Chili con Corpses
Stiffs & Swine
The Battered Body
Black Beans & Vice

Hope Street Church Mysteries

The Path of the Crooked
The Way of the Wicked
The Graves of the Guilty
The Root of All Evil
Fate of the Fallen

Antiques & Collectibles Mysteries

A Killer Collection
A Fatal Appraisal
A Deadly Dealer
A Treacherous Trader
A Devious Lot
A Killer Keepsake

Carbs & Cadavers

ELLERY ADAMS

Chapter One

Cheese Puffs

James Henry wrapped a towel around his formidable stomach and stepped onto the bathroom scale. He hesitated before looking down. He hadn't weighed himself in over a year, but his new pants were growing tighter and tighter, and several of his belts no longer fit at all.

Finally, he steeled himself for the results and peered down, but he couldn't see the numbers because the round, protruding flesh of his belly completely blocked his view. *This is what it must feel like to be eight months pregnant,* James thought glumly.

He leaned forward, trying to read the scale without making the numbers on the dial jump around too much as he shifted his weight. When he was actually able to make out the results, James leapt backward off the scale as if it had suddenly caught fire. He frantically dried the bottoms of his wet feet and the sides of his calves, assuming that an extra million ounces of water must have been clinging to his body in order to produce such a number. Exhaling heavily, James stepped back onto the scale and once again examined the truth laid out in bold black-and-white digits: 275 pounds. He was more than fifty pounds overweight.

James sat down on the toilet and put his face in his hands. Over the last few months, he felt like he had been laid out at the bottom of an open grave while shovelfuls of dirt were thrown on top of him. First, his wife filed for divorce after a three-year separation so that she could marry a hotshot lawyer, then James's mother died, forcing him to move back home to care for his sour, reclusive father, and now, on top of everything else, James was fat. The two things he had loved most — his job teaching English literature at the College of William and Mary, and his wife, Jane — were both gone. Now he was an overweight, divorced, thirty-five-year-old loser living with his father.

"I've got to *do* something about myself," he moaned aloud. "I've *got* to go on a diet."

After completing the traumatic task of weighing himself, James got dressed and trudged downstairs to make breakfast. He cracked three eggs into a bowl and mixed them vigorously with milk. The sound of the liquid slapping about in his mother's stainless steel mixing bowl gave him a small measure of comfort. Next, he poured the pale yellow mixture into a sizzling frying pan, and then sprinkled the cooking eggs with parsley and a dash of garlic salt. He popped two bagels into the toaster oven and poured two glasses of orange juice while keeping an eye on the frying pan. When the surface of the eggs began to look crinkled, resembling a piece of plastic wrap, James expertly flipped the omelet and then covered its surface with a thick layer of shredded cheddar cheese. The toaster oven beeped. James pulled out the perfectly browned bagels, spread a generous layer of cream cheese over each crisp half, and then slid them neatly onto two chipped plates. He divided the omelet in half with the spatula, pushed a half onto each plate, and then called his father.

"Pop! Breakfast!"

Jackson Henry shuffled into the room wearing his usual attire: a faded plaid bathrobe over a pair of denim overalls. He glowered at the food laid out on the counter, his furry eyebrows nearly touching as he bent over to examine his bagel more closely.

"What kind are these?" he growled, picking up his plate and carrying it over to the table. He continued to study the bagel, squinting at it distrustfully.

"Cinnamon raisin," James replied, spearing a forkful of egg. "Why?"

Jackson sat down at the kitchen table and scraped his chair loudly across the linoleum floor as he moved his thin frame closer to his plate. He began to pick raisins out of his bagel like a petulant child.

"I told you, I only like sesame seed," he grumbled, tucking a paper napkin into the neck of his shirt.

James sighed. "The store was out of those, Pop. I'll get sesame seed next time." He inhaled the pleasant aroma coming from his own bagel as he lifted it to his mouth. He loved the smell of cinnamon.

When James was a boy, his mother would have made homemade cinnamon rolls on a dreary October day. They would be waiting at his place for him, warm and fresh from the oven, with rivulets of icing cascading down their high walls of succulent dough. James would come home from band practice, and Jackson would arrive after a long, satisfying day's work at Henry's Hardware & Supply

Company, to be met by the scent of cinnamon filling the entire house. James would drop his instrument case, kiss his mother on the cheek, and sit down at the kitchen table to a delightful treat.

It was the small things, like the aroma of cinnamon, or the feel of her dented mixing bowls, that made James miss his mother's presence the most. She had died in August, just two short months ago, leaving him to care for his father. Physically, Jackson was perfectly healthy, but over the last decade he had become more and more reclusive. After his hardware store was bought out by one of the big chain stores, something in Jackson seemed to wither up and die. He began to leave all of the errands that required a drive into town to his wife. Instead, he'd tinker about in the back shed for most of the day. James's mother complained that her husband barely talked anymore. He came inside for meals, which he rarely finished, and to sit in front of the TV in the evenings. The only programs he'd watch were game shows. He no longer read the newspaper or seemed to have any hobbies.

James had always assumed his mother would live to a ripe old age. She was vivacious and full of life, constantly working on some charitable venture or volunteering at the local elementary school. She walked three miles every morning and had never smoked a day in her life, so when she had a sudden heart attack in her sleep, James was completely stunned. He was also devastated. Not only had he lost his beloved mother, but he also knew that her passing marked the end of his life as a college professor. He couldn't leave his father to fend for himself, nor did he feel right putting him in a nursing home. James was an only child and his mother would have wanted him to move back to Quincy's Gap to care for his father, so he did.

After reluctantly handing in his resignation to the English Department Chair, James packed his old Bronco with his belongings—mostly books—and returned the key to his cozy brick townhouse to the rental agency. He took a final walk through the streets of historic Williamsburg, venturing out early in the morning before the crowds arrived, and marveled over how charming it was. Standing on the sidewalk, he tried to capture an image of the trees lining the gravel road leading toward the campus of William and Mary. As the minutes passed, the morning sun set the autumn leaves ablaze, bidding James a fiery farewell.

Turning away from the life he'd come to know, he filled up a takeout mug with Sumatra Blend at the coffeehouse, and then drove four hours west, to the hometown he only visited during Christmas and summer breaks. Boasting one main street and a population of two thousand Virginians, Quincy's Gap was a picturesque burg nestled in the heart of the Shenandoah Valley. Tucked at the foot of the Blue Ridge Mountains, it was a pastoral, tranquil place where farms formed an emerald-and-saffron checkerboard and horses roamed over hilly pastures.

In the middle of these farms, the town sprouted. Quincy's Gap was a tidy square of historic clapboard and brick buildings. Beyond the town proper were two strip malls. One featured a Home Doctor, the mammoth hardware store, and a Dollar General. The second housed the Winn-Dixie, the video rental store, a nail salon, pet groomers, and an Italian restaurant. Other than Dolly's Diner and the drive-in movie theater, which only operated during the spring and summer months, all of the shops and eateries were on Main Street. The tiny side streets housed the municipal buildings, lawyer and medical offices, and three homes listed on the National Register.

James Henry had returned to Quincy's Gap just in time to fill the vacancy of head librarian for the county's main library branch. His salary was sharply reduced from what he had earned at William and Mary, but his living expenses were too. James moved into his old room, lovingly maintained by his late mother as a shrine to her only child. Every toy soldier, comic book, baseball glove, and even the tattered posters of various rock 'n' roll icons were still Scotch-taped to the walls, as if James were planning to bring a son of his own home to play in his childhood room. But James had no children. What he had was a lot of heavy baggage—both emotional and physical.

His life-altering move had taken place almost two months ago, and James had come to believe that returning to Quincy's Gap signaled the end of any chance of happiness. He would grow old in a place where he had spent torturous years as an awkward boy, followed by four more years as a solitary, unpopular teenager, and finally, as an unmemorable college student returning home during semester breaks.

Staring at his half-eaten bagel, James snapped out of his self-pitying reverie. He shifted his weight on the uncomfortable metal chair with the cracked seat cushion and tried to read a historical novel about a boy growing up in Afghanistan. He had a few minutes to spare before heading to work, and he desperately wanted to know if the boy would win the coveted kite contest so adeptly described by the author. As James read, Jackson scraped his chair noisily away from the table and shuffled back to the den, leaving half of his egg uneaten and a completely pulverized bagel on his plate.

It began to rain just as James finished his breakfast. Licking globs of cream cheese from his fingers, he peered out at the gray skies, checked his watch, and then fixed himself a tuna sandwich for lunch. He carefully wrapped the sandwich in tinfoil along with two dill pickle spears, grabbed an apple and a snack-sized bag of cheese puffs, and packed them all into his leather tote bag. Hesitating, he took a second bag of cheese puffs from the pantry and added that to the tote as well.

James loved cheese puffs. They had been his favorite snack for as long as he could remember. As a boy, he ate them at the movies, in front of the TV, and while doing homework. At the library, he fed himself cheese puffs with his right hand so that his left would be clean enough to turn the pages of whatever library book he was reading during his lunch break. Even when he was a college professor, he liked to enjoy a treat while grading essays, and had often gotten the orange dust on his students' papers. James was well aware that he had earned the nickname of Professor Puff, and though he hated the idea that the moniker had a double meaning, the satisfaction he received from the cheesy, crispy crunchiness of cheese puffs far outweighed what his students called him behind his back.

"Pop!" James called over the sounds of contestants screaming on *The Price Is Right*. "There are some cold cuts in the fridge. You can fix yourself a sandwich for lunch. And there's a can of beef and barley soup in the pantry too."

Jackson didn't reply, but James knew there was nothing wrong with his father's hearing. In fact, he had grown accustomed to his father's silence. Jackson hadn't had much to say since he sold the hardware store, and when he did speak, his words were usually critical. These days, he rarely opened his mouth unless he wanted to issue a complaint. James preferred his father during one of his quiet moods. He wondered how his mother had put up with such morose company, but then again, she had had a way of bringing out the best in everyone.

Heading out to his Bronco, James ignored his reflection in the glass of the storm door. His handsome face looked swollen and weighed down by a rapidly enlarging double chin. He carried his extra weight well—it was evenly distributed over a big-boned, six-foot frame, but his stomach bulged far out over his waistline, and his jowls were becoming a distraction. People no longer noticed his intelligent, golden-brown eyes, sincere smile, aquiline nose, or soft waves of nutmeg-colored hair. They became hypnotized by the shaking flesh on his cheeks, sliding their library books across the checkout desk in a bit of a stupor.

"Good Morning, Professor Henry," was the chorused salutation James received ten minutes later at the library's front door. It was the same greeting he heard every day since he had taken the job a month ago. Francis and Scott Fitzgerald were identical twins. Aside from a retired schoolteacher who worked part-time, the Fitzgerald twins were the library's only other staff members. They clearly loved their jobs and were always waiting to be let in by the time James arrived at eight forty-five.

The twins were long-limbed, brainy bibliophiles who were given up for adoption at birth and spent most of their lives living in a series of foster homes. Luckily, they had never been separated, and the last of their foster homes, which was the one they lived in throughout high school, was a unique place. Their foster parents, Mr. and Mrs. Sloane, owned a bookstore and were die-hard fans of early American literature. The Sloanes believed that fate had brought them together. After all, the brilliant young men were named after one of the Sloanes' favorite writers.

Francis and Scott were encouraged to attend the local community college, and the Sloanes helped them apply for scholarships. The boys were so thorough in applying for grants and scholarships that they both earned bachelor's degrees without incurring any debt. Immediately after graduation, they searched for library jobs across Virginia, hoping to be hired together. The only place where they found two positions was in Quincy's Gap. The former head librarian had hired them and the twins had been happy ever since.

Francis raised a lanky arm to hold the door open for James and his brother, who bobbed his head in gratitude, causing his curls of unkempt hair to bounce. The young men had attractive faces hidden behind thick glasses. When they weren't reshelving books or helping patrons, both would be peering intently at computer screens or rifling through the pages of books. James took an instant liking to Scott and Francis. He was amused by their quirkiness and admired their proficiency and punctuality. So far, things had run smoothly at the King Street Branch.

Perhaps living in Quincy's Gap wouldn't be all that bad, James thought hopefully as he tried to put the morning's negativity behind him. The presence of the tidy stacks of books and the Fitzgerald brothers' boundless optimism always gave him solace when he was feeling down.

"More cheese puffs, Professor?" Francis asked as James transferred his lunch from his tote bag to the staff fridge.

James nodded, slightly embarrassed.

"I'm a sour cream and onion chip man, myself."

"Poor choice, F. Salt and vinegar is clearly the superior chip," Scott said.

"Oh! Customer!" Francis exclaimed, hurling his lunch onto the rectangular table where the three men took turns eating lunch and reading. He strode out to the circulation desk while Scott carefully arranged everyone's sandwiches in a neat row inside the refrigerator. James could hear Francis whispering to someone even though there were no other patrons in the library. Once the clock struck nine, the twins would speak in hushed tones until their shift was over at five.

Francis poked his head back in the staff room. "There's a lady waiting for you, Professor. She says she needs to ask you about hanging a notice on the lobby bulletin board."

"Certainly," James said. He was on the verge of reminding the twins that they could call him by his first name, but he had told them several times, and they seemed determined to call him "Professor." Truthfully, James liked the title. It made him feel dignified and more significant than a small-town librarian each time one of the brothers uttered the word.

As he approached the circulation desk, he observed the woman leafing through the latest edition of *People* magazine. She looked up from the glossy pages, gave James a warm and friendly smile, and extended a small hand. "Hi! I'm Rosalind, the art teacher up at Blue Ridge High." James returned the young woman's handshake, studying her round face as he introduced himself. He couldn't help but notice that Rosalind was round all over. She had large brown eyes, skin the color of café au lait, big breasts, a thick waist, and wide hips hovering above a pair of short, plump legs. Her hair was glossy and black, except where the beams from overhead lights were painting it with filaments of silver. James wondered how Rosalind had managed to arrange her hair so that it was held in place by two lacquered chopsticks, but he didn't think it was polite to ask. Instead, he looked back down at her petite hands, one of which held a neon pink flyer.

"I was wondering if I could hang this in the lobby," she said in a loud voice before immediately slapping her hand over her mouth. "Sorry." When James shrugged to indicate that he wasn't upset, Rosalind relaxed. "Mrs. Kramer, the librarian who was here before you, was such a witch. If you didn't whisper, she'd pretend to misplace the books you wanted to check out. She wouldn't hang anything on this board that wasn't related to 'the literary interests of Quincy's Gap,' which basically meant the personal interests of Mrs. Kramer. She wouldn't even let the Girl Scouts put up signs for their cookie sales. I'm glad you're here now." Rosalind smiled, revealing her perfect teeth. "You're already so much nicer than old Mrs. Kramer."

"Thank you." James returned her smile. "Let's see what you've got there, Rosalind."

"Rosalind is what my Brazilian mother calls me. You should call me Lindy. All of my friends do."

At that moment, James would have hung a flyer calling for a book burning. No one had even approached James as a possible friend since he had moved back home, and the word itself burned pleasantly through his memory. It spoke of a social life, of events that included boisterous parties, restaurant dinners, and conversations punctuated with doses of raucous laughter. James took the pink flyer and immediately tacked it up on the bulletin board, reading it as he pressed pushpins through the soft flesh of cork.

Are You Feeling Out of Shape?
Not So Pleasantly Plump?
Downright Miserably Fat?
Join Our New Supper Club!
We Plan to Get Fit Together!
We Meet Every Sunday Night!
Make Friends!
Lose Weight!
Call Lindy at 555-2846

"What do you think?" Lindy asked.

James creased his brows and decided not to point out what he felt were an overabundance of exclamation marks. "I'm afraid I don't know what a supper club is."

"Oh, it's when a bunch of people get together to cook a meal and talk and form friendships. Some clubs have a theme, like cooking light, or sampling exotic foods from different parts of the world. My sister lives in Atlanta, and she's in a supper club that focuses on pairing wine and food. I came up with the idea that Quincy's Gap should have one where people can lose weight together. Like a dieters' club but more fun. I know I'll never get into shape on my own." She cast her eyes on the ground and mumbled, "And Lord knows I have to stop making excuses."

"So you're just beginning to recruit people?" James asked quickly. He didn't like how Lindy had suddenly become deflated.

"No, no." Lindy perked back up. "We have four members already. Actually, we tried to meet last week to decide what kind of food we were going to eat—you know, like what our theme would be—but two of us wanted to count calories like Weight Watchers, and the other two wanted to follow a low-carb diet like Atkins or the South Beach Diet. What we need is another member to be our tiebreaker."

James made a sympathetic noise. He disliked indecisiveness as a rule, but he also didn't relish the thought of being a tiebreaker.

"Wait!" Lindy grabbed his arm, her wide eyes gleaming. "Why don't *you* join our club? You're new to town." She picked up his left hand and pointed at his ring finger. "And it looks like you're not married. This would be a great way for you to make some friends!"

Taken aback by Lindy's unbridled enthusiasm, James hesitated. It would be nice to make a few friends, but he was also a bit offended that Lindy saw him as someone who clearly needed to diet. Glancing down at his protruding belly, he knew she was right, but it still made him grumpy to think about his weight.

Lindy dropped her hand from James's arm and said, "I didn't mean to offend you. I just thought you'd like to join us."

Her tone was so soft and gentle that James relented. "I'll give it a try. I've turned into a decent cook over the last few years, but I don't know much about diets."

Lindy's face filled with delight. "Don't worry about that! We'll figure something out together. Let's see, today's Friday. It feels weird not to be in school, but we've got parent-teacher conferences, and no one ever wants to meet with the *art teacher*." Lindy shook her head as if to cast off her annoyance and returned to the subject at hand. "The supper club is meeting Sunday at my place. We're having a lunch meeting this time since we haven't worked out any of the food details yet. Let me write down directions for you."

"Thanks." James smiled. "Who else is in the supper club?"

"There's me, Lucy Hanover, who works for the sheriff's department, Bennett Marshall—he's a mailman—and Gillian O'Malley. She owns the Yuppie Puppy."

James considered the name. "Is she a pet groomer?"

"You got it." Lindy handed him the sheet of directions. "You must know Lucy. Didn't you grow up here? You two must have gone to Blue Ridge High together."

James squirmed. "I did, but I wasn't much of a socializer. I was pretty quiet back then. I *did* play in the band," he added with a mix of pride and embarrassment. "French horn. I might know her if she had been in the band, too. Otherwise, I pretty much went straight home after school . . ." He trailed off, wondering why he was babbling about his lack of social activities as a shy teenager. But then he realized he felt comfortable with Lindy. It was a pleasant feeling.

Lindy seemed to grow pensive for a moment. "I don't think Lucy was in the band. But who cares? Even if you didn't know each other in high school, you can get to know each other now. In fact, we'll all be getting to know one another. That's the beauty of a supper club."

"Should I bring anything?" he asked, relieved that the subject of his lack of friends from the "good old days" was over.

"No need. We're just going to have sandwiches while we decide what kind of food we'll be cooking for the next meeting. See you Sunday at noon. It was nice to meet you, James Henry."

"Nice to meet you, too, Lindy." James stole another glance at the pink flyer and then returned to his duties at the circulation desk. Without realizing it, he was humming softly under his breath. The Fitzgerald twins looked at each other over a rolling cart filled with books and smiled. They had never heard their boss hum before. It was a pleasant sound.

• • •

It was a crisp, sunny weekend morning and homecoming Saturday to boot. The counter at Dolly's Diner was empty, but Dolly laid out silverware at every place. James could see that she expected to do a booming business before closing shop early in order to watch the Blue Ridge Red-Tailed Hawks "put a whupping to those braggarts from Jefferson High," as Dolly so aptly phrased it during lunchtime a few days ago. According to Dolly, the Jefferson Cougars had pummeled the Hawks last year, and the football fans from Quincy's Gap were looking for a little revenge. Dolly counted herself among the most loyal Hawks fans of all time.

After casting her eyes in a satisfactory manner over the countertop, Dolly wound her cloud of white hair into a tight bun and peered into the horizontal mirror behind the gleaming rows of clean glasses. James shared the same belief as most of the townsfolk—that Dolly looked like a cross between a sumo wrestler and Mrs. Claus. Much like Santa's wife, Dolly was beloved by all. She was the mistress of her own domain and treasured three things above all else: her business, her husband, and gossip, though not necessarily in that order.

James could feel Dolly's eyes boring into his back as she stood behind the counter and waited for the coffee to finish. He sensed that Dolly had decided it was high time she learned something more interesting about the new head librarian. She questioned him relentlessly whenever he came in for a meal, which was often because the food was delicious, but James Henry had skillfully avoided her most personal questions thus far. He was friendly and polite, of course, but close-lipped when it came to answering any queries outside the realm of work or food. Dolly was not so easily put off, however, and James steeled himself for another round of bluster and evade.

Dolly ambled over to the booth where he sat, appearing to be deeply engrossed in a novel. "You want some more coffee, hon?" she asked, holding the steaming pot up in front of her ample bosom.

James looked up, blinking, like someone who has just driven out of a dark tunnel into the bright daylight. "Pardon? Oh, yes, please. Sorry, Dolly. I was completely absorbed in this book." His act didn't fool the wizened mistress of the diner for a second.

"So," Dolly began, preparing to squeeze new tidbits out of the librarian before he could escape. "I remember your mama telling me about you getting married a few years back." She waited, withholding the coffee until James responded. "How come your wife isn't here with you?"

"I *was* married," James muttered, absently turning a page of his book. "We just got divorced this summer."

Dolly clucked in sympathy and then filled his cup. Instead of leaving, she studied him carefully. "In that case, you ought to be socializing with folks, not sitting here reading. How you ever gonna meet someone with your nose stuck in a book?"

James shrugged, recognizing that Dolly was one of those women who liked to make a project out of matching up all the single people she knew. "It's a good book," he said lamely, wishing she would drop the subject.

Dolly waved off his answer and made a dismissive noise by pushing air out through her closed lips. "Pffah. There are plenty of nice women your age that would love to get to know you better. Why, I know . . ." Dolly trailed off, her attention suddenly caught by some movement out the front window. "Sakes alive! Here comes the parade! They're all gonna want to eat here, and I don't have all the pies out yet. Clint!" She bustled off, calling for her husband, who was safely out of range in the kitchen.

"You got lucky that time," said the young waitress who came

over in Dolly's wake to clear James's empty plates. She was tall and fair with freckled skin and had thick, ash-blonde hair pulled up into a high ponytail. She stood there, smiling at James.

"That was the best stack of strawberry pancakes I have ever tasted." James exhaled, feeling his belt groaning across his bulging waist. "I'm eating all the junk I can before starting my new diet," he told the girl, just to make conversation. He had made a terrific mess with the syrup and felt guilty watching her scrub the sticky droplets from the tabletop while he sat there reading.

"We don't want to get your book stuck," she said kindly. Her name tag read *Whitney* and was pinned on the simple white apron she wore over her jeans.

"Did you go to Blue Ridge High?" James asked.

"Yep. Go Hawks!" she said with false enthusiasm.

James put his crumpled napkins on her tray. "Homecoming parade not your thing?"

"Nah. Plus, I could use the hours. I'm attending James Madison University part-time. I'll need all the cash I can get just to pay for two classes."

"Good for you." James nodded in admiration. "What's a parade compared to a college education? Do you know what you're planning to major in?"

"Business." Whitney handed James his bill. "I can't wait to get out of this hick town, and I figure a business degree is my ticket to a better life," she added with a surprising amount of vehemence. "If I can ever afford to *complete* my degree, that is."

"Whitney!" Dolly called. "Can you help Clint slice the meat loaf? I think we are about to be as packed as feathers on a rooster in a few minutes."

James looked around the diner. Aside from him, there were only two other clients enjoying a late breakfast at Dolly's. The midday sun was making its way into the restaurant, glinting off the exotic souvenirs Dolly and Clint had brought home from their travels around the world. Dolly's husband, Clint, had been in the Coast Guard for almost twenty years. He had been stationed in Guam, Honolulu, the Philippines, Alaska, and up and down both coasts of the United States. Each time Clint was given personal leave, Dolly got to choose a new country for them to visit. Now the evidence of their global wanderings was forever preserved on the diner's walls and rafters.

From his booth, James could reach out and touch an enormous sequined sombrero, a porcelain Mardi Gras mask, an African walking stick with a carved snake curling up the handle, a rusty tin sign reading *Banheiro* (meaning "bathroom" in Portuguese), a cricket bat, a beautiful black silk kimono spread out to show off its embroidered green dragon with the forked tongue, and a corkboard covered with artistic labels from French wine bottles. James tried to sit in a different booth each time he visited in order to admire a fresh collection of treasures before he began his ritual of eating and reading.

As he scanned the room, James noticed one of Lindy's neon pink flyers posted on the bulletin board by the front door. A young man in a rather ragged-looking letter jacket was examining it. As James watched, the man yanked the flyer off the board and held it out to Dolly, who was wiping an already gleaming countertop.

"What's this?" he yelled across the quiet diner. "An ad for the Fat Loser Club?"

"You hush up, Brinkley Myers," Dolly scolded without looking up from her scrubbing. "Some folks need a little help getting into shape. There's no need for you to be putting them down."

"Well, I hope *you* don't join in. We all love you just the way you are," the young man named Brinkley oozed with false charm while eyeing Dolly's chest.

Dolly flashed him an amused grin. "Now, you hang that back up on the board like a good boy," she ordered and then disappeared into the kitchen.

Ignoring her, Brinkley shoved the paper into his jacket pocket and then plunked himself down in a nearby booth. James studied the young man from behind his coffee cup. Brinkley was tall and muscular, except for the first hints of a promising beer gut, and looked to be in his mid-twenties. James was unsure why he was still wearing a high school letter jacket, but assumed that he was a former high school jock who wanted to show his support for the football team. He had a square jaw covered with blond stubble and a full head of curly, reddish blond hair. The unkempt hair combined with deep-set dark eyes gave him a roguish Hollywood look.

Draining his tepid coffee, James wondered if Brinkley had kept the flyer because he was planning to join the supper club. James certainly hoped not. The young man seemed to possess a cocksure and slightly malicious aura. Turning away from Brinkley, James took a twenty out of his wallet and laid it on the table. Neither Whitney nor Dolly was anywhere to be seen, so he decided to finish the chapter he was reading while waiting for his change.

Outside, the hum of a large group of people intensified as the front door of the diner burst open and the noise of the crowd erupted into the calm room. Dozens of people came streaming into the restaurant, laughing and cheering. All of them were wearing red and black hats, scarves, or sweatshirts. James recognized the two shades as the school colors of Blue Ridge High.

Several boys wearing letter jackets crowded into the booth next to him, elbowing one another and yelling loudly at another group of boys sitting at the largest table across the aisle. They all seemed to pay homage to Brinkley before settling down in their seats. A great deal of backslapping and high fives were exchanged between the high school boys and the lone adult clad in a matching letter jacket.

Dolly bustled over to the posse of boys with an enormous smile, beaming with pride at the rambunctious teens. "Well, gentlemen. I've made a special meat loaf to get y'all good and ready for tonight's game. What's needed today is meat and mashed potatoes and a bit of tail whupping. What do ya have to say to that?"

The boys let out a communal holler and banged their fists on the tabletops.

"Just lemme have your drink orders, and then I'll be back with your food. I think y'all should have milk—good for your bones—especially when you've got to stand up to some of those Jefferson linebackers. Of course, I know some of you are addicted to ole Dr. Pepper, so I'll let you decide. But if I were your mama, I'd make you pick the milk."

Dolly flipped open her pad and began scribbling down drink orders. James tried to catch her eye, but she was fussing over the football players like a mother hen, so he looked around for Whitney instead. However, Whitney clearly had her hands full taking care of the group at the counter, so James grabbed the bill and his money and maneuvered around the cluster of excited boys clotting the aisles between the booths.

As he struggled to pass the three booths where the football players milled about, a middle-aged woman with hair bleached beyond blonde into a platinum white jabbed him in the side with her bony elbow.

"Sorry," he said. The woman didn't say a word, but grudgingly stepped aside to let him pass.

At the counter, Whitney was busy serving drinks.

"I'd better pay up," James told her, handing her the money. "I think you're going to need my booth. Looks like you've got one or two football players here."

"Damn right!" exclaimed a man at the countertop as he butted into the conversation. "Those boys are going to play their hearts out tonight. Yes, sir. There's nothing better than a night game in October. Nothing better." He thumped the countertop with his palm in order to emphasize his point. James thought he detected a hint of whiskey on the man's breath.

Other patrons at the counter nodded their agreement and then began discussing which game over the last several years had been the coldest. As Whitney handed James his change, Brinkley Myers suddenly appeared behind his right shoulder.

"Hey, Whit," he greeted the pretty waitress as James pulled a five-dollar bill out of his pile of change and set it down in front of Whitney.

Whitney politely thanked James for the tip and pointedly turned away from Brinkley. She poured glasses of ice water and served them to two men at the other end of the counter without raising her eyes. Seemingly unfazed by her rudeness, Brinkley shrugged his shoulders and turned away.

At that moment, James noticed Whitney throw Brinkley a menacing look as the younger man leaned over to chat with one of the customers at the counter. Her eyes blazed with anger for just a flash before she marched off toward the kitchen, her ponytail whipping back and forth like a pendulum.

"You gonna watch the rookies throw some touchdowns tonight, Brinkley?" one of the men asked. "Think anyone's gonna break your record?"

Brinkley puffed out his chest. "For most touchdown passes thrown in one game? No way. No one's going to do that, but hopefully some Cougar *necks* will get broken!"

The men at the countertop applauded. The man sitting in front of James reached around and clapped him on the back, pinning him in place. James was content to be stuck in the midst of the townsfolk's enthusiastic camaraderie. Normally, he would be uncomfortable in the middle of such a raucous and unfamiliar crowd, but everyone seemed to accept his presence as natural. James smiled shyly at the men and women seated around him. Then Whitney returned, bearing plates of meat loaf with sides of mashed potatoes swimming in brown gravy. Brinkley once again tried to get her attention, but she continued to ignore him.

"So you think we might win tonight?" a woman asked Brinkley as she waited for her food to cool.

"Yes, ma'am." Brinkley nodded and then raised his voice, his eyes boring into Whitney's turned back. "I've been looking forward to this game all season. I think we're *due* this game. Sometimes it's just time to get what you're owed. Do you all know what I mean?"

The woman beamed at him. "So you think our boys are going to get lucky?"

"Why not?" Brinkley shrugged. "I sure plan to get lucky pretty soon. Right, Whit?"

The sexual implication was lost on the woman, but several of the men at the counter guffawed heartily and exchanged high fives with one another. The pleasant spell James had been under was instantly broken by the men's coarse response. He felt embarrassed for Whitney and gave Brinkley his most disapproving stare. The young man returned James's look with a flippant grin.

As Brinkley moved to pass by James, he leaned over and whispered, "I bet you've never had a girl as fine as that. Maybe it's because you look like you swallowed a few watermelons. You need to hit the gym, old man, or people are going to start calling you Buddha and rubbing your belly for luck." Brinkley gave James a pat on the belly and strode off to the booth where the football players and his meat loaf were waiting.

Trembling with anger, James watched as the boys held out a playbook for Brinkley to examine. They had obviously asked the former player to join them in hopes of reviewing their plays before the big game. Anyone could see that they viewed Brinkley as a living legend, and Brinkley savored his role.

More and more people crammed themselves into the diner. James had had enough of both the crowd and the gross display of hero worship for such an obnoxious young man. By the time James could finally squeeze himself out the door, with people pushing past him to get in all the while, every seat had been taken. He suddenly noticed that there were no children present at Dolly's, but once he stepped outside he realized why. All of the children and their parents were continuing to march down Main Street. Curious as to their destination and eager to have his spirits buoyed after Brinkley's disparaging remarks, James followed along.

At the edge of town, one of the side streets had been blocked off and a miniature amusement park had been erected. James spotted a petting zoo, pony rides, popcorn and cotton candy machines, as well as several thrill rides, including a tiny roller coaster and a spinning ride that was guaranteed to make the kids who had overindulged on cotton candy good and sick. There was also a row of carnival games where parents could spend inordinate amounts of money for their child to win a stuffed animal worth a fraction of the cost of the game.

James watched a little girl run up to a female clown wearing an enormous blue and white polka-dotted bow tie and floppy pink shoes and politely ask for a balloon animal. The clown smiled silently and then made a grand show of blowing up and twisting a yellow balloon into the shape of a poodle. The little girl was thrilled, and James watched her run back into her parents' arms with a tinge of envy. He wondered if he would ever have the opportunity to experience fatherhood.

James lingered around the children a bit longer, not wanting to return to the quiet of his house and the grumblings of his father. Finally, he strolled back down Main Street toward the parking lot where he had parked his truck. The street was littered with a variety of small trash from bubble gum wrappers to cigarette butts, but James knew that the town's maintenance crew would restore cleanliness and order before the day was out. After all, weekends meant the arrival of horse people and tourists—the main source of revenue for the bucolic but isolated town of Quincy's Gap. The horse people would compete in local shows or purchase animals from one of the Quincy's Gap horse farms, while the tourists would visit the Civil War sites, historic homes, and apple orchards, or simply drive through the countryside in order to view the vibrant foliage. With the golden sunlight streaming through the pear trees, and the carnival atmosphere pulsing in the air, James was feeling more at peace with his hometown than at any other time since his return.

Back at home, James found that Jackson had locked himself in his shed and had closed all the shades so that James had no idea what he was up to. James didn't even bother telling his father that he was home. He doubted the old man would even notice until dinnertime. In the kitchen, he fixed himself some decaf, settled on the sofa to read, and then paused for a moment and briefly considered attending the football game. James wasn't very interested in sports, but it might be a topic of conversation at tomorrow's supper club lunch, and James didn't want to appear uninvolved in one of the autumn's biggest events. Then again, since he was nearing the book's thrilling conclusion, and it was bound to be uncomfortably cold at the game, he decided that he might as well stay put.

After spending a peaceful afternoon reading and munching on cheese puffs—he easily polished off a jumbo-sized bag—James decided to cook a hearty pot of stew for dinner. As he was peeling carrots, his father opened the back door and shuffled wearily into the kitchen. Ignoring James, he fixed himself a cup of coffee and headed into the den. The sound of the television interrupted the tranquil silence. James heard his father channel surfing, but after a time Jackson found a rerun of *Family Feud*.

James sighed in annoyance. He was tired of listening to game shows and fed up with his father's moodiness. When the stew was ready, he brought a bowl into the den and placed it on a TV tray. Jackson never turned his face from the screen. His eyes were red and puffy, as if he had not slept well recently.

"What were you doing out there all day, Pop?" James asked in concern.

Instead of answering, Jackson pointed at James's shirt. "You got orange stuff all over you again. Ain't you ever heard of a napkin?"

James looked down at the familiar orange dust. "It's from the cheese puffs. It was my last bag. I'm going to start a diet tomorrow."

His father shook his head in disbelief and then focused on the television once more.

"Stupid, stupid," he muttered, and James didn't know whether he was referring to the contestants, who couldn't seem to get any of the answers right, or to his son, who never seemed to get anything right either.

Chapter Two

Coffee Cake

James went to the early church service. He hadn't been to church in years and felt like an impostor sitting in the polished pews among the genuinely devout members of the congregation, but he was happy to be in the same church he'd gone to every Sunday when he was a boy.

None of the other worshippers seemed to share James's tendency to become distracted during the sermon. As he had when he was little, James found himself staring at the scenes of the apostles depicted in the stained glass windows. It was difficult to hear the sermon in the first place, because a man in the front pew kept coughing. It wasn't a subtle cough, but a loud, wet, racking cough. James was certain that at any moment, the man's entire lung would be deposited in the hand that he was coughing into. James wished he had a water bottle to pass to the poor soul.

Sitting up, he tried to pay more attention to the minister. The sermon was entitled "How You Can Be More Giving," and James thought he really should take the message to heart, but he had already given up so much in order to care for his father, and he felt that the level of gratitude being shown to him by his remaining parent was greatly wanting.

As the sermon continued, the room felt warmer and warmer, and the roof of James's mouth grew exceedingly dry. He slid down the pew so that he could reach a hand into his pants pocket without attracting notice. Deep inside that pocket, nestled in a collection of loose change and keys, was a mint. Just as James began the agonizingly slow unwrapping of the mint, pausing each time his fingers created too much noise in untwisting its crinkly casing, the minister paused for a moment of prayer.

James stopped working at the mint's stubborn wrapper, afraid that the congregants seated beside him would realize he had had no idea that the sermon was done. As he jerked his body upright, the loose coins in his pocket spilled out on the wood pew and rolled to the floor. James thought the reverberated tinkling of his falling coins could surely be heard in China. Several of the old ladies seated in front of him pivoted in their seats and gave him reproachful glances.

Stooping to collect his change, not because he wanted the money but because he wanted to hide the red flush of embarrassment that had crept up his neck and covered his fleshy cheeks, James was prevented from seeing that the collection plate had arrived at his pew. Just as he straightened, his fist closing around the wayward coins, his neighbor held out the large brass plate to him.

Here is my chance to redeem myself, James thought, smiling. He would put a generous contribution into the offering plate and then no one would pay him any more attention. He pulled his wallet from his back pocket and opened it hastily, aware that his neighbor was still holding on to the heavy plate. Her friendly smile soon rearranged itself into an impatient frown, and would soon morph into an outright scowl if James did not produce some money quickly. To his horror, only two singles lay tucked in the folds of his wallet. James had forgotten to go to the bank. And naturally, his checkbook was at home. Because he only used checks to pay bills, he never carried it on his person.

Looking around wildly, he finally accepted the plate from his neighbor. The woman continued to pointedly stare at him, clearly waiting for him to place money in the plate. In fact, James had taken so long with his offering that everyone in his pew was looking at him. The hymn, which was usually repeated three times during the collection, had now begun its fourth repetition. Whispering began. In a panic, James pulled out the two singles and folded them into a roll, hoping that his neighbors would be fooled into believing there were bills of a higher denomination within the roll. At the last second, he unceremoniously plopped in his loose change as well.

As he handed the plate to his neighbor, he felt like his face was on fire. The man he handed the plate to shook his head in what James felt was a very un-Christian display of disgust, and the service continued. James was so flummoxed during the final hymn that he sang louder than usual and continued to attract odd glances from those seated around him.

When the service finally ended, James decided to make a hasty break for the door and vowed to wait at least until Christmas, or possibly until Easter, before returning to church. Just when he thought he might safely reach the exit, Dolly appeared out of the blue and hooked her arm in his.

"Why, Professor Henry!" she exclaimed as if she hadn't seen him in years. "I don't think I saw you at the game last night."

"No, I didn't make it," James mumbled. He was probably the only person in Quincy's Gap to have missed the game. Other than his father, that is.

"You should have been there! Blue Ridge won, don't you know? And guess how close the score was?"

"I can't imagine. One touchdown?" James asked, looking longingly at the front door. It began to recede as Dolly tugged him in the opposite direction.

"Not even! There was only one field goal separating us from defeat!" Dolly continued to gush about the prowess of the home team as she cut a swathe through a group of parishioners. She maneuvered James toward the refreshment table, where several ladies were removing coffee cakes from white bakery boxes and cutting them into neat squares. "Now, Professor, you've just *got* to try Megan's coffee cake. It is *simply* out of this world!" Dolly collected a plate and fork and handed them over to James. "Megan owns the Sweet Tooth, the candy store and bakery. I don't think it was open yet when you were visiting last Christmas. And guess what?" She lowered her voice to a conspiratorial whisper. "She's single, but she's got a daughter," Dolly plowed on. "Not to worry, the girl's out of high school. Should be living on her own by now anyway. How do you feel about kids?"

James cut off an enormous piece of coffee cake with his plastic fork and hastily shoveled it into his mouth, guaranteeing that he would be unable to reply. However, he was unprepared for the savory sensation of that bite of coffee cake. All at once he tasted brown sugar, almonds, vanilla, and a powerfully strong jolt of sugary icing. Relishing every chew, he had to close and open his eyes a few times to be sure that he hadn't actually died and gone straight to coffee cake heaven.

"Good, eh? I told you, honey." Dolly punched James playfully in the arm. "That woman can bake! I've also heard that she can't actually cook worth a damn—just sweets, mind you—but you two could work that out. Let me introduce you."

James finished his coffee cake in three bites and then made a big show of checking his watch. Thankfully, it was eleven forty-five. He needed to get going if he wanted to arrive at Lindy's by noon, and James made a point of being punctual.

"I can't right now, Dolly." He pointed at his watch. "I'm actually supposed to meet someone in fifteen minutes."

Dolly didn't bother trying to mask her interest. "Oh, ho! And who is this *someone*?" she demanded, refusing to release his arm.

James didn't want to offend Dolly, and he could hardly drag himself away while she was physically restraining him, so he looked around for a distraction. Not seeing any, he was forced to fabricate something on the spot.

"Is that Clint over there, talking to Luanne Lovett?" he asked slyly.

That did it. Dolly swiveled her head back and forth like an owl. Luanne Lovett was a celebrated flirt. Having just divorced her third husband, she was said to be on the prowl for number four. With a Rubenesque body and a show of girlish naiveté that women could instantly recognize as pretense but men could not, Luanne had become a threat to long-term marriages throughout the county. James hadn't actually seen either Clint or Luanne, but he knew that Dolly would forget about her matchmaking goals the second she heard the vixen's name. As he'd expected, she elbowed her way through the crowd, leaving James free to make for the exit.

Driving to Lindy's, he reflected that he was lucky to have eaten that wonderful coffee cake before officially starting his diet. From now on, he would stick to whatever foods his new friends decided they should eat. He was ready to do anything to lose some weight.

At the next red light, he checked his reflection in the rearview mirror. Brushing coffee cake crumbs from the front of his shirt, he chuckled. He would never succeed in losing weight if he were involved with the woman Dolly had wanted him to meet. It would be impossible to turn down her baked goods, especially if they were as delicious as that cake.

Lindy's house was a small gray bungalow within walking distance of Blue Ridge High. The yard consisted of a square of tidy green lawn, neatly trimmed shrubs, and a flower bed bursting with raspberry asters and the last of the summer Salvia. Red ceramic pots filled with ochre-colored chrysanthemums flanked the front door. Several other cars were parked along the curb in front of Lindy's house, and the sight of a tan Jeep and a mail truck made James nervous for a moment. Lindy seemed nice enough, but what would the other members of the group be like? Would they warm to him? Would they want to befriend a divorced librarian who lived with his father?

Suddenly, James felt like retreating. He'd never excelled at making new friends. In Williamsburg, he had left his social life in the hands of his capable wife. Most of his friends were just spouses of her friends, but they had all gotten along just fine. Now that he was on his own, he worried that he had little to offer this group of strangers.

Before he could entertain more second thoughts, a car pulled up behind his truck. Its front bumper was so close that he was now effectively boxed in. There was no turning back, so James got out of his truck and prepared to greet the driver. A woman with what James could only describe as a bird's nest of orange hair alighted from the compact sedan and waved at him.

"I'm Gillian!" she called. She approached him with hurried steps, as if she'd been waiting for ages to finally meet him. "You must be James Henry."

They shook hands. Gillian gave her tangled locks a shake, inhaled a great gulp of air, and smiled up at the sky. She then gestured at the house. "Shall we?"

James followed closely behind Gillian, noting that she had a barrel-shaped torso supported by a pair of shapely, toned legs. Her billowy tent shirt and tight purple leggings emphasized the fact that she was as wide in the waist as she was in the hips. On top of the oversized shirt, Gillian had arranged two voluminous shawls in bright purple and blue woven with strands of sparkling silver. The shawls hung down her back and followed in her wake like two kite tails. With her orange hair, aquamarine eyes, sapphire shirt, and purple leggings, Gillian was like a walking rainbow. James had never seen anyone like her. She reminded him of pictures he had seen of hippies dancing at Woodstock, except that all of those hippies were waif-thin; Gillian, with the exception of her legs, was not.

Gillian rang the doorbell. Inside the house, Lindy called out,

"Come on in!" so James and Gillian obeyed. Lindy met them in her tiny front hall carrying a bowl of potato chips. James eyed them hungrily.

"Chips?" Gillian immediately frowned. "I thought we were starting a diet."

"These are baked, not fried. And anyway, we haven't decided which diet we're doing, so we're just having sandwiches for lunch." Lindy turned her friendly smile toward James. "Lucy and Bennett are already here. I've just laid out bread and lunch meat on the kitchen counter, so we'll fix ourselves sandwiches and then get down to brass tacks."

As James walked into the kitchen, a short and stocky African-American man with a toothbrush mustache and close-cropped hair stopped spreading mayo on his bread and held out his hand to James. "Bennett Marshall, U.S. Postal Service carrier. Pleased to meet you."

"You too. James Henry. Librarian."

Bennett cocked an eyebrow. "But some of your mail reads 'Professor,' doesn't it?" He cleared his throat. "Sorry. I'm not your carrier and shouldn't be discussing your mail in public."

"That's all right. And yes, some of my letters do say that. I used to be . . ." James trailed off, his attention caught by the pear-shaped woman standing behind Bennett. She was busy folding three slices of turkey on top of a piece of bread and did not realize that James was overtly studying her. He briefly took in her oversized flannel shirt and the black leggings encasing her round hips and thighs, and then his gaze lingered on the profile of what seemed to be a very pretty face. Whoever she was, this woman had beautiful hair. It fell down to her shoulders and was the color of melted caramel, and James would have loved to run his fingers through it. He was lost in a fantasy of doing exactly that when the woman suddenly raised her eyes. James was mesmerized by their unusual shade of blue. They reminded him of bachelor's buttons, his mother's favorite flower. James felt something stir to life inside of himself as the woman smiled at him.

"I used to be a professor," he finally finished answering Bennett's question, though his shy grin was directed at the woman with the cornflower eyes.

"James Henry, this is Lucy Hanover." Lindy pointed back and

forth at the two of them with a knife smeared with yellow mustard. "Behave yourself or she'll have to arrest you."

"Hi," Lucy said, raising her plate in greeting. "Don't listen to Lindy. I'm just an assistant over at the sheriff's department. I don't even own a pair of handcuffs." Her teasing expression quickly turned serious. "It's a dream of mine to be a real deputy someday, but I've got an uphill road to climb before that can ever happen." She looked at the window as if seeing herself in the sheriff's brown and beige uniform, and then turned back to James. "But we all have goals to reach, don't we? That's why we're here, and we're glad you've joined our group, James."

"Thanks." James made himself a ham and cheese sandwich and then sat down next to Bennett at the kitchen table. The space was small, but it gave the group's gathering a feeling of intimacy and coziness.

Gillian was the last to take a seat at the table. She folded her hands together in a *namaste* gesture and bowed at each of her dining companions. "This food is a gift from the universe. May we all be worthy of it." Then, taking an enormous bite of her sandwich, she released a rapturous moan. James stole a glance at Lucy and saw her grinning wryly. Gillian swallowed her food and reached up for one of Lindy's pink flyers, which had been wadded into a tight ball and tossed next to a ceramic napkin dispenser. "What's with this?" she asked. "Looks like the result of hostile energy."

Lindy shrugged. "I was angry. Someone decided to edit my flyer— probably one of my students. I'm sure they thought it was funny, but *I* don't. I found it in my mailbox."

Gillian smoothed out the crumpled sheet and read the revised version aloud.

Are You Feeling Like a Total Lard?
Do You Look Like a Bowling Ball?
How about a Beached Whale?
Join Our New Loser's Club!
We Meet in the Grocery Store (near the donuts)!
Make Friends with Other Losers!
Lose Dignity with Losers!
Call Lardy Lindy at 1-8OO-EAT-MORE

"Very creative." Gillian nonchalantly tossed the flyer into the garbage. "Though clearly not destined to be the next Shakespeare."

"I saw that kid, Brinkley Myers, mowing the lawn across the street," Bennett said, gesticulating with his sandwich. "I bet it was him. He always looks like he's up to no good—he's just got one of those faces. And to think he was messing around with your mailbox. That's serious business."

"It wouldn't surprise me if I found out he was the guilty party," Lindy said. "Brinkley was one of my worst students. Ever. He thought he was so great at football that he didn't have to apply himself to any of his academic subjects. I was stuck being his academic advisor. What a nightmare! He barely graduated and now he's mowing lawns. Guess he might be a little bitter." She shook her head. "He still wears that letter jacket all over town. And yet, he thinks *we're* losers? Ha! Pass me the chips please, Bennett."

"That might be the last sandwich with three slices of American cheese and regular mayo you have for a while," Bennett pointed out. "That is, if we go on your Weight Watchers plan. If we decide to follow my idea of—"

"Gillian wants to do Weight Watchers, too," Lindy interjected.

"Absolutely! I just *cannot* eat all of the meat they have on those low-carb diets. I'd feel utterly vile." Gillian shivered dramatically, curls of her orange hair bobbing in front of her eyes.

"Are you a vegetarian?" James asked.

"I eat some chicken and fish, but I'd *really* like to be a full vegetarian. I can almost *sense* the pain of those innocent animals. Gillian paused to compose herself and then continued. "My problem is that if I don't get enough meat in my diet, I end up eating too many heavy starches like bread and potatoes. It all sticks right to me. I don't even have a *dent* to indicate a waist anymore. I'm like a walking marshmallow."

The rest of the group nodded empathetically. "I hear you," Bennett said, wiping the potato chip grease shining on his fingers onto his paper napkin. "I used to be a lean, mean, wrestling machine, but all that muscle has turned to flab. Know why? Because I eat during my deliveries. Lots of snacks from the 7-Eleven. My route is long and that means lots of snacking."

"What do you eat that's so bad?" Lucy asked.

"Donut holes mostly," Bennett answered. "You know, the little ones that come in a box. I just pop them right in. I eat a whole box every day, and I am not a tall man." He turned to James. "You can carry some extra weight pretty well. Me, I can't."

Bennett's comment resonated with Lindy. She raised her hand in the air and waved it about. "I'm short, too! My deal is that I can't stop eating candy. I keep bite-sized pieces in my drawer at school as a reward for kids who help me with various jobs. Tasks like unloading the kiln, cleaning the paintbrushes, et cetera. The problem is, I eat just as much of it as I give away." Lindy patted her stomach. "I've eaten myself out of all the clothes in my closet. I've *got* to do something." She lowered her voice. "I have a confession to make. I'd love to catch the eye of our new principal. He's Latino and so handsome . . ." She got a dreamy look in her eyes and then seemed to come back to reality. "But he looks right through me whenever we meet in the hall. I want to make him look twice—to see the Lindy I have inside me. She's beautiful and sexy and confident."

"Hear! Hear!" Gillian raised her cup of water in salute to Lindy's declaration.

Feeling safe enough to contribute, James decided to volunteer his particular food addiction. "I'm a cheese puff man. Once a bag is open, I just can't stop eating them. I like the flavor well enough, but I lose control when I get started. The truth, and this is the real problem, is they actually make me feel good. They're an escape. And I need all the escapes I can get these days."

Everyone was quiet for a moment, and James wondered if he had confessed too much with that last statement. Lucy looked at him kindly with those lovely blue eyes and nodded in understanding. He felt his heart pounding beneath his ribs.

"I know exactly what you mean," she said. "For me, it's frosting. You know, like birthday cake or cupcake frosting. When I've had a really bad day, I'll actually eat it right out of the can. It's gross, I know, but that sweet taste just makes me forget about whatever is going wrong in my life. Until later. Then I feel really terrible for eating like a pig. I keep saying that I want to become a deputy, and I know I have the brains to do the job, but until I can control myself, I'll *never* have the body for it. And every time I even think about passing any kind of physical, I feel so lousy that I might actually go back and eat more frosting." She sighed. "It's a pretty vicious cycle. And even though I want to stop my behavior, I don't seem to have the power to put the brakes on my horrible habit."

Everyone bobbed his or her head in agreement. They'd all experienced the intense feelings of pleasure followed by the waves of powerful guilt Lucy had described.

"I have an issue with peanut butter cups," Gillian whispered. "I sit there, trying to meditate, to enter a state of *zen*, but I can't." She turned to James. "I do a lot of yoga. Anyway, I attempt to reach a deep meditative trance, but instead of visualizing emptiness, I start picturing peanut butter cups! They literally float in front of my vision until I have to have one! I'll never achieve enlightenment at this rate." Gillian was being serious, but the other four people around the table chuckled.

"So now that we've shared our challenges, we have two other items to cover today." Clearly hoping to move along to a more proactive dialogue, Lindy said, "We need to choose a diet plan, and then decide where to meet for our first official supper club meal. Gillian and I want to follow Weight Watchers. Bennett and Lucy want to try a low-carb diet. I'm afraid it's up to you, James. You're the deciding vote."

James shifted in his chair. He had been feeling completely comfortable a moment ago, but now he was being put on the spot. He really didn't have a preference as to which diet they followed—he just wanted to be involved with a group that he felt he could trust. James looked at each expectant face. When he gazed at Lucy across the table, he noticed that she had a faint peppering of freckles across the bridge of her nose. She gave him a shy smile.

In the end, James picked the low-carb diet. He didn't think he had the discipline to count points or calories. He knew he could probably enter the information online, but the idea still put him off. More than that, he had an inexplicable desire to please Lucy. If voting for the diet she favored made her smile at him again, then that was reason enough.

"I vote for low-carb," he said firmly.

Lucy and Bennett happily exchanged high fives and Bennett then clamped James on the shoulder. "You're all right, my friend."

"Since I'm thrilled with the choice, we can meet at my place for the first supper club meal next week," Lucy said.

"Just as long as you put those dogs of yours outside," Bennett grumbled. "I can't even get near her mailbox," Bennett explained to James. "She's got three of the most terrifying German shepherds known to humankind, and I am not afraid of dogs."

"Forget about the dogs. This is so exciting!" Lindy exclaimed. "We're embarking on a journey together, and we're going to have so much fun helping one another lose weight!"

"But how will we know what to eat?" Gillian looked put out.

No one said anything for a moment and then James spoke up, feeling more confident now that his decision had been so readily accepted. "We have several low-carb diet books at the library. Cookbooks too. I'm sure I could print out some menus from the Internet, so I volunteer to figure out what meal we should eat on Sunday. I can contact each of you and tell you what item to bring."

Lindy retrieved a pad of paper and a pen from one of her kitchen drawers. "Why don't we exchange emails and phone numbers? Is James's plan okay with everyone?" They all agreed and thanked James for his initiative. "And I think that whoever offers their house for the meeting should have a pass from having to cook," Lindy continued. "It's enough to have to clean up before and after our meal."

"Oh, this is *such* a thrill!" Gillian cried. "I truly hope we can lose some weight together, but it won't be easy. Do you think we need a slogan or a name or something to psych us up?"

Everyone grew silent as they tried to conjure a witty moniker for their supper club group.

"There are five of us. How about the Fab Five?" Lindy offered.

Lucy shook her head. "That's taken. Besides"—she spread her arms out to encompass everyone at the table—"we're not exactly fabulous. Not yet."

"Yeah, more like flabulous." Bennett cackled.

"So instead of the Fab Five, we're the Flab Five," James mumbled, grinning to himself. Everyone turned to stare at him and then four round faces lit up with laughter.

"That's it!" Lindy shrieked. "That's what we are! And when we've knocked off the flab, we'll change our name. We need to earn that name change though. Really, seriously earn it. Together." Lindy put her hand in the middle of the table. "Put your hand on mine if you are willing to be a member of the Flab Five and pursue a low-carb diet until your personal weight-loss goals have been met."

They all stacked hands on top of Lindy's. James was last, and as his hand covered Lucy's, he felt the warmth of the room and the people seated around the table fill up an empty space within him. It had been so long since he had shared any feelings of true companionship that he believed he might actually grow tearful. Quickly withdrawing his hand, he covered up the emotions welling inside by clearing his throat. "I'll prepare a list of which foods we're allowed to eat during my lunch break tomorrow. You can all stop by the library at the end of the day and pick one up. This way, we'll be eating low-carb foods during the week. Maybe we can share how much we've lost when we meet again next Sunday."

"If we've lost anything," Gillian said glumly.

Just as all of them were pondering the enormity of their individual tasks, a siren screamed outside the window and a parade of three brown cars with lights blazing zipped past.

"That's the sheriff! And Keith and Luke and—!" Lucy exclaimed, jumping up. "I'm going to call over to the station and see what's going on. Can I use your phone, Lindy?"

"Sure." Lindy gestured toward the wall phone in the kitchen. As the sirens moved off in the distance, she mused out loud, "You know, while we're all here we should talk about some ideas for exercise." Bennett groaned. "Seriously," continued Lindy as Lucy listened to a loud voice coming over the phone line. "Maybe we could meet at the high school track and walk or something."

"I don't know," Gillian replied, tossing the end her scarf over her shoulder. "We all have such different schedules. And I am not a morning person like you folks."

"What about you, James?" Lindy peered at him hopefully.

James didn't answer. He was too distracted by Lucy's puzzled facial expression. She looked completely bewildered. He got up from the table and moved closer to her.

"Is something wrong?" James asked softly.

"I'm just talking about a little cardiac activity, people," Lindy plowed on. "It's not like I'm saying we should sign up for a marathon." Seeing the abject curiosity on her friends' faces, she fell silent. Everyone was watching Lucy.

Lucy put the phone down and shook her head in confusion. "It's really odd. I got the station's answering machine." She grabbed her coat, her eyes reflecting both concern and a twinkle of anticipation. "Maybe the sheriff needs help. I'd better get down there. This could be my chance to prove myself indispensable. If there's anything worth reporting, I'll call you guys and let you know what it is." With a quick wave, Lucy hurried out to her car.

The remaining foursome exchanged perplexed looks.

"Something major must have happened," Lindy said. "Otherwise, why would every deputy on duty respond?"

"What are you suggesting?" Gillian asked, eyes wide.

"You know," Lindy whispered. "Something bad. Like a robbery. Or arson. Maybe even murder." She put her fingers to her lips. "I wonder if our local boys are trained to handle something like that. Maybe they'd have to get help from some cute forensic guys from Harrisonburg or Charlottesville. Maybe *Unsolved Mysteries* or *CSI* would want to do a story based on our little town . . ." She trailed off, absorbed in her own fantasy.

"That's ridiculous. We don't have that kind of violence in Quincy's Gap, Lindy. It's simply impossible." Gillian tried to sound doubtful, but her voice caught a little on the word "impossible." She pulled out a crystal pendant from the depths of her shirt and began to rub it.

Bennett calmly folded his napkin into a tiny square. "Well, homicide rates in the South have increased more than in any other part of the United States, especially when guns are involved. We may be a small town, but we're a small Southern town. Statistically, I guess we're due." He turned to James. "Statistics are my hobby."

"You're so interesting, Bennett," Lindy said. "I think you'd be a great character for a detective show. A crime fighter with a mind stuffed full of facts and figures."

"You really think so?" Bennett looked pleased.

James noticed that the group's initial concern had gradually turned to excitement as the speculations grew. He was ashamed to think that he was also feeling a little thrill over the possibility of a Quincy's Gap mystery, but he had to admit to himself that he was even more interested in what Lucy was doing at this very moment.

"I wonder where those patrol cars were headed," he said.

"I can tell you that." Bennett pointed toward the mail truck parked outside. "I've got a police scanner in there. If anything's going on, we can listen in."

The foursome practically ran to the mail truck. Though it was only parked at the end of Lindy's front walkway, they were all short of breath after hustling their normally sedentary bodies at such a rapid clip.

Bennett hopped into the driver's seat and began to turn dials on the scanner. There was a great deal of static and the voices were garbled. Eventually, the white noise disappeared long enough for them to make out the words "Sweet Tooth" and "901H."

"A 901H," Bennett muttered darkly.

"What? Is that bad?" Gillian demanded shrilly, grabbing hold of Bennett's arm.

"It's a code. Most law enforcement agencies share a common set of codes which—"

"But what does it mean?" Gillian shook his arm.

"It's a call for an ambulance," Bennett replied, glancing nervously at Gillian's fingers, which were curling around his forearm in a vise-like grip. "A request for the paramedics to come to the Sweet Tooth in order to collect a dead body." He let loose a sigh. "Looks like the sheriff and his crew got there too late to help the poor soul."

"A body in the bakery? I hope it's not Megan Flowers or her daughter." Gillian released Bennett and put her hands over her heart. "I can't just sit here! Let's find out what's happened!"

Bennett's eyes lit up. He had never actually seen the codes he could so skillfully translate on his police scanner being put into action. "Hop in, folks. It's against regulations to have you in here, but I can bend the rules this one time."

As they sped off downtown, Gillian said, "I hope Lucy stayed at the station. It's obvious that she's dying to wear a uniform, but the Sweet Tooth wouldn't be the best setting for her to volunteer her investigative services."

Bennett seemed lost in his own thoughts. "Who knows what kind of situation the sheriff is dealing with right now? All we know is there is a body involved."

"It's not *what* he's investigating that Gillian's worried about, Bennett, it's *where* he's investigating. I hope Lucy is staying put at the station, answering phones and the like," Lindy added as they raced well over the speed limit toward Main Street.

"What would be the problem with her meeting us at the bakery?" James asked. He felt someone should defend Lucy's ambition to become a deputy. "She must be as curious as the rest of us."

Lindy looked at him as if he were dimwitted. "James, we just started a diet. We've got to keep Lucy as far away from the Sweet Tooth as possible. The place is filled with frosting!"

Chapter Three

Chocolate Chip Cookie

Bennett was accustomed to driving a mail truck bearing the weight of thousands of letters, hundreds of magazines, and dozens of packages, but the painful squealing of tires as his official vehicle of the United States Postal Service turned the corner of Elm and Main streets made him cringe. Apparently, four overweight human bodies shifting around the interior were harder on the truck's axles than all the mail delivered during the Christmas season.

"Hurry!" Lindy yelled. Her long hair whipped about her face like a licorice-colored tornado, and her round cheeks were tinged pink with expectation. Bennett had his window cranked down in order to escape the overpowering scent of Gillian's patchouli perfume, but Gillian constantly leaned over his headrest in order to ask impatient questions about the conversations taking place on the police scanner.

"They're saying that there are two women inside the Sweet Tooth," Bennett shouted over the wind. "Megan and Amelia Flowers. The police are going to question them."

"Good, they're obviously alive and hopefully unhurt," Gillian said. "But what about the identity of the dead person?"

James couldn't make out a single word coming from the scanner. All of its jumbled noises sounded like kids screaming at each other underwater.

He looked out his window at the quiet town. Church services had ended, and most folks ate a large midday meal at home and then spent time crossing jobs off their honey-do lists, tending to the fall gardens, or taking leisurely strolls. Very few businesses were open on Sunday, but James knew that some people would wander into town for an afternoon treat from the bakery or to pick up fresh bread for a sandwich supper. Whatever happened at the Sweet Tooth would soon be public knowledge. Nothing ever stayed private in Quincy's Gap for long. Perhaps that was why he and his new friends hoped to learn the news first. It would give them something exciting to talk about at work Monday morning.

Barreling down Main Street, the mail truck made record time before finally slowing to a crawl near the bakery. Three sheriff's cars with blue lights flashing had parked helter-skelter along the curb, indicating how quickly they had arrived at the scene.

"Nice work, Bennett. We made it here in three minutes. It looks like we even beat the ambulance." Lindy clapped Bennett on the back. "We'd better park next door, in that back lot behind the stationery store."

"Good idea," Bennett agreed, maneuvering the truck into the gravel lot. "Look! There's Lucy's Jeep!"

The mail truck groaned to a halt, and its four passengers clambered out. Sticking as close as possible to the cement wall on the alley side of the bakery, they crept toward the back door. Lindy, who was leading the curious foursome, turned the corner into the bakery's parking lot and then leapt backward, right onto Bennett's big toe.

"Ow!" he yowled.

Lindy clamped a hand over his mouth.

"Sorry," she whispered, making frantic gestures indicating everyone should retreat. "Lucy is standing right outside. She's talking to one of the deputies. Listen."

Sure enough, voices floated to their corner of the building. The town's Sunday afternoon tranquility, defined by a noticeable lack of traffic noise, allowed their eager ears to hear the strained conversation taking place just outside of the bakery's back door.

"Look, Keith," Lucy was saying in a pleading tone. "I just want to observe, to see if I can learn something. I know you've heard me mention that I want to take the deputy's exam in the near future and I—"

"I thought you were joking!" The man named Keith laughed maliciously. "Come on, Lucy. You'd never pass the physical. Not in a million years! Besides, being a deputy is a *man's* job."

"I don't think so," Lucy replied heatedly. "There are plenty of women in law enforcement and in the Armed Forces as well. They—"

"Are in far better shape," Keith interrupted her once again. "Now, I'd love to debate the topic with you, Lucy, but I've got a dead body to examine and witnesses to interview." He paused. "You ever seen a stiff, Lucy?"

"No."

"What makes you think you can handle it? Most corpses are nasty things. There's blood and foul smells and all kinds of bodily fluids involved, if you get my drift. It takes a tough person to get up close and personal to a dead body. Are you tough enough?"

Listening to the deputy's patronizing tone, James suppressed an urge to race to Lucy's defense. Why didn't the jackass just give her a chance? But instead of running to her side, James bit his lip and took a quick peek around the corner of the building to get a look at Lucy's jerk of a coworker.

Keith stood with his hands on his hips and his legs drawn apart in a cowboy-like stance. His red hair glinted in the October sunlight, and, even from a distance, James could see that his face was so obscured with tawny freckles that it was difficult to see the pallid skin underneath. Keith wore mirrored sunglasses that reminded James of the cool cop shows on TV during the seventies, but seemed startlingly out of place in a small Virginia town in the twenty-first century.

"Let me see if I *can* handle seeing a dead body, Keith. If it upsets me, then I won't bother thinking about taking the exam." Lucy's desperation was just shy of pathetic. Her new friends looked at one another, their eyes burning with indignation on her behalf.

"Donovan!" another male voice called out from within the building. "Get your tail in here!"

James saw Keith do a little jump and then hustle inside, leaving the door ajar. After hesitating for a fraction of a second, Lucy pulled a small notebook from her purse, turned to a fresh sheet of paper, and resolutely followed in her redheaded tormentor's wake.

"Come on!" Lindy moved forward, tiptoeing up to the back door.

The heavy metal door had been propped open, and the sounds of a woman's hysterical voice could be heard from within. Aside from the view of cooking equipment and the tantalizing smell of freshly baked bread that curled around the foursome like an alluring, invisible boa, there was nothing to be seen through the doorway.

"The action must be up front," Gillian said. "We can't go in, so let's sneak around to the street side and try to peer in through the display windows."

At that moment, the honk of a nearby horn pierced the stillness.

"Hurry! That could be the paramedics!" cried Bennett as he led the group around the building. "It is! Look!"

The yellow van from Quincy's Gap Fire and Rescue moved

quietly but briskly past them into the bakery's small parking lot. The driver honked again, but the breathless group was too far away to see why he was making so much noise.

The first window they reached took up most of the storefront. Megan Flowers always displayed examples of her decorated wedding cakes in that window, along with a sampling of items she planned to bake throughout the week.

Today, her display shelves had been covered with black and orange crepe paper. Plastic pumpkins were brimming over with miniature banana nut and pumpkin spice muffins. A black cat with glowing purple eyes drew attention to a platter of donuts dripping with white icing and a hefty dose of orange sprinkles. Beneath the shadow of a friendly scarecrow, another platter featured Megan's latest creation: a variety of cookies in the shapes of various monsters. Every cookie looked like it had been slathered with an inch of home-made buttercream. James's eye was particularly drawn to the Dracula cookies. Each pale-faced vampire had two rivulets of bright ruby icing dripping down from fangs fashioned out of white sprinkles.

"I've never seen such a good-looking mummy." Gillian pointed at a cookie.

"Forget him," Lindy said, her eyes wide with wonder. "I'd take that Frankenstein's monster any day. Look at all the black sprinkles forming his hair. I'm about to drool all over the sidewalk."

Bennett tried to see beyond the display, but when he stood on his tiptoes, a shelf crammed with miniature éclairs swollen with custard blocked his view.

"James," Bennett croaked, his mouth dry with longing. "You're the tallest. See anything?"

James finally focused his attention beyond the display of tantalizing goodies. Unfortunately, he could only make out the backs of three people as they stood looking down at something. There were two women and one man. From this angle, James couldn't tell what their gazes were fixed on. He was able to see Lucy, however, standing off to the side, and it was clear that she was fighting to control her emotions. Her lovely face had turned rather gray, and the hand that gripped her notebook was shaking. Someone must have spoken to her at that moment, for she wordlessly nodded and began writing notes with a tremulous hand.

"I can't see what they're staring at. We're going to have to move to the other window," James said to the others. "That will mean going right past the front door, and it'll seem pretty odd if all four of us slink past the door at the same time and suddenly stop to peer in the window."

"Well, the sign still says Open, so it's not at all strange for us to be walking to the bakery," argued Gillian. "And from the look on Lucy's face, I'd say something serious definitely happened inside!"

Crouching as low as they could, the foursome shuffled past the entrance and to the smaller storefront window. The display in this section was mostly an array of breads. Beyond the plump mounds of rye, pumpernickel, egg, and raisin breads, along with a pair of wide baskets filled to the top with dill and rosemary rolls, James was able to get a clear view of the three people whose backs had been turned to him a minute ago.

The first was a burly middle-aged man with an enormous mustache. He appeared to be questioning a tall woman wearing a red-and-white-striped apron embroidered with the words *The Sweet Tooth*. Her slender arms were folded across her chest in a pose of self-preservation, and her eyes reflected both fear and confusion.

As James watched, she slid an arm around the waist of a younger, more curvaceous version of herself. The younger woman had dull blonde hair that fell like a curtain over her eyes and her gaze was locked on the floor. She held a rolled-up magazine in her right hand, tightly enough to cause her knuckles to turn white, and had her left hand shoved deep into her apron pocket.

"That's Sheriff Huckabee. He's talking to Megan Flowers and her daughter, Amelia," Lindy whispered before James had a chance to ask the names of the three people.

Though he didn't know Megan or Amelia, James remembered Huckabee. He had been a deputy when James was in high school and had often been visible at athletic events at the school. Sometimes the crowds could get a little rowdy at football games, and the presence of a few deputies helped maintain order. James remembered Huckabee because of the unique name and because the man resembled a walrus. With his wide girth, slow gait, and remarkable mustache, the comparison had been made by many Quincy's Gap residents.

James leaned forward until his nose was a millimeter from the window glass and raked his eyes over the small area of floor. He was able to see through an opening between a loaf of rye and a loaf of whole grain bread. As James watched, a paramedic pivoted to retrieve an instrument from his case. In the seconds it took for the EMT to search his bag, James had an unobstructed glimpse of the object that had set Lucy's hands to trembling. It was such an alien sight that James's mind was slow to identify it.

He was looking at the body of a man. A man he'd just seen two days ago at Dolly's Diner. James recognized the worn letter jacket immediately, as well as the unkempt hair, the wide shoulders and muscular arms.

Brinkley Myers had collapsed on his stomach with his head turned toward the window. His open eyes were glazed, and his nose and mouth were covered with smears of fresh, bright blood. Tiny droplets still leaked from his left nostril. The blood dripped slowly, like water from a leaking faucet. A pool of crimson had formed around his face and head, widening into an ellipse that contrasted with the black-and-white-checkered linoleum.

"I couldn't stop the bleeding!" Megan cried, loud enough for all the supper club members to hear. She brandished a wad of blood-soaked dish towels. "I tried. I really tried!"

Beside her, Amelia's face crumpled, and she began to cry. As her mother tried to comfort her, Amelia hid her face in her hands.

James had a hard time concentrating on anything other than the inordinate amount of blood on the floor, but then he spied what looked like a shattered cell phone near Amelia's foot.

"That's Brinkley Myers," Lindy whispered. "I'd say that he's definitely dead."

"From what?" asked Gillian. There was a noticeable quaver to her voice. "He's so young. And I've never seen so much blood."

"Maybe it came from a wound on his head. There's no blood near his chest or legs. Point of fact, it seems like he had a nosebleed that just wouldn't quit." Bennett clucked his tongue in sympathy. "That'd be an awful way to go."

The others remained silent as they checked Bennett's theory by casting their eyes once more on Brinkley's inert form.

"What's that in his right hand?" James asked, unable to get an unobstructed view over the shoulders of the paramedic.

"I can't tell," said Bennett. "Can you see, Lindy? Hurry, they're about to place him on a gurney."

Lindy sucked in a sharp breath. "I see it! I'd know that tasty morsel anywhere. It's one of Megan's famous cookies; a 'chocolate chipped and dipped.' Those cookies are so—" The rest of her statement was cut short by the sudden appearance of Sheriff Huckabee's face in the window. He did not look at all pleased to see four civilians with their noses pressed against the glass. Waving them off with a brusque flick of his hand, Huckabee drew the green shades over both windows and then turned the store sign over from Open to Closed.

James stepped back and turned to his dumbfounded companions. "Guess the show's over," he said. "I don't know about the rest of you, but I've just seen my first dead body, and I feel kind of weird. Pretty unnerved, actually."

"Yeah, me too," Bennett muttered. They all stood on the sidewalk in motionless silence.

"Let's go back to my place and have some coffee," Lindy suggested. "I don't think I'll be able to settle down without talking this out. It would be nice to have some company."

Nodding in silent agreement, the foursome walked back to the mail truck like a troop of automatons. James's mind was buzzing with all that it had just absorbed.

"Fine time for us to start a diet." Gillian let loose a crazed little laugh. She twisted the rings on her fingers around and around. "In a few days we're *all* going to wish we had one of those cookies."

Lindy cast an uneasy glance at Gillian. "Stress is making you talk like that. It's okay. We're all feeling out of sorts. Who wouldn't after seeing what we just saw?" She patted Gillian's arm and then sank back against the seat of the mail truck. "I never liked Brinkley Myers," she said with a drawn-out sigh. "But at least his last meal was a good one."

Chapter Four

Dry-Roasted Peanuts

Coffee at Lindy's had not lasted long. All of the supper club members found that they needed some time alone to process the fact that a young man had suddenly died. True, he was a distasteful young man, but he belonged to the Quincy's Gap community nonetheless. He was one of them, and now, he was gone.

Monday came and James was relieved to be at work, where he busied himself researching acceptable foods for a low-carb diet plan. He grew quickly confused between the definition of low carbs, good carbs, complex carbs, simple carbs, and bad carbs. Everywhere he looked he seemed to run across an overwhelming number of phrases mentioning the term "carbohydrates." Frustrated, James decided to pursue the good-carbs, good-fats approach, as at least the adjectives put a more positive spin on the mountain of depravity he and his new friends were about to climb.

After skimming through several books, James realized that he had already exceeded his daily allowance of carbohydrates by having a bagel for breakfast. True, he had skipped his regular layer of cream cheese and had used a generous measure of strawberry jam instead, but he had innocently added on even more bad carbs cleverly disguised as sugar.

"How can they expect anyone to lose weight with all of these conflicting menus? This book says no fruit, this book says only berries, and this one says eat fruit every day." James snapped a weight-loss book shut and stared at the cover. A shirtless man with washboard abs, and a pair of biceps that looked like cannonballs concealed beneath a layer of skin, smiled at him. The Greek god had forearms that Popeye would have envied, and a busty blonde model wearing only a sports bra and a minute pair of spandex shorts clung to his left one, gazing at her bronzed diet-mate with a look of unadulterated rapture.

In order to keep his fingers occupied during his lunch break (so that they would not be tempted to buy a package of cheese puffs from the lobby snack machine), James surfed the Internet. He was able to obtain a vague idea of which foods the supper club should be eating. As he made notes, he became more and more confident about their plan. Energized, he had just begun to type up a complete shopping list followed by a catalog of acceptable snacks, when Lucy entered the library.

Unbeknownst to James, Francis and Scott had already left for the day. Their boss had been so preoccupied with his computer research that when the twins called out, "Until tomorrow, Professor!" before leaving for the day, he only grunted in reply, being completely absorbed viewing yet another website for low-carb dieters. Normally, James would have recognized that the workday had come to an end by telling the twins that they'd done good work and wishing them a pleasant night.

Even when Mrs. Waxman, the part-time librarian in charge of the evening shift, arrived and began to assist a group of boisterous high school students at the reference desk, James remained engrossed in his task. So it was Mrs. Waxman who greeted Lucy.

"Hello, Lucy," Mrs. Waxman whispered. "Haven't seen you in here for a few weeks. What true crime books are you reading these days?"

Mrs. Waxman had taught eighth-grade English at the Thomas Jefferson Middle School for so many years now that no one could remember who had occupied the position before she moved to town. She'd taught both Lucy and James and remembered the names of every one of her students, as well as the reading habits of every library patron within a three-county radius.

"Hi, Mrs. Waxman." Lucy smiled. "I'm still working on that Ann Rule paperback."

"I bet you finished those M. C. Beaton novels, though," Mrs. Waxman chuckled. "I think you have a crush on that fictional detective."

"Hamish Macbeth?" Lucy shrugged. "He *is* a dog lover, but he's too tall and skinny for me. Plus, I'm not really attracted to red-heads."

"My, aren't we particular?" Mrs. Waxman clicked her tongue in disapproval. "How old are you now, Lucy?" she asked.

Lucy blushed. She knew where this conversation was headed, and she did not want to admit that she was thirty-five and had never come close to walking down the aisle. Not even as a bridesmaid.

"Actually, I haven't come to check out books this time, Mrs. Waxman. I'm here to see, um, Professor Henry."

"James is in his office." Mrs. Waxman called everyone by his or her first name, regardless of title or occupation. Dr. Morris, the town vet, was still Emily, and Reverend Beasley of the First Baptist Church was, and always would be, Mike Jr. "He's doing something on the computer. Go on back."

Lucy tapped lightly on the door separating James's tiny office from the shelving area behind the circulation desk. James started in his chair. "You startled me." He put his hand over his heart.

"Sorry." Lucy offered a shy grin, pointing at the wad of papers James clutched in his hand. "Is the diet already making you a bit tense?"

James looked down at his hand and then put the pile of papers on his desk. Smoothing the wrinkled edges with his fingers, he said, "Actually, I was so busy this afternoon that I kind of forgot about being hungry. Of course, I've had about five diet sodas, and none of them were decaffeinated, so I'm a little jittery."

Lucy sat in one of the office's uncomfortable wooden chairs. "This chair reminds me of school," she said, thinking glumly of the advice Mrs. Waxman had been on the verge of doling out. Lucy had heard it many times before from the older women in Quincy's Gap. They all told her that she shouldn't set her sights so high when looking for a man, but Lucy wasn't going to settle. She wanted an amazing man, and she didn't want to defend her decision to Mrs. Waxman or anyone else. Realizing that James was staring at her, she smiled again. "How did the research go? Are we going to survive this diet, or will we be eating carrot sticks and Swiss cheese for the rest of our lives?"

"Actually, it's not that bland. There are lots of foods on our list that are pretty good. Of course, it helps if you like any vegetable known to man, which I don't."

Lucy shrugged. "I like potatoes."

"Yeah, who doesn't?" James laughed. "Fried; scalloped; baked with cheese, chili, and sour cream; hash browns with ketchup; tater tots—"

"Stop!" Lucy begged. "All I had for lunch was a Caesar salad with grilled chicken, and I'm starving."

"I know. Right now, I could eat a miniature pony. I had a tuna salad sandwich without the bread. Man, I already miss not sinking my teeth into a piece of toasty bread." James consulted his food sheet and grinned approvingly at Lucy. "At least what you had for lunch was good. Did you eat the croutons?"

"Yes," Lucy admitted sheepishly. "I wasn't supposed to, was I?"

"No, but you didn't know that. Next time, you'll pick them off." He handed her a stapled packet of menu ideas. She flipped through some of the meals and groaned. "There are so many fish dishes on here. I'm not a big seafood fan."

"That's okay," James said, coming to sit down next to her. "You can make the same recipes using chicken."

"You did all this today? That is so wonderful, James. Thank you." Lucy looked into his eyes, and he held her lovely gaze for a long moment. Feeling a small spark pass between them, they both became slightly flustered and suddenly feigned great interest in a crumb or speck of lint on their shirts. James scrambled to think of something to say to restore a sense of normalcy.

They were saved from any further awkwardness by the appearance of Lindy and Bennett. As they came into the office, chattering away about the coolness in the air and what they had eaten for lunch, James dragged two of the plastic chairs from the kitchen area into his office. When Gillian arrived a few minutes later, James gallantly offered his own chair. Everyone seemed genuinely impressed with his work.

"Why, James. You've done so much!" Lindy gushed. "You've made this incredibly organized. We won't have any excuses not to succeed now, except that we all have to start cooking."

"That's going to use up a great deal of my precious reflection time." Gillian sighed dramatically, curling a strand of orange hair around her finger. "Still, I'm getting a really powerful vibe that we're all heading toward a more positive place."

Bennett cleared his throat. "I see some menus here, but what can we snack on? Scientific data has me believing that a diet including five smaller meals is more successful than a diet of three large meals."

James was so busy basking in the joy of having four friends gathered around his little desk that he almost didn't hear Bennett. When the words finally sank in he leapt up and grabbed a sheaf of paper from his printer tray. "I almost forgot. Here's a list of suggested snacks."

The Flab Five's "Good" Carb Snack List

Celery sticks with Swiss cheese
1/2 cup low-fat cottage cheese (add chopped tomatoes or cucumbers if you want)
Cucumber slices with feta cheese or sugar-free ranch dressing
4 ounces nonfat yogurt
Hard-boiled egg
Beef jerky
Hummus (no pita! Use a vegetable for dipping instead)
Low-fat ham or turkey slice rolled up with a slice of mozzarella
Mozzarella string cheese (2)
Two pieces Canadian bacon
Granny Smith apple wedges with 1 tablespoon natural or light peanut butter
Dry-roasted peanuts (about 25)
Almonds (1/4 cup)
Pistachios (about 30)
Fat-free, sugar-free pudding
Sugar-free Jell-O (1 cup)
Sugar-free popsicles
Sugar-free gum
Sugar-free hard candy
Diet soda
Coffee with fat-free half-and-half
Artificial sweeteners

"What about all those low-carb bars I've seen at the grocery store?" Lindy asked. "They look delicious—like a nice, tasty candy bar."

"You'd have to check the calories," James said. "Any bar with more than a hundred and fifty calories isn't going to help us. Plus, they're pretty expensive."

"Where, in Buddha's name, is all the fruit?" Gillian demanded, shaking her list.

"I think we're supposed to go light on fruit until we lose some weight," James said. "This is kind of our put-it-in-high-gear snack list. We can add more foods once we've lost some weight."

"I don't think sugar-free gum is going to get me through an afternoon of art class with twenty-five hormonally imbalanced seniors." Lindy rubbed her temples and moaned.

"And not many of these are good for eating in my truck." Bennett frowned. "Did you know that there are thirty-two thousand motor vehicle accidents a year caused by drivers distracted by either talking on their cell phones, reading, putting on makeup, eating, or drinking? That's why I need something that goes in nice and easy." Bennett opened his mouth in a wide "O."

"Look, everyone. Are we giving up before we even get started?" Lucy stood and put her hands on her formidable hips. "No one said this was going to be easy."

James reddened, feeling that Lucy was defending him and not just their diet plan.

"You're right," Lindy said. "And I really appreciate all of your hard work, James. After yesterday's freaky event, I've just felt off-kilter and more than a little distracted. It's been hard to concentrate on starting this diet." She turned to Lucy. "Is there any word on what happened to Brinkley?"

Lucy sat back down in her chair. "After you guys left, we had to wait for the medical examiner to make his way to us from Rockingham County. Sheriff Huckabee went on home and left Keith—Deputy Donovan—and Deputy Truett to wait with the body. They interviewed Megan and Amelia, too. I was there for everything." Lucy sounded proud. "I know I was only taking notes, but they've never let me remain at a scene before."

Gillian shuddered dramatically. "The poor Flowers women! I should bring them some homemade chamomile tea. It's very soothing. How are they holding up?"

"Fine, I guess." Lucy hesitated. "Though there's one thing Amelia did when she thought no one was looking that I keep turning over in my head. Something that just doesn't sit right."

"Which was?" Lindy asked, leaning forward in her chair.

"When Keith was busy questioning Megan, I saw Amelia sneak back to the front to look at Brinkley's cell phone. Doesn't that seem odd?"

"Where was the other deputy? Wasn't he supposed to be guarding the body?" Gillian scowled in disapproval. "How could a person lose focus at such a significant time?"

"Honestly, I think he succumbed to temptation. One of Megan's mummy cookies was practically hanging out of the display case. I guess it had been caught in the sliding door and was just asking to be saved from falling to the floor. I saw Deputy Truett dart over, grab the cookie, and duck into the restroom. I guess he went in there to eat his mummy." Lucy shrugged. "I can't say that I blame him. I could polish off a few dozen of those right now. Did you notice how much icing each cookie had?" The others murmured in agreement, immediately caught up in fantasies involving cookies shaped like famous monsters.

"Where were you all this time?" James asked quickly. He was afraid he might start drooling if they didn't change the subject. "Did you see us?"

"Just your backsides as you hustled off to the parking lot." Lucy giggled. "Don't worry, I'm not mad. I tore down there faster than a speeding bullet, so I can hardly blame anyone else for being curious." She resumed her narrative. "Anyway, I was taking notes while Keith interviewed Megan. He took her to the kitchen and they both sat down near the ovens. Amelia followed, clinging to her mom like a baby chimpanzee. But after a few minutes, she excused herself, saying she needed to get some air. With Deputy Truett holed up in the bathroom, Keith didn't notice Amelia heading to the front instead of through the back door for her breath of fresh air, but I did."

"Didn't she notice you?" Gillian asked. "Do you have the gift of camouflage?" She grew excited, tugging on her violet overshirt. "I've read about people who can fade into their surroundings by remaining perfectly still. They—"

"Sorry to let you down, Gillian, but I was behind the display cases trying to find my pen. Once I'd gotten it from where it had rolled into a floury corner, I stood up and saw Amelia pick up the cell phone. Unfortunately, her back was turned to me, and I couldn't see what she did with the phone. Keith was being his usual charming self to Megan, and she was too distraught to notice Amelia was near the body. It all happened very quickly."

Bennett's eyes shone with interest. "How did Amelia seem after examining Brinkley's phone?"

Lucy grew thoughtful. "When she headed to the back again, I could tell that a huge weight had fallen from her shoulders. Kind of like when a huge pile of snow goes sliding off a rooftop. Of course, she tensed up when she looked down at that pool of blood, but who wouldn't? Lord knows I've never seen anything like that before."

"The human body holds about five liters," Bennett casually informed them. He pointed at a plastic liter bottle of Diet Coke sitting on the break room's countertop. "That's five of those, folks."

"Having that amount spread out on the bakery floor had the ME pretty flustered." Lucy also gestured toward the bottle. "He showed up a few minutes after I saw Amelia steal a glance at the phone and got right to work. But he was totally stymied. He told the deputies that he couldn't figure out what had caused the blood loss and refused to hazard a guess. He ordered the paramedics to deliver the body to his lab, and they were all gone soon afterward."

"In that case, can we assume that neither Megan nor Amelia bludgeoned him to death with a rolling pin?" Lindy sounded a trifle disappointed, and the others regarded her curiously. "Well, let's face it: the guy was a total jerk."

"Certainly to women," James agreed, and all eyes turned toward him. He filled them in on the belittling remarks Brinkley had made about Whitney, the sweet young waitress at Dolly's Diner.

"She's a good girl!" Lindy cried indignantly. "A top-notch student and a hard worker to boot. Her daddy had to quit his job last year because of health issues, so Whitney stopped going to college full-time and started taking shifts at Dolly's in order to help out with household expenses. I always chat with her when I'm there. How many kids these days would be so selfless?"

"None that I've seen. They're far too entitled." Gillian sniffed in disapproval. "That's why I work with animals. They're as loving and spiritual and selfless as you can get."

"I don't know if I'd call Lucy's three hounds of hell loving. I could think of several other adjectives for them," Bennett mumbled, and then his stomach growled so loudly that everyone stared at him. "No donut holes today," Bennett said, looking embarrassed. "See? My gizzard is staging a revolt."

His friends laughed in sympathy. Their own stomachs were also complaining over not having received their daily doses of fatty carbohydrates and sugary treats.

"So there's no indication of what caused Brinkley's death?" James asked Lucy once the room had grown quiet again.

She shook her head with an air of regret. "Besides one powerful nosebleed, it's a mystery. The ME did send a blood sample to the lab in Charlottesville, but it could take a week or longer for them to send him the results. They have to go with their priority cases first, and I doubt Brinkley Myers will qualify as a priority."

"What kind of case does qualify?" Lindy asked. "This one seems pretty unusual to me. After all, Brinkley was young and healthy."

Lucy shrugged. "I guess it would have to be viewed as a suspicious death. We've never had something like this happen since I've been working at the sheriff's department, so I'm not exactly sure. Who knows? Maybe the lab won't be busy and we'll know before I see you all at my house on Sunday."

Lindy turned to James and raised her brows playfully. "Okay, Mr. Drill Sergeant Henry, what are we having for dinner on Sunday?"

Lucy looked at him expectantly. James could feel his heart beating faster as he shuffled through the menu packet he had created. He glanced up briefly, noting how the light from the fluorescents turned her blue eyes a deep indigo. "Ah, it's here on page six. This is the full menu and includes what item each person needs to bring. I wasn't trying to be bossy, but I thought if I gave us all assignments, then things would be clear to everyone." His hesitated. "I found this website on running a supper club, and I was following its suggestions to the letter, but if it's too restrictive . . ." He trailed off.

"Oh, James!" Lindy was instantly apologetic. "I was just teasing you with the drill sergeant comment. You've done a terrific job, and, speaking for all of us, I'm glad we were able to recruit you. We'd still be trying to decide on a diet plan if it weren't for you." She reached over and squeezed his hand. "Now, since I don't have a single one of those snack items at home, I'm heading to the grocery store."

"Man cannot live on celery alone," Bennett said and then frowned. "Actually, I hate celery. I'm going to pick up some cheese and a whole mess of peanuts."

"Me too," echoed the others as they shuffled out of the office, wishing James a good night and warmly thanking him again for the menu packets.

James was so unaccustomed to praise that he just stood behind his desk, soaking up the moment. The library was quiet. Most of the high school students had received the information they needed to complete their projects and had gone home. Mrs. Waxman was busy flipping through the pages of *Time* magazine as James walked past her with a cheerful wave.

"Have a good night, James," she said in her librarian's whisper. Her smile was filled with warmth.

Outside, darkness had fallen among the pine trees. "I believe I will have a good night," James told a sky speckled with glittering stars. "This is the beginning of an all-new James Henry."

And with that, he headed to his car, walking a little taller, like a man with a purpose.

Chapter Five

Sirloin Steak

Later that week, James was using the table in the staff break room to repair a hardback copy of *The Old Man and the Sea*. He lovingly applied a thin line of glue along the inside gutter and then carefully replaced the page that had fallen out the day before. Closing the book, he wrapped a rubber band around it, and set a brick covered in muslin on the top cover so that its weight would help set the glued page. Scott, who'd given him several lessons in book repair, sat beside him using fine-grade sandpaper to rub away ground dirt smudges from the page corners of a copy of *Tender Is the Night*.

"There you are, Mr. Hemingway. A nice new protective cover for your masterpiece." James handed Scott a copy of *The Sun Also Rises* to be placed on the reshelving cart.

"Think you could ever run with the bulls, Professor Henry?" Scott asked, pushing his heavy glasses back onto the bridge of his nose.

"Not unless they counted me as one of the bulls," James replied grumpily. It was only Thursday, and he felt as though he couldn't survive another second without having a bag of cheese puffs or a slice of pepperoni pizza. He was irritable and hungry, and felt completely devoid of energy.

"The F. Scott Fitzgerald books must be in the best shape out of our entire collection," James said.

"We try," he said. Still beaming, he glanced across the room to where his twin brother sat manning the reference desk. "Those novels see so much wear because they're on the reading list at Blue Ridge High. Imagine, a Fitzgerald classic every year! What a great school that place must be."

James nodded absently, wishing a patron would arrive with a challenging question so that he might be distracted from his powerful cravings. Sadly, there were no interesting queries at all, and by eleven thirty the stillness of the library began grating on James. He strolled restlessly to the lobby, telling himself that the books for sale needed to be straightened. Of course, it just so happened that he had a perfectly unwrinkled dollar bill inside his wallet that would slide effortlessly into the snack machine's slot in exchange for a bag of crunchy, orange-hued heaven. Checking over his shoulder to make sure the twins were occupied, James fed the money into the machine and desperately punched the E6 button until the splendid thumping sound announced the delivery of a parcel of cheese puffs.

"It's just a snack-size bag," James muttered defensively to the vacant lobby. "A precious, salty, delicious snack-size bag."

Slipping outside, he sat down on the front steps and, heedless of the cold, began to devour the bag's contents. He crunched blissfully, examining the blazing red, orange, and gold leaves on the maple and oak trees dotting the library parking lot. James felt an incredible sense of elation from having permitted himself to indulge in his favorite treat, but the contents of the bag disappeared all too soon. He stared longingly at the bottom of the bag, probing in the creases for any remnants. Having eaten every crumb, he balled up the evidence, stuffed it in the lobby trash can, and was just about to suck the orange dust from his fingertips when Francis came outside.

Without thinking, James frantically wiped his hands on the back of his pants as Francis leaned on the stair railing and blinked in the sunlight like a bat who'd just emerged from his cave.

"Nice day," Francis said, his breath hanging in the air like wet lace.

James agreed, rubbing off more of the orange dust stuck in the webbing between his thumbs and index fingers.

"Do you remember the Halloween Carnival from when you lived here?" Francis asked. There was a strange hint of anxiety in his voice.

"Sure," James said. "All the local businesses can enter a float for a chance to win a cash prize."

Francis shuffled his feet. "Mrs. Kramer would never let us enter a library float. She said we didn't have the necessary funds in our budget, even though Scott and I came up with a design that would only cost three hundred dollars to build."

Sensing where the conversation was heading, James smiled. "So you two want to enter a float in this year's parade?"

"Yes, Professor, we sure do."

"Let me review the budget for this month, but I'm sure we can come up with a few hundred dollars. I think it would be great to have the library represented. We're an important part of this community."

"I suspected you'd be more open-minded. In fact, Scott and I have already prepared a drawing to show you." Francis proffered a roll of paper.

James unfurled the drawing and examined it carefully. He was impressed by what he saw. "This is terrific. Really terrific, Francis. Are you certain that you and Scott can build this on your own? It's not too . . . adventurous?"

Francis looked sheepish. "Actually, we started construction last year in hopes of changing Mrs. Kramer's mind. We just need to add some final touches, like special effects, and we could finish it off in no time. Thanks, Professor! I can't wait to tell Scott the good news." Francis bounded up the steps and went inside. A few seconds later, James followed.

At lunch, he stared at his chef's salad, suddenly feeling very guilty about cheating on his diet. His favorite snack would definitely fall in the category of a high-carb, high-calorie no-no.

"You're really sticking to your plan, Professor," Francis said as he entered the kitchen. He folded his long, lanky form into the chair opposite James and began to eat one of his three peanut butter and banana sandwiches while reading the latest paperback release by Piers Anthony. James was still unenthusiastically picking at his salad when Scott arrived and switched places with Francis, who had consumed his entire meal within five or six minutes. Scott ate two salami and cheese sandwiches, a bag of pretzel twists, and a jelly donut while speed-reading the October issue of *Popular Mechanics*.

Midway through his donut, Scott wiped his sugar-speckled lips with a napkin and shot a nervous glance at his boss. "Sorry, Professor Henry. I guess it's kind of mean to be eating this kind of stuff in front of you."

"Don't worry, Scott." James sighed. "Just be glad you have the metabolism of a goat."

Scott guffawed heartily. "Because their stomachs have four chambers? Good one, Professor!" He cocked his head to the side. "But did you know that hummingbirds have the fastest metabolism of all animals? I wouldn't want that. If we were like that, we'd have no time to do anything except eat. No reading, no video games, no nothing. Just food, food, food."

At that moment, the phone in James's office began to ring. James was still hypnotized by Scott's last phrase, but finally he bestirred himself, muttered, "The life of a hummingbird sounds pretty good to me," and got up to answer the phone.

"James? Do you have a second?" Lucy asked after they'd exchanged greetings.

The black cloud that had been orbiting James's head disappeared with a poof. "Of course," he said. "What can I do for you?"

"The lab results came back." Lucy paused. "I kind of eavesdropped on Sheriff Huckabee while he talked to the ME in Rockingham. All I heard was the sheriff repeat the word . . . hold on." James heard the rustle of paper. "Sorry. Here it is. Coumadin. Do you know what that is?"

"No idea."

"Well, I can't look it up from work or they'll wonder what I'm doing. Plus, I have to type up the incident report and all of the interviews, even though Keith is supposed to do his own." James could almost feel Lucy shrug at the other end of the line. "Guess it's better this way, because I get to stay in the loop. Do you have time to conduct a quick Internet search? I don't want to keep you from—"

"No problem. The library is quieter than usual today," James assured her. "And though I'm not positive, Coumadin sounds like the name of a drug. Give me a sec and I'll grab a *PDR*."

"A what?"

"It's a hundred-pound book called the *Physicians' Desk Reference*. Stay here. I'll be right back." James set the receiver on the desk as gently as if he were placing a bird's egg back in its nest. He grabbed the blue tome from the reference section and returned to his desk, his lethargy completely gone. Glancing through the index, he spotted Coumadin under the heading "Blood Modifiers." He picked up the phone again. "Lucy? Looks like it's a kind of blood thinner." He scanned the microscopic font describing Coumadin's uses. "Comes in tablet form or can be injected. If I'm translating this medical-speak correctly, it looks like people are mostly given Coumadin after they've had heart valve replacement or after suffering a heart attack. I believe that's what *myocardial infarction* means."

"Weird," Lucy said after a moment. "I doubt Brinkley had heart problems. He was a football star in high school, and after graduation, he mowed lawns all day long. Doesn't sound like someone with a heart condition to me. What would Coumadin have to do with his sudden death?"

"I don't know. It doesn't make much sense to me either."

Lucy seemed to be lost in thought. After a pause, she sighed. "I'll have to just wait and see, I guess. Continue to sit here and answer phone calls about lost pets or flat tires until one of the *real* deputies gives me a report to type or something." Her voice trembled a little, as if she might begin to cry out of sheer frustration. When James failed to respond, she said, "Thanks for your help. See you Sunday," and was gone.

James held the receiver aloft until a recording blared from the earpiece suggesting that, should he like to make a call, he should hang up and try again. James put the phone down and thought back to the many times when his wife had been upset about something that had happened at work, and how he'd never succeeded in comforting her. He'd tried. He'd listened to her complain and offered suggestions and sympathy, but if she started to cry, he'd go mute. He always seemed to shut down in the face of a woman's tears. James didn't know whether Lucy had been on the verge of crying or not, but he knew his knee-jerk reaction of stunned silence had taken a hold of him when Lucy most needed to hear him speak. His inability to think of the perfect thing to say to her upset him. He was going to have to be especially attentive and charming on Sunday to make it up to her—two character traits he had never been known for.

James was just about to return to the circulation desk, when Scott tapped him on the shoulder.

"You've got something on your pants, Professor."

Looking down at his clean khakis, James saw nothing amiss.

"On the back." Scott pointed at his own flat derriere.

James craned his neck over his shoulder and still saw nothing. Excusing himself, he went into the men's room and turned his back to the mirror. There, on his wide bottom, were two perfect handprints made of orange dust. James sighed and dampened a paper towel with water. Rubbing at his pants while watching himself in the mirror, he noted that tiny dots of white paper towel were now sticking to his pants along with the orange dust. He moved closer and closer to the mirror above the sink until his rear end was practically hanging in the bowl. He was so focused on his reflection that he didn't hear the door to the restroom open.

An older man took three steps forward and then stopped. He gasped in shock at the sight of the head librarian thrusting his buttocks toward the mirror. The man mumbled something about "weirdos and perverts," turned on his heel, and exited with haste. James groaned. He'd never be able to look that patron in the face again.

This is my punishment for cheating on my diet, he thought.

• • •

Over the weekend, James tried to stick to the plan. When Sunday evening rolled around, signaling the end of a gray and rainy week that seemed to have dampened the spirits of everyone in Quincy's Gap, he decided to stop by Dolly's Diner and pick up one of her famous After Church Pot Roast specials for his father's dinner. The diner was abuzz with a pleasant combination of music and the hum of lively conversation. Silverware clinked, people chatted between booths, and Dolly bustled about, laughing with enough gusto to make her mighty bosom shake beneath her "Kiss My Okra" apron. She bagged James's order and pinched his cheek before sending him on his way.

At home, Jackson eyed the takeout container with a frown. "What's this?" he demanded, sniffing the lid as if the package was filled with fresh manure.

"Pot roast." James opened the fridge. "There's a bowl of Caesar salad in there for you, too. I'll be back around tenish."

"You got some kind of hot date tonight?" Jackson cackled gleefully. "Maybe she could come over and fix our leaky roof instead of you wastin' your money throwin' food down her neck."

"I told you, Pop. I'm in a supper club," James said as he glanced at the two plastic buckets sitting on the counter. He'd used them to catch the water seeping in through the ceiling of the upstairs bathroom and hallway. James knew that the entire roof needed to be replaced, but he didn't have enough money in his savings account to pay for it. In fact, he was completely supporting himself and his father on his librarian's salary. Jackson never offered his son any money and didn't even glance at the bills in the mail pile, most of which were in his name. James didn't know if his father even owned a credit card anymore.

"There are five of us altogether. There will be *three* women at the meeting tonight, and they're all lovely and intelligent and happy to call me friend," James added proudly.

Jackson's caterpillar-like eyebrows crawled higher on his forehead in a mocking expression. "Oh, yeah, the *Fat* Club."

"Not for long, Pop. We'll have a new name soon enough." Hurt by his father's nastiness, James reached for his raincoat. It was an old coat, left in his closet during a visit home several years ago. James now found that he couldn't zip it all the way. Jackson smirked and anger whirled up from deep with James. It swirled like a tornado until he opened his mouth and yelled, "At least I'm getting out of the house! What are you doing with you life, Pop? Do you think Ma would have wanted you to sit inside that shed doing God knows what? Or waste the rest of your life watching game shows? *You're* more of a ghost than she is, and she's the one who died!"

Both men were taken aback by the fury in James's voice. He had never spoken to his father in such a tone. Jackson's eyes flashed with a mixture of ire and pain, and before his father could deliver one of his scathing responses, James fled.

Because of the exchange with his father, James was the last one to arrive at Lucy's house. He was still fuming, and he kept replaying how he'd screamed at his remaining parent until he felt both ashamed and liberated at once. His father was obviously having trouble dealing with his wife's death, and James should be more sympathetic. And yet he had spent a lifetime accepting his father's criticism and dour moods without saying a word, and he was simply growing tired of being treated like an uninvited houseguest. Especially when he, James, was taking care of everything on his father's behalf.

James breathed in deeply and tried to expel what Gillian would call his negative energy. It was time to join his friends. Sitting in the truck, he took a moment to study Lucy's clapboard farmhouse. It was painted a cheerful butter yellow and had teal-green shutters. Two large planters filled with sedum and marigolds flanked the front door and an ancient maple tree dropped fiery leaves all over the front steps leading up to the small porch, where Lucy had installed a porch swing and a pair of white wicker rockers. Three lopsided pumpkins squatted on the porch swing, covering up several large rust-colored stains. The house and the outdoor furnishings all looked like they could do with a fresh coat of paint.

Mail was overflowing from the black metal mailbox affixed to the front door and dead leaves blew across a ratty doormat. The word "Welcome" was so faded that only the "l" and the "o" were discernible. The lawn had an air of neglect and Lucy's dormant azalea bushes were in dire need of pruning.

As James approached the house using an uneven brick walkway pocked with weeds, a ferocious chorus of barking erupted from behind a chain-link fence. This barricade surrounded a seemingly endless backyard, where dense woods suddenly swallowed the dandelion- and thistle-speckled lawn. Lucy materialized at the front door and held the screen door open for him.

"Come on in." She smiled thinly. James noticed that the skin beneath her eyes looked swollen, as if she had been crying or had had too little sleep. He wondered if the diet was taking a big toll on her.

"I like your house," James said brightly, trying to boost her spirits.

"Thanks. It was my grandparents' place. Built in 1939." She beckoned him to join the others in the kitchen. "They raised four kids in a two-bedroom house. I've managed to fill it up all by myself, though. I'm kind of a pack rat."

"Don't forget your roommates, the Hounds of Hell," said Bennett, coming forward to greet James. "What are their names again?"

"Benatar, Bono, and Bon Jovi, after the three greatest band leaders of the eighties." Lucy's eyes twinkled for a second. "The best decade of music in history."

James wasn't so sure of that, but wisely decided to keep quiet.

Lucy's kitchen was decorated in shades of blue and white. She collected blue pottery roosters and had an array of ivory-colored cow creamers displayed on a baker's rack. There were a number of dirty dishes in the sink, and a pile of *Cosmopolitan* magazines looked like they had been hastily dumped on top of the refrigerator.

Gillian was preparing their side dish—faux mashed potatoes. Every few seconds she stopped stirring in order to yank the bottom of her mango-colored turtleneck over her love handles. Yet, no matter how much she tugged, the shirt was too short. It snapped up after each tug like a roller shade. Whenever she raised her arm to stir the mashed vegetable, a pale fold of skin would poke out above the waistline of her pants. Finally, Gillian gave up and let her flesh hang out.

"I *am* among friends," she murmured to herself.

"What's actually in this dish, Gillian?" Lindy gazed into the steaming pot, unconsciously pulling her own shirt down over her round bottom. "It smells really good."

"It's in this menu packet James made for us. See?" Gillian pointed to the recipe.

The Flab Five's Phony Mashed Potatoes

1 head of fresh cauliflower
1 1/2 teaspoons minced garlic
1 teaspoon rosemary
1 tablespoon whipped cream cheese
1/4 cup grated Parmesan cheese
A generous sprinkle of salt and pepper
1/8 teaspoon chicken bouillon powder
1 tablespoon of butter substitute such as Smart Beat or Smart Balance

Boil cauliflower for five to six minutes until soft. Drain water. Using a potato masher or large spoon, mash the cauliflower while slowly adding in the rest of the ingredients. Don't use an electric mixer or food processor — it won't taste as good. Plus, mashing by hand burns calories! Makes 4 servings.

Gillian paused in her mixing. "I was only supposed to use one tablespoon of butter substitute but I used two. I really like the flavor of butter."

Bennett placed two bottles of diet soda on the counter. "You look like you could make this in your sleep."

Gillian beamed. "I actually did a trial run last night because I was feeling a little anxious about cooking for others." She cast a sideways glance at the packages of red meat sitting in the sink. "In fact, I doubled this recipe. *I* will not be partaking in the shameful consumption of innocent animals this evening," she added theatrically.

"Super. James and I will split the extra steak." Bennett nudged James in the arm. "Right?"

Lindy scowled at Bennett for being insensitive and patted Gillian's shoulder. "Looks like you've done a great job with our side dish. Bennett and I shared the cost of the meat, but I was in charge of prepping the steaks. I just coated them with a Southwestern meat rub, and now they're ready for the grill. I picked the ones with the least amount of fat. Bennett, did you bring the herb butter?"

Bennett bowed with a toothy grin. "I surely did, ma'am. Half cup butter substitute, one teaspoon rosemary, one teaspoon parsley, and a sprinkle of garlic salt. I then rolled them into balls with a spoon. They'll melt nice and fast on those hot steaks. That is, if the dogs don't attack me on the way to the grill."

"Don't worry, I'll protect you. Grab those tongs and let's get out there. I'm starving." Lucy led Bennett to the deck, where her grill was warmed and ready to cook their sirloin steaks.

A few minutes later, the supper club toasted their first meal together with glasses of diet soda. They agreed to put off the discussion of their weight-loss progress (or lack thereof) until after the meal. As they ate Caesar salad, cauliflower mashed potatoes, and steak with herb butter, the conversation naturally drifted toward the most interesting event of everyone's week: Brinkley's death.

"So what's new with the Case of the Has-Been Football Star, Ms. Sheriff?" Lindy asked Lucy.

Without warning Lucy's lip began to quiver. She looked utterly miserable and was clearly trying to get a handle on her emotions. A pregnant silence descended over the table as the four friends stared at Lucy.

Lindy put an arm around Lucy's shoulders. "Lucy, honey. What is it?"

Lucy sniffed and tucked a strand of hair behind her ear. "I'm sorry. I really don't mean to ruin our time together. I've been trying to act normal all night, but, oh, I might as well tell you. The sheriff plans to arrest Whitney Livingstone tomorrow on suspicion of murder."

"What?" Gillian squeaked, dropping her fork onto her empty plate with a clatter.

"The only reason she's not in jail right now is that the sheriff is hosting a family reunion tonight. First thing tomorrow, though, he's going to pick her up."

"That's absurd!" Lindy banged her fists on the table. "That girl wouldn't hurt a soul! Are you saying that Huckabee actually believes that Whitney is Brinkley Myers's killer?"

"The man must be suffering from delusions," Gillian said.

James looked at Lucy. "Do the sheriff's suspicions have anything to do with Coumadin?"

"Isn't that a drug?" Bennett asked and frowned at James. "What do you know about this that we don't?"

James hastily explained Lucy's telephone call on Thursday and gave a brief definition of Coumadin and its uses.

Lucy released a mournful sigh. "The problem is, Whitney's daddy is the only person in Quincy's Gap currently taking Coumadin. He had a massive heart attack earlier this year and needed emergency surgery. I remember Mrs. Livingstone telling me that her husband had required a heart valve replacement. According to Donovan's interview with the pharmacist, Mr. Livingstone was prescribed Coumadin following that surgery. According to Donovan's notes, the blood thinner would help prevent clots from forming on Mr. Livingstone's new valve. Donovan believes Whitney gave Brinkley the entire contents of her daddy's bottle."

James shook his head in disbelief. "So Whitney's father used the drug, and Whitney wasn't fond of Brinkley. Those are pretty circumstantial pieces of evidence. There were no eyewitnesses, right?" Lucy shook her head. "How can an arrest be made on such insubstantial facts?"

"There's more," Lucy said, clearly reluctant to continue.

"Let me hazard a guess," Bennett said. "It was what she said yesterday at Dolly's that did her in, wasn't it?"

Lucy looked at him in surprise. "How did you know?"

"I was there," Bennett said. Seeing the perplexed expressions of his tablemates, Bennett hurried to explain. "I only work until noon on Saturdays, and I always go to Dolly's for lunch after my shift. I had a package to deliver to Clint so I went in through the kitchen door. I could see Whitney working behind the counter. She was waiting on three customers. Two of them were football players who were apparently loading up on huge cheeseburgers before last night's game, and the third was Lucy's favorite person since Milli Vanilli, Deputy Keith Donovan."

"Who, in this strange and wonderful world, is Milli Vanilli?" asked Gillian, momentarily distracted from the main narrative.

"Pseudo-rock star brothers from the eighties. They had cool hair, hot bods, and got busted for lip-synching during a live show," Lindy replied. "Go on, Bennett."

Bennett took a swallow of Diet Dr. Pepper and continued. "As Whitney was handing a check to the football players, one of them asked if she missed Brinkley. She looked as though she wanted to shoot missiles from her eyeballs, but she kept her cool and said, 'No, why should I?' and then got busy brewing a fresh pot of coffee. From what I gathered from the rest of their conversation, those boys thought Whitney was one of Brinkley's girlfriends."

"Ha! Whitney is way too good for a jerk like Brinkley!" Lindy said.

"That's about what she said, in slightly cruder terms," Bennett said. "But the boys wouldn't let up. They taunted her, saying, 'Brinkley told us that he was going to meet you behind the movie theater so you could give him what he had coming.'" Bennett tugged on his toothbrush mustache. "My mama would have put all those boys over her knee if she heard the rest of what they hinted at."

"And Deputy Donovan just sat there and let those boys insult her?" James asked. It was a man's duty to intervene when a young lady was being disrespected. Then James remembered how the deputy had done nothing to stop Brinkley's insinuating remarks to Whitney on Homecoming Day.

Lucy's face was flushed with anger. "The man is a walking toad. As the town's foremost chauvinist, Donovan was probably enjoying every minute of it. He loves to see any woman put down."

"If we could all just learn to love one another!" Gillian wailed.

Ignoring this outburst, Bennett turned to Lucy. "He did seem to be wearing a sheep-eating grin."

"So is that what prompted the sheriff to target Whitney?" James asked. "A bunch of boys gossiping about their buddy and his supposed love life?"

"No," Lucy said very softly. "Whitney leaned over the counter and grabbed one of the boy's shirts. She practically pulled him out of his chair, she was so spitting mad. She yelled, 'I'm glad that son of a bitch is dead! I hope it was slow and painful and bloody as hell!'"

There was a long stretch of silence.

"She said all that right in front of Donovan." Lucy gave her friends a mournful look. "And then he finds out about her daddy's Coumadin, and, well, Whitney's in a heap of trouble."

"So she hated Brinkley for how he treated her." Lindy threw her hands in the air. "Who wouldn't? That doesn't mean she killed the boy."

"I've got to find a way to help her." Lucy cast a desperate glance around the table. "Any ideas?"

"Do you have access to the prison cells? Could you talk with her privately after she's brought in?" James asked.

Lucy raised an eyebrow. "I think so. Why?"

"The more we all know about Whitney and her relationship to Brinkley, whatever it was, the more we'll be able to form a clear picture about them. I don't think we'll be of much use without knowing the real story."

"That's true," Bennett agreed. "But aside from trying to clear this little lady's name, we need to put our sights on who could have given Brinkley the Coumadin instead of Whitney."

"Exactly!" Lindy cried. "Do you know when someone supposedly slipped him blood thinners, Lucy?"

"Yes, sometime during his meal at Dolly's Diner. I read the ME's report. It was just sitting on Donovan's desk, and while he was out for one of his two-hour lunch breaks, I had a chance to take notes on all the important points." Lucy smiled a little at the memory.

"I'll ask Dolly if she noticed anyone near Brinkley's food after Clint plated it. You never know," Bennett said.

"And I'll discreetly question a few of my current students to find out who Brinkley's enemies were," Lindy said.

"And who he hung out with," Gillian added. "I know the mamas of these high school boys come into my shop. The Yuppie Puppy is a hotbed for gossip. If I bring up Brinkley's name, I'm certain to hear some *very* colorful tales."

James wanted to prove his willingness to assist, but he couldn't think of a useful suggestion. "Do you want me to come with you to see Whitney? I could bring her some books and magazines to read." He cleared his throat. "And give you moral support."

"Great idea, James! I'll send along some prayer beads and a healing crystal. That girl's going to need all the help she can get," Gillian said.

Lucy smiled. "Thanks, guys. I feel so lucky to be in your company tonight. I may have only lost two pounds this week, but look what I've gained. Four amazing friends."

"Two pounds is wonderful!" Lindy shouted. "I lost four."

"Make that three for me," Gillian added.

"Me too," said James. "Bennett?"

Bennett's dark eyes twinkled. "Five big ones!"

"Good for you, Bennett. Though, truth be told, I guess I was expecting a more dramatic loss," Lindy said. "Still, I cheated once or twice this week. Being on a low-carb diet is much harder than I thought it would be."

James listened as his friends admitted to having cheated on their food plans by eating their favorite treats at least once.

"What about you, James? Any cheese puffs?"

"Four snack bags," he confessed. "I felt really hungry in the middle of the afternoon, and I didn't want celery, or an egg, or whatever I was supposed to have. I wanted something that tasted really good. Something satisfying."

"Amen to that. Speaking of cravings, what's for dessert, James?" Lindy asked hopefully.

"Sugar-free chocolate pudding."

There was a collective sigh of resignation.

"We should be proud of this week's weight loss," Gillian said while they ate their pudding. "But I think we could do even better."

"We need to start exercising," Lindy said.

"I've been reading this book," Gillian went on. "It's called *Filling Your Life With Light*. The author suggests that when you make any kind of life-altering goal, you should use something physical to keep you on track. Most people need visual reminders of what they're trying to achieve. But I—"

"What kind of reminder would we use?" Lindy quickly asked before Gillian could get too much wind in her sails.

Gillian clasped her hands together as if in prayer. "We could all bring a piece of clothing to our next dinner. Something that we can't wear now, but hope to fit in within, say, two months."

"What would your special garment be, Gillian?"

"Oh, I have this psychedelic tank top that I got on a trip to San Francisco. The thing is, it's got horizontal stripes." She placed her hands around her torso. "Right now, I am a human barrel supported by a pair of legs. I want smaller arms and a waist that is narrower than my hips, not the other way around. When I have a waist again, I will wear that top."

"Okay." Lindy smiled. "I've got something I'd like to wear one day as well. This is a great idea, Gillian. I like the idea of fitting into clothes as our goal instead of seeking certain numbers on the scale."

"Whose house should we go to next week?" James asked, hoping his voice gave no indication of his inner turmoil. Eventually, he would have to invite the supper club members to his place. That would mean introducing the Flab Five to his father, and he was not looking forward to that meeting.

"We can use mine," Bennett offered. "It's small, but there's room enough."

Lindy put a hand on top of Lucy's. "Please email us after you talk to Whitney. We'll all do everything we can to help her, and that means we might need to get together before next Sunday."

"After James and I visit her tomorrow, I'm hoping to have something new to share with Sheriff Huckabee. Something that will prove Whitney's innocence."

"If she's innocent," James said very quietly.

Not quietly enough, however. Four pairs of eyes made it very clear that he had just ended their evening on a most unpleasant note.

Chapter Six

String Cheese

Quincy's Gap had only one jail. It had occupied the basement of the old brick courthouse since the early 1800s. James had dawdled at the library, unable to decide which books or magazines would be appropriate to bring to an incarcerated young woman. Finally, he'd appealed to the twins for help and now carried a paper grocery bag filled with beauty and celebrity magazines, as well as a copy of Mitch Albom's *The Five People You Meet in Heaven.*

"That's to give her hope," Francis had said when he handed James the book.

"Good luck, Professor Henry." Scott had spoken gravely, as if his boss were headed off to war. "We've known Whitney for years. Not well, you know. But she likes fantasy books and science fiction, and we talk about that kind of stuff with her. There's no way that girl hurt anyone."

"Yeah. She's always been really nice to us," Francis had added, implying that not all women their age were as kind as Whitney.

"I'll make sure to send her your regards," James had said before leaving the library.

At twelve thirty, Lucy appeared at the top of the white slate steps leading up to the courthouse. She wanted to spend a few minutes with Whitney before Keith Donovan returned from lunch. Keith was treating himself to a meal at the Italian restaurant, Il Pomodoro, to celebrate his excellent police work. If Keith returned to discover that Lucy wasn't seated at her desk, ready to answer the phone or attend to his smallest whim, he might discover that she was visiting Whitney. For now, Lucy wanted to keep her investigation hidden from Keith.

"Being head librarian has a distinct advantage over my old job," James said as he and Lucy stepped into the courthouse lobby. "I can take an extra-long lunch break if I want without having to rush back. My teaching schedule at William and Mary wasn't that onerous, but my office hours and the endless number of department and staff meetings often made me feel trapped. Here, I can take a two-hour lunch if I want and make up that hour later in the afternoon. And it's nice to leave knowing the library is in good hands."

"I wish I had some of that freedom," Lucy said wistfully. "But let's worry about getting Whitney hers first."

James followed Lucy down a dimly lit stairwell leading to the basement. There were storerooms, filing areas, and holding cells in the chilly space. A sleepy deputy sat at a wooden desk guarding the entrance to the cells.

"Good morning, Glenn." Lucy offered the man a dazzling smile. "I brought you some Krispy Kremes. You been here all night?"

"Yep." The young deputy sat up straighter and examined the box of donuts. "Chocolate frosted. Thank you, kindly."

"Professor Henry, this is Deputy Glenn Truett. Glenn, Professor Henry has brought Whitney some magazines and library books. We'd like to take them to her and see how she's doing. That okay?"

Glenn was already happily occupied with his breakfast. Wiping his hands on a paper napkin, he did his duty by taking a quick glance through the bag of books and magazines. He paused for a long moment to admire a photo of Angelina Jolie in a low-cut dress on the cover of *Cosmopolitan*, then led Lucy and James to Whitney's cell. She was in the third cell to the right. The other cells were empty, save one. A middle-aged man splayed on a narrow cot occupied the last cell to the left. He was snoring like a locomotive, and a rank smell of stale beer and body odor snuck out from between the bars of his cell.

"Wilbur's sleeping off another one?" Lucy asked in a conspiratorial whisper.

"Yep. Gotta keep him away from his old lady when he gets like this. How's ten minutes, Lucy? It's not officially visiting hours yet." Glenn unlocked Whitney's cell. The young woman had her face buried in her hands and did not even look up as the barred door slid open with a squeak.

"Ten minutes will be just fine, thanks." Lucy gave Glenn another grateful smile.

"I'll give a holler when it's time," Glenn called over his shoulder, hustling back to his box of donuts.

"That's some willpower, Lucy," James said with admiration as they waited for the deputy to return to his desk. "Having Krispy Kremes that close to you."

"Believe me, I was very tempted," Lucy said under her breath as they stepped into the cell. Lucy leaned over the cot and put a hand on Whitney's shoulder.

"Whitney," she whispered. "Look at me, hon. We don't have much time."

The young woman reluctantly met Lucy's eyes. "I already told the sheriff that I didn't kill Brinkley." Whitney's face was blotchy from crying. "I don't know who did, but it wasn't me."

"And I'm here to tell you that I believe you. Of course, I'm not a deputy, but I'd like to help you. We both would. You've met Professor Henry, right?"

Whitney sat up a tad straighter and managed a small smile for James. "I'm glad you've come, but I'm not sure what you can do for me." She gave a resigned shrug.

"You're wondering how we can help, right?" Lucy said and then signaled for James to take a seat on a stool in the corner of the cell. "We don't know either, and we can't promise to get you out of here, but we'd like to try. In order for this to succeed, you'll need to be totally honest with us, okay?"

James was impressed by Lucy's gentle, forward manner. He watched Whitney's shoulders relax and her creased forehead slacken as she placed her trust in them.

"The whole town knows that Brinkley Myers was a horse's ass, pardon my language," Lucy began. "And that afternoon at Dolly's, before the football game, he was harassing you, right?"

Whitney nodded.

"Did he do stuff like that all the time?" Lucy asked.

"Only when he had an audience," Whitney said. "He didn't have much to say to me when no one else was around. He was a show-off. If he didn't have an audience, he wouldn't bother acting out, ya know?"

"Sure as the crow flies." Lucy paused for a moment. "I'm sorry, but I have to know. Were you and Brinkley ever an item?"

"God, no!" Whitney was clearly appalled. "I may not be in school full-time now, but I'm going to finish college and get a good job. I'm only going to date men who have the same ambitions as me. Brinkley wanted to do as little work as possible and still act like the town's greatest gift." She clenched her fists. "Trust me, the only feeling I have ever felt toward Brinkley Myers was one of disgust. I hated the guy, but I didn't kill him."

Lucy put up her hands in a placating gesture. "Just checking. I didn't really think you were together. Not for a second. You're a class act, Whitney." She smiled. "Okay, back to homecoming Saturday. Did you serve Brinkley his meal?"

"No, Dolly did. I was busy behind the counter for most of my shift. The professor was pretty much my last table on the floor."

Lucy shot James a curious glance and then focused on Whitney again. "Do you know what Brinkley ordered?"

"Everyone had the same order. Meat loaf, mashed potatoes with gravy, and collard greens. That's what Dolly always serves for homecoming. No one is allowed to order off the menu. Dolly is very superstitious about that meal. She says that we always win if the whole town eats her meat loaf before the homecoming game."

"That's true." Lucy laughed. "I had forgotten all about the Victory Loaf." She grinned. "And neither Clint nor Dolly bore any grudge against Brinkley?"

Whitney waved the suggestion off. "You know them, they love everybody."

"Isn't that the truth?" Lucy nodded in agreement. "How about other young women your age? Was he ever obnoxious to your peers?"

Whitney looked down at her hands. "I imagine so, but I don't know which girls in particular."

"Hmm." Lucy gazed around the cell, unseeing. "Guess it still keeps coming back to your daddy's pills. You never touched them?"

"Never." Whitney's voice grew steely. "Daddy keeps them in his bathroom, and I wouldn't go through his things, let alone steal them and then use them to commit murder."

Lucy allowed silence to fill the cell. Finally, she turned to James. "Professor? Can you think of anything else we should be asking Whitney?"

James shook his head, feeling immensely useless. He handed Whitney the bag of books and magazines.

"Hang in there," he said kindly, and gave her a paternal pat on the back.

Abruptly, Whitney clamped a hand on his arm and squeezed, as if trying to communicate her fear and desperation through touch. "Thanks so much for coming. It's really nice to know that a few people believe that I'm not, that I could never . . ." Her eyes welled up with tears.

"Time's up!" Glenn barked down the short hall.

"I'll be back, Whitney. You won't be here long. Not if we can help it." Lucy gave the younger woman a hug.

Glenn shut and locked the cell door and then led them back down the corridor, jingling his key ring and humming as he walked.

Having consumed three donuts, Glenn was now more interested in Lucy's visit than he'd been before. "What were you and our prisoner chatting about?" he asked, picking his teeth with a toothpick.

"Just books," James blurted quickly. "Whitney's a voracious reader."

The spark of curiosity in Glenn's eyes died immediately.

"Good thinking," Lucy said when they were safely out of earshot.

James felt a rush of pleasure. "It was nothing," he said and smiled at her.

When they reached the lobby, they were both out of breath from having climbed the steep steps from the basement. Lucy pushed a damp lock of hair from her cheek and said, "I've got to go back to work, but would you be willing to meet me afterward to pay a visit to Whitney's parents?"

"Do you think they held something back? Something they didn't want to tell the sheriff?" James wanted to accompany Lucy again, but he didn't like the idea of causing Whitney's parents more pain.

"It can't hurt to talk to them. We've got to learn every detail if we want to have a complete picture of what happened," she said, her face pink with exertion. "That's how all of the world's great detectives work."

Lucy offered to collect James at the library after her shift was over.

Five hours later, he waited in the lobby—hungry, excited, and trying his hardest to ignore the celestial glow of the snack machine. He'd forgotten to pack the green apple and Tupperware of peanut butter meant for his afternoon snack, and his stomach was complaining loudly. James pictured himself inserting a dollar bill into the snack machine over and over again, but he didn't act on his fantasy. Lucy's imminent arrival prevented him from indulging in another bag of cheese puffs. Still, his proximity to his favorite treat was driving him crazy, and so he peeked out the front door in search of Lucy's brown Jeep for the third time.

Fifteen minutes past the time she promised to arrive, Lucy pulled into the parking lot and honked the horn.

Slightly irritated, James opened the door to what appeared to be Lucy's garbage can on wheels. Empty paper cups covered the floor mat, and a pile of papers, fast food bags, and receipts prevented him from even seeing the surface of the passenger seat.

"Sorry," Lucy said, hastily scooping up the debris from the seat and hurling it into the back.

Reluctantly, James climbed in. He was a man who cherished neatness and order. He cast a sideways glance at Lucy. Her caramel hair was pulled back in an untidy ponytail and her turquoise blouse, which was so tight that James could see glimpses of skin in between the straining buttons, had several stains along the neckline. Her fingernails were even but were polished a shade of garish red that had chipped or been chewed off. Studying her from the corner of his eye, James began to wonder if he was really compatible with someone as sloppy as Lucy.

They pulled up in front of the Livingstones' brick house a few minutes later. Lucy had thoughtfully brought some pumpkin muffin tops from the Sweet Tooth as a gift for Whitney's parents.

"They're open for business again?" James asked, pointing at the bakery box.

"Oh, yes. They opened first thing Tuesday morning. Megan's a single mom and can't afford to stay closed, so as soon as she was given permission, she disinfected the place from top to bottom and started baking up a storm."

"And the sheriff? He allowed that?"

Lucy shrugged and reached out to ring the doorbell. "Guess he felt there was no more evidence to be found once the paramedics had removed the body."

James was about to ask what had happened to Brinkley's cell phone when a woman in her late forties with Whitney's ash blonde hair and heart-shaped face opened the front door. Wringing her hands, she took a step back and invited them inside. "We sure appreciate you visiting our gal this morning, Miss Hanover. Not many folks are willing to call us friends right now."

"Please, call me Lucy. This is James Henry, our new librarian. He's also interested in Whitney's welfare." She handed Mrs. Livingstone the box of muffin tops.

"Thank you, kindly." She offered James her hand. "I'm Caroline. Sorry we haven't met yet, Mr. Henry, but I'm not much of a reader." She smiled apologetically and led them to a living room that seemed to belong to an earlier decade. The floral fabric on the sofa, chairs, throw pillows, and curtains was worn, but the room was clean and had a comfortable, lived-in air.

"This is my husband, Beau." A middle-aged man with receding hair and a beer belly pushed himself out of a faded leather recliner and switched off the TV. He gave James a powerfully firm handshake and thanked Lucy profusely for the muffins.

"We told the deputy everything we know, which is basically nothing." Caroline shrugged to illustrate her confusion. "But feel free to ask us anything you want. We'd rather talk than sit here feeling guilty. If only we had the bail money, but we just couldn't raise it . . ." She trailed off, embarrassed. "We're trying to borrow some cash from my sister, but she's got her own share of troubles."

Beau cleared his throat and touched his chest. "We just don't have a nest egg anymore after all of the medical bills."

Lucy clucked her tongue in sympathy. "This might seem like going back a ways, but could you tell us about your surgery? I want to understand every nuance about Coumadin and its uses."

Beau nodded. "Absolutely. It's easier to talk to you two, anyway. That Keith Donovan fellow came in here and started acting like he owned the place. He strutted around like a big shot, trying to scare us into making a confession. We didn't have anything to confess!" He stopped to collect himself. "Me getting mad won't help my little girl, so let me answer your question. As you probably know, I was a roofer. Ran my own business for over twenty years," he added proudly. "Things were going along just swell. We had enough put by to send Whitney to James Madison and were saving up more for my retirement. I wanted to quit early enough to take Caroline to some real nice places. She's always wanted to travel."

James could see Caroline smiling at her husband with a mixture of pride and sorrow.

"One day last spring—I had just come down off the ladder, thank the Lord—when this pain shot up my left arm like an electric shock. Don't remember a thing until I woke up in the hospital the next day, and the doctor told me I'd had a heart attack. He said he gave me a new heart valve, the mechanical kind, and that he had to tell me some bad news." Beau paused, no doubt recalling the exact conversation. His eyes went to his lap, and James could feel the painful memory coursing through the older man. His heart went out to him, but once again he had no idea what to say, or how to gently coax the difficult narrative along.

"It's all right, Beau. I'll take it from here." Caroline put her hand on top of her husband's. "The doc told us that Beau had suffered a stroke during the surgery. His heart was going to be fine, but his balance would never be the same again. They said he could never go up on another roof. They don't even want him to drive. So he sold his business to George Dundy, his right-hand man, and now Beau's working real hard doing odd jobs. Anything to keep us fed and pay the mortgage."

James filled the silence following Caroline's explanation with his first question. "And you've been taking the Coumadin since the spring?"

"Five milligrams a day," Beau said.

"That's a bottle per month?" Lucy asked. When Beau nodded, she frowned. "Is there any chance that you lost one or purchased an extra bottle by accident?"

Caroline laughed at the suggestion. "Mr. Goodbee would have your head if he heard you say that in his drugstore."

"I know he would." Lucy grinned. "Still, you never lost one?"

"No." Beau sighed morosely. "It's the same question that keeps circling in my head. And to be honest, my memory just isn't what it was before that stroke. I didn't tell that deputy that I have some gaps because he'd just use it against my little girl."

Caroline patted her husband's hand again. "Sweetheart, you can't blame yourself for what happened. You didn't bring on your stroke, and you didn't get Whitney arrested." Her voice trembled when she spoke her daughter's name.

"Who else should I blame then?" Beau roared, causing everyone to jump. "Who? My child is in a cell! I'm here, comfy as you please, while my daughter is in jail!" His anger subsided as quickly as it had flared. He collapsed into his chair and rubbed his face with calloused hands. "I'm sorry. I know you folks are trying to help."

"Why don't I make us all some coffee?" Caroline said softly. "A friend of mine went to New Orleans and brought me back a can of the good stuff."

Suddenly, Lucy's eyes lit up. "Wait a minute, Mrs. Livingstone. Did you and your husband go anywhere after Beau was released from the hospital? Any trips out of town?"

Caroline pursed her lips and considered. "I don't think so." She seemed to vanish into the past for a moment and then she snapped her fingers. "Yes! We did go out of town. We went to Baltimore for the weekend for my sister's anniversary party. Remember, Beau?"

Beau shot out of his chair like a rocket. "That's right! I forgot to bring my pills along that weekend. I never packed them!" His excitement was contagious. He turned to his wife. "Do you remember? You reminded me so many times, and I still left them in our bathroom."

"Oh, my stars, I certainly do. We had to go to one of those twenty-four-hour pharmacies to get you a refill."

James could feel the energy flowing through the room. It was as if tiny streaks of lightning were filling every person with the radiance of hope.

"Was Whitney home alone?" Lucy asked, doing her best to sound calm.

"Yes. It was Labor Day weekend, a little over a month ago. Whitney had to work most of the weekend, poor darling, but she didn't want to go to that old-folks party anyway." Caroline sank down on the sofa, the coffee forgotten.

James was riveted. He was also thankful for all the noise because it covered up the sounds his stomach was making. It was nearly dinnertime, and since he hadn't had a snack, he was starting to get so hungry that he was having trouble focusing on the conversation.

"I didn't want to go to that party either," Beau muttered. "I wish we'd all stayed home. Maybe none of this would have happened."

"Do you know if Whitney had anyone over that weekend?" James asked. He had to think of something other than the snack machine at the library and its contents of crunchy, savory cheese puffs.

"I never thought to ask," Caroline said. "She's such a responsible girl. If she wanted to have one of her girlfriends over, she could have done so without checking with us first. We've had to demand so much from her as it is." Caroline's eyes filled with unshed tears. "Do you think this discovery could help?"

"I'll talk to Whitney first thing tomorrow morning—find out if anyone else was in your house that weekend. At least this takes some of the heat off her," Lucy assured the Livingstones. "Someone *else* could have taken that bottle of pills from your bathroom."

"That someone would have had to come here first and then showed up at the diner before the homecoming game . . ." James mused aloud.

"If we can come up with a genuine suspect, they'll have to release Whitney," Lucy said.

Beau and Caroline thanked them both for coming, their faces uplifted with the knowledge that there was hope for their daughter. The couple decided to pay a visit to Sheriff Huckabee in the morning, explaining that they'd remembered a crucial detail. The fact that someone could have gained access to their house and to Beau's bottle of Coumadin could convince the sheriff of Whitney's innocence. Or at least her lack of guilt.

"We never lock the house," Caroline said. "It's one of the reasons we live in a town like this. Most of our neighbors don't lock their doors either."

James nodded. He'd grown up having never seen either parent turn the dead bolt on the front door. And during the summers, the only thing separating the inside from the outside was a flimsy screen door. "Folks shouldn't have to lock their doors, ma'am. Don't change your ways."

Caroline beamed at him and waved goodbye as he and Lucy got into her filthy Jeep.

On the way back to the library, Lucy handed James two sticks of mozzarella string cheese.

"Thought you might like a snack."

"Would I? I'm dying!" James devoured one immediately. Lucy did the same. "You know, you're really good at talking to people," he said as she pulled up next to James's old Bronco. "Really. You've got a gift."

Lucy's face glowed with pleasure. She flashed him one of her beautiful smiles, and he forgot all about the slovenly condition of her car.

"We make a good team," she said. "I talk, you listen. You have a gift, too, James. Your presence. You don't even need to say anything. It's like your humbleness, or something. Everyone feels comfortable around you. Safe. It's a nice feeling."

James was completely tongue-tied. After all, his wife had always told him that he was a dull conversationalist—that he needed to pipe up more at social events. He'd always preferred listening, but Jane claimed that he was too much of a wallflower. She even went so far as to say that no one noticed when he left to go home and she stayed behind.

Now, Lucy was actually complimenting him for simply being himself. He was so stunned by how amazing this made him feel that if Lucy had been standing in front of him at that moment, he might have taken her in his arms and kissed her. But she was in her car, and night had fallen as he stood motionless, the passenger door ajar, trying to think of the perfect response to her compliment.

And then, just like that, the moment passed him by.

"Let me know what Whitney says," he murmured to fill the silence. "Give me a call at work."

Lucy assured him that she would. She gave James another smile, but he noticed that it lacked the brightness of her previous smile. Not only that, but her eyes were no longer shining with happiness.

With a brief wave, Lucy drove away without looking back.

Chapter Seven

Candy Corn

There hadn't been a murder in Quincy's Gap since 1913. A few days before Christmas, Barnaby Forrester lost his entire fortune in a high-stakes poker game to one Robbie MacDougal. The game took place at the town's only tavern, and may not have culminated with Forrester shooting MacDougal in the chest with his shotgun had the other man not laughed in his face and called him a fool. Forrester, who had pumped himself full of whiskey for hours, had nothing left to lose, so he grabbed the innkeeper's gun and stopped MacDougal's winning streak for good.

The Shenandoah Star Ledger printed the story of Forrester's crime on the front page for a week straight. It had taken ninety-three years for another murder headline to occupy that prominent position in the county's only daily paper.

Murphy Alistair, reporter and managing editor, had printed the headline LOCAL FOOTBALL STAR SLAIN! in big, bold letters above her cover story. She splashed photos of Brinkley over the next three pages, as well as interior and exterior shots of the Sweet Tooth and a file photo of Megan from the bakery's grand opening. Every day since she'd heard the codes on the police scanner, Murphy had been fervently researching and writing about the untimely death of Brinkley Myers. When Whitney Livingstone was arrested, Murphy's zeal escalated. She'd been waiting for something newsworthy to happen in Quincy's Gap, and now it had.

"Murder," she whispered to herself as she examined a photograph of Whitney. It was a class photo from Whitney's grade-school years. Murphy had chosen to print the image because Whitney wasn't smiling. Instead, she was gazing at something off to the right, and her expression was troubled.

"Perfect." Murphy smiled wickedly and placed the photograph facedown in the scanner. "You should have said 'cheese' like all the other kids, Whitney. Now I've got to show everyone that you were a disturbed ten-year-old."

To say that Murphy was disappointed to learn of Whitney's release would be an understatement, but she was ready and waiting when the young woman was given her freedom Tuesday morning.

Whitney and her parents had just exited through the courthouse doors when Murphy leapt toward them, snapping photos with her digital camera and hurling a barrage of questions until Beau stepped in front of his daughter. Approaching Murphy with an enraged snarl that could have stopped a charging bull in its tracks, he covered the camera lens with his hand. He leaned so close to Murphy that she could smell his spearmint gum.

"Ms. Alistair, my girl has been through enough. We'd like to get her on home, and we'd like you to stop printing pictures of her. If you don't, we're going to visit a lawyer." He gently pushed the camera downward. "This is not the time for your questions. In fact, you're the last person any of us want to see, let alone talk to."

"*The Star Ledger* readers have a right to know what's happening in their county, Mr. Livingstone. And your daughter was falsely accused, right?" Her eyes widened in mock concern. "Don't you want to set the record straight on her behalf? Otherwise, folks might continue believing that she had something to do with Brinkley's murder. If Whitney would tell me her side of the story, I'm sure I could help convince the members of this community that it was all just a big misunderstanding."

Caroline pushed past her husband. "The sheriff and his men jumped to conclusions. So did *you* when you wrote that article about our daughter. Anyone with a lick of sense knows that Whitney would never commit such a terrible crime."

"Of course not!" Murphy exclaimed, switching tactics. "I realize that now." She craned her neck and spoke directly to Whitney. "Miss Livingstone, it must have been horrible to have spent time in jail. Especially when no one in a position of authority would listen to your protests, or believe in your innocence. Would you like to comment on the treatment you received while you were incarcerated?"

"I didn't smile in that school photo because I saw a friend of mine trip as she was passing our classroom door," Whitney said, her eyes flashing with anger. "That's why I looked *troubled*. And that's my only comment."

The Livingstones walked briskly away from the foiled reporter.

"I'll call you at home. I'd just like to get a few quotes!" Murphy called after them. Scurrying inside, she hoped to corner the sheriff or one of the deputies and ruffle them enough to get them to give her a juicy quote about the lack of developments in the Brinkley Myers murder case.

"Or are they sitting around eating donuts and not working on the case at all?" she asked the empty air. Suddenly, her mouth curved into a malicious grin. Nothing stirred up her readers like the belief that their tax dollars were going to waste. "I like that angle. I think I'll run with that on page two of tomorrow's edition."

• • •

As the workweek marched on, another of Murphy Alistair's headlines shouted at James as he tidied the newspaper rack. From WAITRESS FALSELY ACCUSED! on Tuesday to IS QUINCY'S GAP SAFE? on Wednesday, the headlines had everyone in the town on edge.

Emails among the Flab Five flew back and forth like witches on brooms. The first was from Lucy, describing her brief visit to Whitney's cell prior to her release.

> *Dear Fellow Flabs,*
>
> *I saw Whitney this morning and was able to ask if she was alone in her house the entire time her parents were away. She said she worked most of that weekend, which is what her parents said too. Still, I asked her again if she'd had any friends over. She denied it, but there was something in the way she said "no" that makes me believe she's hiding something. I don't know why she'd lie about that to me, but my gut (and it's big enough to know!) feels that something's not right about her story. I got the sense she was protecting someone. A friend? A boyfriend? Lindy, do you remember who Whitney was close to back in high school? It's only been two years since she graduated. Maybe she hangs out with the same crowd.*
>
> *Hope to see you all at the Halloween parade Saturday night. Should we meet somewhere and watch it together?*
> *Lucy*

Lucy's reference to the Halloween parade reminded James that the twins had filled out the paperwork and were officially entering a float in the parade contest. Suddenly anxious that the float wouldn't be ready in time, James left his office and went in search of the twins. He found Scott dusting shelves in the audio/video section.

"We seriously need to update these audiobooks, Professor." Scott pointed at the scant number of plastic book boxes with his duster. "We haven't added a new release to this section since the late nineties. Mrs. Kramer didn't believe in patrons listening to books instead of reading them, and we only have this many because people donated them."

James looked at the scant number of titles and nodded in agreement. "We have several elderly patrons who prefer to listen to books. Especially if they've suffered vision loss. And our large-print section isn't much better."

"Moms like the audiobooks, too," Scott added, nudging his glasses back onto the bridge of his nose. "Sometimes it's hard for them to sit down and read a book aloud to their kids. With a book on tape, their kids can work on their listening skills while the moms get stuff done around the house, like folding laundry or cooking dinner."

"You have amazing insight into the habits of our patrons." James gave Scott a fatherly pat on his scrawny back. "How's the float coming along?"

"Things are going according to schedule, Professor," Scott said, beaming with pride. "We've been working on it until late at night."

James noticed telltale shadows beneath Scott's Coke-bottle glasses. "Listen, why don't you and Francis work half days for the rest of the week? I think the float is great publicity for the library, and you two shouldn't be spending all of your free time building it."

"Really?" Scott blinked in surprise. "But how would that affect our . . ." He looked down at his boat-like feet, clearly trying to phrase his question delicately.

"Your paycheck won't change. I can handle a few solo afternoons. Tell Francis that you can both take off after lunch." James lowered his voice even more than his typical library murmur. "It'll be our secret."

"Yes, sir!" Scott saluted, his face aglow with happiness.

As he dusted the top shelf on his tiptoes, James heard him whisper to the empty space surrounding the audiobooks, "We're going to win that money. Then we'll get more audiobooks, more videos, and maybe, just maybe, a few decent computers!"

On the way back to his office, James surveyed his domain. He loved every inch of the library, but Scott was right. Some of the sections were in desperate need of new titles, and the computers and printers had to be updated. The budget wouldn't allow for any of those things, but if the library float attracted new patrons, perhaps more people would join the Friends' group and the donations would start trickling in.

Lost in dreams of transforming the library, James returned to his desk. He sat down, thinking of how fortunate he was to work with the talented and kindhearted Fitzgerald twins, and then saw that a new email had appeared in his in-box.

> *Dear Dietmates,*
>
> *If we can help Lucy discover the identity of the person Whitney is covering for, then those good old boys down at the sheriff's office might just treat her with respect. I have no idea who Whitney had over at her house that weekend, but I do know that Whitney and Allison Shilling, of Shilling's Stables (you know, the richest family in Quincy's Gap), were best friends when they were seniors at Blue Ridge High.*
>
> *Speaking of friends, it seems like Brinkley had a bunch of girlfriends but really only hung out with one guy. This boy was on the football team with Brinkley. His name is Darryl Jeffries. He works at the gas station over by the highway entrance.*
>
> *That's all the news I have. Did you all see the headlines in the* **Star** *this week? That woman has gone completely nuts!*
>
> *Let's meet outside of Dolly's Diner to watch the parade together. I'll bring us some snacks so all the candy thrown from the floats won't tempt us.*
>
> *'Til then,*
>
> *Lindy*

By the time Saturday arrived, James was worn out. Covering for the twins had been harder than he'd expected. For the first time, he'd had to lead the children's story times. On Wednesday, reading *The Square Pumpkin* to a dozen costumed children under the age of five had been easy. Helping them create and decorate their own square pumpkin trick-or-treat bags had been a huge challenge. Cutting and gluing seemed to be Herculean tasks for his pint-sized audience, and James had never conceived the mess a small child could create when handed a bottle of Elmer's and a bowl of glitter. The craft had barely gotten under way and there was orange glitter covering every surface area of the children's trick-or-treat bags, their clothes, the table, the chairs, and the floor.

And when one of the kids said, "You look like a nice round pumpkin, Mr. Henry. I'll just draw you instead of the square pumpkin," James was mightily tempted to abandon the whole project. Luckily, the mothers all pitched in and helped. They assisted with the coloring and gluing, brought children to the bathroom for hand washing, and passed out Dixie cups of orange Kool-Aid and square pumpkin cookies (graham crackers covered with orange frosting, a smiling licorice rope mouth, and candy corn eyes).

Francis had made the treats during his lunch break the day before, carefully wrapping them with cellophane and hiding them in the fridge inside a brown grocery bag so as not to tempt his boss. James was not to escape temptation so easily, however. A five-year-old girl dressed as Raggedy Ann called him over, removed the candy corns from her cookie, and placed them delicately in James's hand.

"I don't like those," the little girl said in her high, sweet voice. James stared at the candy corns like they were gold nuggets and silently willed himself to carry them to the trash can. The girl looked at him expectantly. "Mommy says not to waste food because there are hungry children in . . . a place I can't remember. Will you eat them so I don't waste them? Pretty, pretty please?" She gazed up at him with imploring eyes, the circular spots of makeup on her cheeks glowing apple-red.

"Of course." James smiled and popped the candy into his mouth.

Relieved, the girl bit into her treat. "Fankoo," she mumbled through a mouthful of cookie, spraying graham cracker crumbs all over the carpet. Her mother, who'd observed the entire exchange, beamed at James as if he had suddenly sprouted wings and a halo.

James conducted two children's story hours on Thursday, followed by an adult book discussion on Alice Hoffman's *The Ice Queen* on Friday. During the book club, two of the older women got into a heated argument over who wrote the fairy tale about the Snow Queen: Hans Christian Andersen or the Brothers Grimm. The rest of the women took sides, and before James knew it, they were bickering about everything from the best brand of laundry detergent to the president's economic policies. After playing referee to the bevy of squabbling women, James was ready to call it a week. He'd done the work of three people, and he sincerely hoped the Fitzgerald brothers were creating a float that would make it all worthwhile. Being so busy had kept him from the snack machine, however, so even though he'd eaten a few candy corn, he'd managed to stay away from his beloved cheese puffs for a record-setting five days.

The scale reflected his good behavior on Saturday morning, and he was delighted to discover that he'd lost another three pounds. That gave him a total of six pounds in two weeks. James had expected a more dramatic loss, but he also knew that he hadn't been totally disciplined when it came to the food plan, and he still wasn't exercising.

Downstairs, Jackson waited for his breakfast. He sat at the kitchen table and studied his son through hooded eyes. The moment James reached for the frying pan, his father held up a gaunt arm and hollered, "Goddamn it all! You're *not* makin' me more eggs! Are you tryin' to kill me? 'Cause if you are, I'd just as soon you used my Colt to do it."

James doubted his father's ancient revolver still worked but decided against starting an argument over the old gun. "What would you rather have, Pop?" he asked his father as pleasantly as possible.

Jackson's furry eyebrows creased in thought. Suddenly, a malicious twinkle appeared in his eyes. "I reckon I could do with some blueberry pancakes."

An inaudible moan escaped through James's lips. He loved blueberry pancakes, and his father knew it. "You're deliberately trying to sabotage me, Pop, but it's not going to work. I'm going to cook myself a scrambled egg with mozzarella and salsa, and then I will make you pancakes. That way, I won't be hungry anymore, and therefore, won't be tempted by them."

"Suit yourself. Call me when the good stuff's ready." Jackson shuffled into the den and turned on the Game Show Network. "And don't forget to melt butter over mine while my pancakes are still hot!" he ordered from the other room.

Muttering to himself, James savagely broke one egg after another into the mixing bowl. He kept repeating the motion until he had half a dozen eggs floating in the bowl. Looking at the half-empty egg carton, James cursed.

"What kind of man releases pent-up anger by cracking eggs?" he murmured to the bowl and began to whisk the eggs so savagely that they sloshed over the rim and onto the counter. But cooking settled him down again, and the smell of melting cheese soon had him drooling. James ate a leisurely breakfast, and only when he was satisfied did he fix his father a stack of homemade blueberry pancakes.

"Pop, your breakfast is ready!" he called and then hurriedly left the house. No matter how much he'd enjoyed his eggs, he still wanted a bite of fluffy, buttery pancake. Luckily, showing his father that he wouldn't be derailed was more important than succumbing to his desires, and he felt so empowered that he spent the next few hours doing yard work.

Driving into town that afternoon, James felt a sense of excitement that he hadn't experienced since he was a young boy. Halloween had always been his favorite holiday. He'd spend days dreaming of a night defined by seemingly endless candy gathering. James's mother allowed him to stay out until ten o'clock on Halloween night; nine o'clock if the holiday fell on a school night. Like James, she loved Halloween. Every year, she lined their dirt driveway with a dozen jack-o'-lanterns carved with an array of different expressions ranging from silly to downright fearsome. Jackson always helped with this time-consuming project, and although he grumbled about scraping out the pumpkins, he loved to stand with his wife and son at the end of their road and gaze at the row of glowing faces.

The jack-o'-lanterns made the Henry house a favorite stop for trick-or-treaters, and once a year James enjoyed a brief flash of popularity with the kids at school.

"Sweet pumpkins," they'd say, and for a few delicious hours, James would feel accepted by the in-crowd. Even in November, the pumpkins continued to draw attention from passersby. The day after Halloween, James and his mother would turn the faces on the pumpkins around and decorate the uncut orange skins with wooden turkey heads and plastic feathers. For the next three weeks, a line of colorful turkeys flanked the Henrys' driveway. By Christmas, the pumpkins were gone, and so was James's tenuous popularity. Like Cinderella at midnight, he returned to being the shy bookworm he was for the rest of the year.

Of course, there would be no line of carved faces this year. James hadn't even bought a pumpkin and didn't want to pick up any Halloween candy until the last second, knowing he would be unable to resist eating some. As he got closer to town, he slowed down to admire the decorations adorning the houses bordering Main Street. He saw skeletons swinging from low tree branches, cardboard tombstones with glow-in-the-dark epitaphs, figures of witches on broomsticks flattened against tree trunks as if the two had collided, electric eyes peering from the bushes, hairy black spiders creeping along picket fences, and strings of purple lights shaped like bats spiraling up lampposts.

Every storefront in town was decorated for Halloween. Paper ghosts announced special sales in the window of the stationery store, while a line of motorized vampires asked for blood donations as they popped out of their coffins in the bay window of Goodbee's Drug Store. James slowed down to about ten miles per hour as he pulled up next to the Sweet Tooth so he could get a good look at the delectable things he wouldn't be eating this holiday. Fortunately for him, traffic was practically at a standstill as drivers cast about for parking spots before the parade got under way.

Megan Flowers always did an exemplary job decorating her window for each and every holiday. In honor of Halloween, she'd draped a row of shoeboxes with orange crepe paper so that a variety of bugs made out of chocolate cakes with licorice stick legs could crawl across the line of sight of even the smallest child. Black widow spider cakes with Red Hot markings headed the line, followed by a millipede with gumdrop legs. James almost crashed into the car in front of him as he spied the troop of chocolate ant cakes covered with chocolate sprinkles. Each ant carried one of Megan's famous meringue bones on its back, destined for a hive made of mounded brown sugar. Every Halloween, Megan made trays of "skeleton bones" out of meringue, and to the children's delight spattered them with cocoa powder "dirt." It wasn't truly the Halloween season until the bones were piled up inside Megan's giant plastic cauldron.

James met Lindy and Bennett at their designated spot in front of Dolly's Diner. As soon as everyone settled into their folding chairs, Lindy showed them Murphy Alistair's latest headline: IS THE HALLOWEEN PARADE SAFE?

"Gillian would say that this woman is spreading too much negative energy with this kind of writing." Lindy slapped at the paper.

"And she's having the time of her life doing it." Bennett laughed. "That reporter hasn't had an event this exciting since Trent Riggsby's sow bit the judge's finger off at the State Fair a few years back."

"I remember that!" Lindy squealed like the pig in question. "Oh, here comes Lucy. Scoot over a bit, will you," she asked James, indicating the tiny space between their chairs. "Lucy hasn't lost *that* much weight yet."

"Hey!" Lucy greeted her friends and placed her chair in the spot created by Lindy and James.

"Where's Gillian?" James asked.

"She's sharing a float with the ladies from Shear Elegance, the hair salon next door to the Yuppie Puppy," Lucy said.

James searched Lucy's face for a trace of what she might be feeling after their awkward goodbye the other evening, but she seemed to be her usual sunny self. "Well, we've got the best seats in the house," he said, smiling at her. He was incredibly relieved when she returned his smile.

At the far end of Main Street, the band from Blue Ridge High began playing "The Monster Mash." The Halloween parade had officially begun.

"Look! Here comes the first float!" Lindy shouted happily.

As was the tradition, the Dolly's Diner float came first. Shaped liked a giant pumpkin pie, the float lumbered down the street. Dolly, dressed up to resemble a generous dollop of whipped cream, shouted and waved to the crowd while Clint, who was zipped into a giant fork costume, tossed out coupons wrapped in rubber bands. James unwrapped his to discover a coupon for one dollar off the price of any item. Lindy groaned when she saw that hers was for a free dessert with the purchase of an entrée. As the float went by, they all clapped and cheered. Bennett jumped up and down, hoping to get Clint to toss him a coupon.

"I feel like I'm ten years old!" Bennett yelled when he caught one and zealously unwrapped his prize. "Free coffee with breakfast? Perfect." He tucked the coupon into an empty mailbag.

"Free stuff brings out the kid in everyone," Lucy said, pointing at the next float. "Here comes Gillian!"

Like most of the floats, the one Gillian shared was a decorated flatbed trailer. These were drawn by either car or tractor, and Gillian's float was being pulled by a black pickup truck bearing the sign "Beauty Queens on Halloween" in glittering purple. The float's platform was populated by a coven of witches and their dogs. Steaming cauldrons, birdbaths filled with neon potions, and dogs with purple-tinted fur sat at the feet of women with hooked noses and waist-long black hair. Each witch had lime-green talons that she used to throw out pieces of Mary Janes to the noisy crowd.

"Why Mary Janes? Most kids hate these." James watched the yellow and red candy wrappers zipping through the crisp air.

"Mary Jane Pulasky owns Shear Elegance. I guess this is her way of telling everyone her name." Lucy picked one up off the street in front of her feet. "I'm kind of glad I don't like them. I'm not tempted by this one bit."

"I do!" Lindy held out her hand. "I may as well tell you, I'm going to eat some candy today. It's a celebration, after all."

"Me too," James agreed heartily.

The next float was sponsored by Blount Realty. It featured a two-story miniature Victorian with patches of gray paint and purple trim. The house, which had a faded "For Sale" sign posted near the cracked front steps, was clearly haunted. Bare trees with spiky branches led up to a crooked door and cracked glass windows. Ghosts flitted back and forth around the graveyard in back of the house, and spooky noises such as high-pierced screams and boards creaking emanated from within. A woman dressed as a dead

Victorian bride tossed marshmallow and peanut butter ghosts to the throng.

Troy Motors followed the haunted house. Instead of a float, their entry was an antique black car. It looked just like the bizarre vehicle used in *The Munsters* TV show. The car was complete with a curtained "coach" section where Lily and Marilyn Munster sat waving while the show's theme song played from speakers hidden inside. The car even had the red leather jump seat in the back for Eddie and Grandpa Munster. The pair hurled chocolate vampires to the furthest rows of bystanders and reminded people to shop Troy Motors. The owner of the dealership, Bradford Troy, was Herman Munster. He drove the hodgepodge on wheels, blasting a comical horn and pretending to drive off the road as he turned around to blow kisses at Mrs. Munster.

Right behind the Troy Motors vehicle was the Sweet Tooth float designed by Megan and Amelia Flowers. Gasps and exclamations of delight from the children preceded the float well before it came into view. The entire float was a mammoth trick-or-treat bag, which had been turned on its side so that its contents spilled across the float's platform. The treats were giant-sized in scale. Candy bars as big as stepladders stood on end, sticks of gum as large as mailboxes littered the floor, and, with the help of invisible wire, candy corns the size of beach balls dangled in space. Every piece of candy looked good enough to eat.

Megan Flowers, who wore an angel costume, stood on one side of the float, throwing out toothbrushes and dental floss to a chorus of boos. Amelia, dressed as a sexy devil in a skintight Lycra suit, tossed out fireballs and swung her tail in a flirtatious circle. Every motion she made charged the air with sexual electricity. She coyly posed with her pitchfork and blew playful kisses to the young men watching her with slack-jawed expressions.

"Get a load of Amelia!" Lindy exclaimed. "She always turned the boys' heads in school. You can all see why."

James and Lucy both stared at Amelia's long, shapely legs, tiny waist, and high, firm breasts. Her form-fitting suit showed off her perfectly rounded rump as she reached into a papier-mâché fire pit to grab another handful of fireballs.

"And she works in a bakery, too. It's just not fair," Lucy muttered under her breath. But she didn't stay dejected for long. By the time the Sweet Tooth float had moved farther down the street, her face was aglow with anticipation again.

The floats continued to pass by. Goodbee's Drug Store featured a mad scientist with bubbling potions and a group of children modeling the Halloween costumes for sale at the store. Home Doctor, the town's home superstore, the very one that put Henry's Hardware out of business, featured a pumpkin field with enormous glowing jack-o'-lanterns bobbing up and down in time to "Bad Moon Rising" by Credence Clearwater Revival. A scarecrow presided over the pumpkin field, waving a pair of mechanical arms and laughing maniacally. The scene was rather creepy because there were no humans on the float. It was all automated and, like the superstore, felt a little alien in the small-town parade.

At long last, the library float came into view. When James saw it, his eyes widened with wonder. Pulled by an old tractor, the Shenandoah County Library float was entitled "The Magic of Words." The Fitzgerald brothers had built several books the size of small cars out of plywood. Standing on top of one of the open books was the Headless Horseman from *The Legend of Sleepy Hollow*. The fearsome rider, astride a real black horse, held a menacing jack-o'-lantern in the crook of his arm as he pointed an accusing finger at the townsfolk. On top of another book was the monster from *Frankenstein.* James certainly hoped that the misshaped and stitched figure was a dummy as bolts of electricity seemed to be jolting the figure right off its metal lab table. The last book was what excited the crowd the most. Standing upward, so that people behind the float could read the title on the spine as well as on the front cover, the text was the much-beloved *Harry Potter.* On top of the pages, Francis had dressed himself as Harry and sat astride a broomstick. Waving to the cheering masses, he flew in an arc around the book, dispensing Tootsie Pops as he pretended to chase the Golden Snitch.

Bennett caught one of the candies and showed it to James. There was a tiny piece of paper wound around the lollipop stick. Another lollipop landed right on James's lap, and he peeled off the strip of paper.

"'A recommended read for those who dare to be scared,'" he read aloud.

"What book did you get?" Lucy asked, holding out an orange Tootsie Pop.

"*Faust*," Bennett said with a shrug. "Never heard of it."

"Mine's *Picture of Dorian Gray*." Lucy frowned. "I've never heard of that one either, but I'm curious now. I think I'll check it out."

"Me too," Bennett said. "What a brilliant idea."

James didn't think he could contain the pride swelling within his heart. The library float was fantastic, and the reading suggestions distributed by way of lollipop were nothing short of magical. All of the spectators were pointing at their slips and discussing the book titles they'd received. Not only had the twins been remarkably entertaining, but they'd also managed to excite literary curiosity.

Before the float could pass by, he applauded as loudly as he could and caught Francis's eye. In Harry Potter's round glasses, Francis looked like a young boy. He winked at James as fog from beneath the Headless Horseman's horse began to roll off the float and drift over the first rows of spectators.

The final float bore the parade queen. Typically a high school senior, the parade queen was elected by her peers and wore a shimmering black velvet robe and a glittering tiara made of amber rhinestones. Two members of her royal court, the Halloween princesses, flanked her golden throne, which was decorated with wheat stalks and bejeweled masks. Standing at the front of the float were the members of the sheriff's department. The men were the symbolic guards of the Queen of Quincy's Gap and raised real swords in salute to their monarch.

"Someday I'm going be up there!" Lucy announced bitterly. "It's always been men on the queen's guard, but a woman can protect people too."

"Of course they can," Lindy said soothingly and then let out an indignant cry. "Who is sitting on the throne? That's not Heather Gilchrist. Why, it's Allison Shilling! But she graduated two years ago! That's not—"

"The float is sponsored by Shilling's Stables," Bennett interrupted, pointing at the logo covering the entire side of the float. "Guess Allison's daddy bought her a crown."

"But she's not even in high school!" Lindy protested.

A woman standing in the row behind them leaned over and said,

"Heather and her two attendants had such a terrible case of food poisoning that they couldn't even stand up. Poor things. Biggest day of their young lives, and they're all home, puking their guts out."

"So who are the queen's attendants?" Lindy asked the woman.

She shrugged. "Trainers from the stables, I suppose."

As the float went by, the entire town followed, preparing to surround the podium where the float prizes would be awarded.

When all were assembled, the mayor, a portly woman with a booming voice, took the microphone. She thanked Blue Ridge Savings & Loan for donating the prize money as well as the table of judges who'd cast their votes for the winning float.

The runner-up prize, a check for one thousand dollars, went to the Sweet Tooth. Megan came forward in her angel costume, thanked the mayor and the people of Quincy's Gap, and then locked her gaze on Murphy Alistair, her face darkening with anger.

"I don't give a hoot what you print in your paper," Megan said while Murphy snapped her picture. "This is the most wonderful town in the whole world, and I can't think of a better, safer place to spend my Halloween!" She then waved at the crowd. "Come see us at the Sweet Tooth tomorrow. I'll have a whole new batch of bones for you all!"

After the applause died away, the mayor stepped forward again, holding up an oversized cardboard check for five thousand dollars.

"And this year's winner, by unanimous vote, is our very own Shenandoah County Library float!"

James let loose a joyful "Hurrah!" and Lucy and Lindy gave him celebratory hugs. Scott, who had managed to extricate himself from his Headless Horseman's garb, bounded up the podium's makeshift stairs to accept the check. He took the microphone from the mayor's outstretched hand and said, "We promise to use this money to create the kind of library this fine town deserves! Come by next month and see all of the new things we're going to have for you folks to do. And don't forget to check out your lollipops for some *real* magic. Francis and I want to thank Professor Henry for letting us build this float! He is the best boss in the world!" Scott held the check high in the air and waved at James.

"That's a ton of money!" Lucy yelled over the cheers of the throng. "You must be so proud."

James popped a chocolate vampire into his mouth. "You know, I don't think I've ever been happier." He smiled as he chewed, the liquid sweetness spreading over his tongue like ambrosia. "And that's not just the chocolate talking."

Chapter Eight

Herb-Roasted Chicken Breasts

"I think Whitney made a bargain with the devil," Gillian declared with her usual dramatic flair during the Sunday night supper club meeting.

In honor of Halloween, Bennett had covered his glass dining table with a black vinyl cloth and placed paper napkins with flying ghosts on five orange place mats. He'd also lit two human-sized skull candles to add to the spooky-but-festive atmosphere. The candles' wicks were located inside the eye sockets, and their flickering light created an illusion of animation within the waxen orbs.

After dining on lettuce wedges drizzled with blue cheese crumbles, bacon bits, fresh ground pepper, and balsamic vinaigrette, the supper club moved on to their main course. Lucy had volunteered to cook the chicken—boneless breasts seasoned with garlic cloves, olive oil, rosemary, parsley, salt, pepper, and lemon juice—and James was pleasantly surprised by how flavorful and tender the entrée turned out.

"I thought this would be like eating a dry rubber band," Lindy confessed. "But this is delicious! Any secrets from the chef on how to prepare this on our own?"

Lucy dabbed at her lips with a napkin and said, "Honestly, I called my mom for a bit of advice. She told me to use fresh herbs instead of the stuff in the jars. She said the closer the food is to the farm, the better it'll taste. As usual, she was right."

Lindy laughed dryly. "I've got one of those mamas, too."

"Wait a minute. Gillian was talking about devils, not angels like our mamas," Bennett said. "What did you mean about Whitney?"

Gillian stared at her forkful of chicken, and then, looking as though she were about to swallow a cyanide capsule, laid her fork down. "No offense, Lucy. I'm sure it's really tasty. I just need to apologize to the spirit of the chicken for eating its flesh before I begin."

"I told you that I bought Amish chicken," Lucy said, clearly miffed. "They're fed an all-organic diet and are completely free range. Shoot, they're probably treated better than my dogs!"

"They probably deserve better treatment than those horrid hounds," Bennett sniggered under his breath. "At least those chickens never tried to attack innocent civil servants."

"Back to Whitney . . ." James prompted after taking a gulp of Diet Sunkist.

"Yes, let's not lose focus." Gillian inhaled deeply and then exhaled through her nose. "After we'd all left our floats in order to hear the mayor present the awards, I realized I'd forgotten my evil eye protector. It's a key chain that I bought a few years ago in Greece—a blue bead painted to look like an eye. Every driver has these beads hanging from their rearview mirrors to prevent accidents, and I had mine tucked under one of our big potion bottles to ensure that there would be no driving mishaps during the parade. And see!" Her face gleamed. "Not a scratch! I bring it every year to protect the vehicles in the parade."

"We're all mighty grateful for the power of your evil eye protector," Lindy teased, but Gillian took her seriously.

"Thank you. It's the least I can do for my friends and neighbors." She bowed her chin and a cascade of marmalade-colored curls fell over her eyes. "So you can understand why I had to return to the float for my luck charm. I always keep it in my car, and I'd be *terrified* to drive without it. It was then that I saw Whitney speaking to someone wearing a devil costume."

"What were they talking about?" Lucy's eyes were lit with excitement.

"I couldn't hear the exact words, but both of them were upset. Whitney looked like she was pleading with the devil, while the devil was waving her hands around like she was really *disturbed* by whatever Whitney told her. Of course, I have no idea who the devil was because she had a mask on."

"How do you know it was a 'she'?" Bennett asked.

"She had the body of a *Sports Illustrated* swimsuit model, for starters. She wore that Lycra suit like it was her second skin. Not an ounce of flab on that woman!" Gillian frowned. "Like I said, I couldn't hear exactly what was being said, but I could tell the voices belonged to women."

James sprinkled salt over the remainder of his chicken. "The devil was Amelia Flowers."

"Yes, sir. Hard to forget *that* outfit." Bennett cackled. "Man, she can take me to the fiery pits of hell any old time."

The women at the table glared at Bennett.

"So Amelia and Whitney might be friends," James quickly suggested before any of the female supper club members could respond to Bennett's comment.

"They are the same age." Lindy stroked her round chin pensively. "I don't remember them hanging out in high school, but maybe Amelia was the unidentified person at Whitney's house Labor Day weekend."

James stood up and carried his plate to Bennett's sink. A tenuous connection between Amelia and Brinkley was tickling at his mind, but he couldn't think what it was. Clearing his head with a small shake, he said, "We need to find out if Amelia was at Dolly's on homecoming Saturday."

"But what would her motive be for killing Brinkley Myers?" Gillian asked. "Why are we even considering pointing the finger at another young woman? Why can't some desperate and crazy stranger have broken into the Livingstones' house and stolen the drugs?"

"Because it's not very likely." Lucy sighed. "I wish it were, but according to my law enforcement textbook, most small-town homicides are committed by people who know the victim and have a motive."

"Still, out of all the nation's homicides, only ten percent are committed by women," Bennett said. "Just playing devil's advocate."

Lucy looked over at him with a scowl of irritation. "How do you know this stuff, Bennett?"

Bennett shrugged. "I like statistics. In my spare time I read books that contain nothing but facts. One day, I'd really like to be a contestant on *Jeopardy!* I think I could give those lawyers and stockbrokers a run for their money." He patted the bulge of his belly and laughed. "One goal at a time though, right?"

"Right," James said with an encouraging nod.

"Listen, I'll go to the bakery this week and find a way to ask Amelia whether she's friends with Whitney or not," Lindy offered. "It would seem a natural line of conversation since I used to be her teacher. She and I always have a good chat whenever I'm at the Sweet Tooth. Of course, ever since we started this diet, I've been trying to stay as far away from that place as possible." She gestured toward the bowl of candy Bennett had set aside for trick-or-treaters. "It's bad enough to be in the same room with that collection of beautiful candy—my biggest weakness."

"Never fear!" Gillian rose, her lemon-colored shirt floating behind her as she marched into the kitchen. "I've made us a special holiday dessert. And don't worry, this treat still adheres to our diet plan."

"Wow!" James exclaimed as Gillian came out of the kitchen carrying a tray. "What exactly is that?"

"Dessert pizza," Gillian replied proudly. "Halloween style. I used low-carb bake mix, cinnamon, and artificial sweetener to make the crust, and sugar-free vanilla pudding with sugar-free candies to make the tombstones."

James could feel his mouth watering as he examined his tombstone. The letters "R.I.P." had been created using chocolate chips, and his name was spelled out with red shoestring licorice. Tiny gumdrops formed a floral design on the top of the vanilla grave marker. Without waiting for anyone else, James took an enormous bite of his pizza. As he chewed, his tongue was immediately accosted by the strange flavor of the crust. In his mind, he had prepared for the taste of a sugary dough like that of a donut or, at the very least, the satisfying richness of French toast. This dough was dry, crumbly, and carried a strange and unidentifiable tang to his dejected taste buds.

"Too many chemicals." Gillian grimaced as she bit into her own dessert. "That's why real sugar tastes so much better. It's a *real* plant. A *real* part of nature. I think we're supposed to eat things grown from our Mother Earth." Her shoulders slumped. "I can't even pronounce half the ingredients in that bake mix. No wonder it tastes awful."

"You did a great job with these, Gillian." Lindy pointed at her own tombstone. "You've saved us from eating a bunch of empty calories, and you displayed creative artistry in decorating these. Thank you for your effort."

"You must be a fabulous teacher," Gillian said, a slow smile igniting her freckled cheeks. "You're a hell of a good cheerleader when any one of us is feeling down."

"Well, let's put our minds on something more positive." Lindy smacked her hands together. "I brought the item of clothing I want to fit into in a few weeks. I'm going to assume the rest of you didn't chicken out on me."

"I hope this means you're going first," James said gloomily.

Lindy grinned. "Sure, I'll go. You men will probably be more embarrassed by what I brought than I will."

"Bring it on, sister," Bennett said and finished clearing off the table.

Before Lindy could speak, the doorbell rang.

"Your turn, James!" Lucy sang out, thrusting the candy bowl into his hands. James opened the door to a pair of teenage boys who were about five years too old to be going door to door asking for candy.

"Give us a shitload of candy or we'll egg your mailbox," the one vaguely dressed as a punk rocker threatened.

"And I'll toilet paper your trees." The second boy bared a pair of plastic fangs. It was the only attempt he'd made at pretending to wear a costume.

James surveyed Bennett's front yard. Even in the dark he could see by the lamppost light that the only trees in the yard were mammoth pines. They would be very difficult to paper.

"Be my guest. I hope you bought enough paper. And a pair of stilts. Or a really tall ladder." James removed the candy bowl from the boys' reach. "I should also warn you that the man who lives in this house works for the United States Post Office. If you tamper with his mailbox, which is a federal crime, you're going to get a hefty fine, and I'd be more than happy to serve as his witness."

"Yeah, right," the rocker scoffed. "You're just a fat lardass who's totally full of crap."

Lucy appeared from nowhere and grabbed the rocker by the oversized shoulder pad of his leather jacket. "Jason Stein, you get off this doorstep by the time I finish this sentence or I will call your father *at work* and let him know you are threatening folks into giving you candy! You too, Bobby Wilcox!"

The boys hesitated for less than a second, torn between

indignation and genuine fear. When Lucy yelled "Git!" they jumped in their shoes and scrambled across the lawn. James watched them as they ran down the street and were swallowed by the shadows gathered at the base of the hillside.

"I was handling them," James said to Lucy. In fact, he'd enjoyed standing up to the teenagers. He'd had so little practice facing down bullies that he resented having this opportunity stolen out from under him.

"Sorry," Lucy replied defensively. "I just thought we could get rid of them faster so we could get back to business."

"Fine, let's go." James sulked all the way back to the table.

"Before I show you my clothing item, I have to show you something else first," Lindy said as James and Lucy took their places. She then slid a glossy eight-by-ten photograph toward the middle of the table. It was a picture of a young woman in a one-piece bathing suit, arching backward into the flow of a narrow waterfall. The woman's body was long and lean. She had waist-length ebony hair and an hourglass figure that Marilyn Monroe would have envied. She also had the same light coffee-colored skin as Lindy.

"That's my mother. She was a famous teen model in Brazil. I'm half Brazilian, but all I seem to have inherited from my mother is her skin tone. My father is a short, round Southerner from a podunk town outside of Birmingham. My parents met in an art history class at Georgetown University and fell in love. Everyone was shocked when they got married, but I think they were even more shocked when I was born. Right away, people could tell I was never going to be a model. In fact, I looked nothing like my mother. By the time I was three years old, I was already overweight, and my father said that I was the spitting image of his own mother. Trust me, being compared to Grandma Bertha wasn't exactly a compliment. I've seen smaller rumps on a water buffalo."

"Where are your parents now?" Gillian asked as she examined the photograph.

"They live in DC. My mother manages an art gallery, and my father does restoration work for the Smithsonian." Lindy reclaimed the photo and shoved it back into her purse. "My mother was always putting me on diets and trying to get me to exercise. Her obsession with my weight drove a wedge between us. My father loved me no matter what I looked like. I tried to teach in DC, but the schools there are too chaotic, and I wanted to escape the constant comparisons to my mother. Here, no one knows me. This is my town, a place where I can be myself."

"You did get her huge eyes and that killer smile, Lindy," Lucy said. "And there are tons of kids who are really lucky that you decided to move to Quincy's Gap."

"Thanks." Lindy rummaged around in her duffle bag–sized purse. "And if you thought I was opening up before, look out." She pulled a black satin bra out of her bag and tossed it on the table.

"Good morning!" Bennett leapt back as if the bra were a coiled rattlesnake.

"I wore this in high school." Lindy held out the slinky-looking bra. "Nice size, dainty shape, alluring demi-cups — to me, it was the kind of thing a movie star or one of the prom queens from school might wear. Right?"

The ladies nodded in agreement. James and Bennett looked at one another in hapless embarrassment.

"This is what I wear now." Lindy yanked a flesh-colored object out of her purse. "This is a full-cupped, reinforced underwire bra, size forty-four double E." She tossed it on the table next to the black one.

James couldn't help but notice that each cup of Lindy's current bra looked like it could successfully hold an entire cantaloupe.

"Watch. This is the scary part." She held up the enormous biscuit-colored bra and then placed the black bra inside of it. "At one time, my bra size was a thirty-eight D. My, how I've grown!" She sat back, hands folded across the round shelf that formed her chest, and frowned at the amazing difference between the two bras.

Lindy's current bra could hold five cups the black bra's size. It was like comparing a pair of oranges to honeydew melons. She picked up the high school bra and held the delicate piece of lingerie over her chest. James could clearly see that only a portion of each breast would be able to fit into the old bra.

"I could never fasten this around my back, either. I'm just too wide now." Lindy dropped the bra back into her purse. "It would take an entire box of rubber bands to close the space between each set of hooks. So that's my goal, my friends. I want to slim down enough all over, but I especially want to get back into that bra. After all, can you imagine me out on a date with Principal Chavez, with things getting kind of hot and heavy, when . . . Bam! He sees my fat lady underwear and drops me like a hot potato."

Lindy's audience of four sat in stunned silence. Fortunately, the doorbell rang, and the supper club members could hear a group of children giggling outside. They could also make out the sudden patter of raindrops hitting the metal roof of Bennett's carport.

"I'll get it!" the men shouted simultaneously and dove for the candy bowl.

"That was very brave of you," James heard Gillian say as she gently covered Lindy's hand with her own. "You've inspired the rest of us to bare our clothing and our souls."

"The rain is really coming down out there." James returned from answering the door to a pack of hobbits hiding under umbrellas. He placed an old belt on the table. "I don't have anything quite so interesting as Lindy, but this is a belt I could wear about five years ago. I *might* be able to use the last hole these days."

"I want to fit into these," Lucy said, holding up a folded pair of pants. "If I can pull these up and zip them, then I might be inspired to keep losing weight. If I lose enough, I can start exercising. Then, I'll be in good enough shape to pass the physical I need to enroll in the deputy training program." She looked down at the faded denim on the table. "Putting on this pair of pants would be a big step toward a whole new me."

Everyone spoke a word or two of encouragement and then turned to Bennett.

Bennett coughed. "Mine's a little embarrassing, too. It's a wrestling outfit. Let me give you some background on this thing. See, I didn't go to college like the rest of you folks. I had to work two jobs straight out of high school to help raise my brothers and sisters. There were eight of us, and I was the oldest."

"So you felt responsible for their welfare?" Gillian asked.

"I didn't *feel* anything." Bennett pulled roughly on his mustache, a flash of annoyance sparking in his dark eyes. "My folks said 'you've got to help,' and that was that. We lived in an even smaller town than this outside of Lynchburg. My folks scratched out a living working on other people's farms. White people's, mostly. Now I'm forty, a bit older than the rest of you, and back then, the black families all still lived on one side of town and the white folks lived on the other. Our neighborhood was growing poorer and poorer, and way too rough around the edges. My folks wanted to move to a better place, but there just wasn't enough money. So I started commuting to Lynchburg College to work as an assistant wrestling coach. I was an all-American wrestler in high school, and I had a whole bag of tricks to pass along to those college boys. The only other job I could manage while coaching was a part-time postal route. That's how I became a mailman."

Lindy pointed at Bennett's uniform. "What happened to your wrestling gig?"

Bennett frowned. "Budget cuts. Not in the football program, of course, but the wrestling was canceled altogether. The sport just wasn't popular enough with the alumni, I guess. Anyway, this is a suit I wore a couple of times to demonstrate moves with my players. I'd look like a pound of soft butter sitting in a hammock if I wore it now. I'd sure like to leave this spare tire on a car somewhere and build up some of that muscle I used to have."

James smiled as Bennett held up the wrestling uniform, gazing at it nostalgically. It looked a bit like a mustard-colored slingshot.

"I ordered a set of weights a few weeks ago," Bennett continued, lowering his voice to a self-conscious whisper. "They were so heavy that they had to be delivered by *the men in brown*. I ripped open this giant box with an *Iron Bodies* label, bent down, and pulled out a pair of thirty-pound dumbbell weights. Meanwhile, a whole pile of those packing noodles flew all over the carport." Bennett scowled. "Took me half an hour to clean those damned things up. Anyway, I started lifting the weights by curling them in toward my chest, but it didn't take long before I had to set them down. There was a time when I would stand in front of the TV, doing rep after rep while watching SportsCenter on ESPN. Man, my arms were once pythons of muscle, and my legs were thick as logs. Not anymore."

"But you started working out as soon as you got the weights. That's great!" Lindy congratulated Bennett.

"Hold the phone, Lindy. Those dumbbells are too damned heavy. Here I thought that loading and unloading that mail truck would have kept me in decent shape, but I have no muscle tone at all." He gestured at his television set. "I also got an exercise video with my weights. It's called *Thirty Days 'Til Iron.* I haven't watched it once. It's still wrapped in plastic."

"I didn't go to college either, Bennett," Gillian said. "But at thirty-seven, I'm smart enough to know that the human mind can accomplish wonders. And if you want to be an ironman, then you'll be an ironman. Me, I just want to look like a *woman.* Right now, I am wearing a girdle under this top." She pulled at her loose shirt and then let go. The sound of elastic snapping back into place caused everyone to blink in surprise. "On top of the girdle, I'm wearing another flesh-restraining shirt. They're like control-top pantyhose for your torso. It's awful. I can barely breathe in all of these shirts, and they make me quite sweaty. I have marks all over my skin every night when I finally take them off, and I *still* look like SpongeBob SquarePants." She held out a tank top with horizontal rainbow stripes and a plunging neckline. "I'd like to wear this and look *good* in it. I have meditated on acquiring the strength to lose weight for months, but it wasn't until I joined this supper club that I felt I'd gained the *fortitude* to reach this goal." Her eyes glistened with tears. "I am deeply grateful for all of your support."

Everyone clasped Gillian's hand or gave her a friendly pat on the back, and then the Flab Five planned their next dinner for the following Sunday at James's house. Gillian would have offered hers, but she was having work done in her kitchen and asked for a week's reprieve. James swallowed nervously as he realized that his private life was about to be revealed to his friends. The leaky roof, torn kitchen chairs, and the knowledge that he had no idea how his father would react had James sweating like a bridegroom. He decided to tell Jackson ahead of time so he could determine how his father might behave well before next Sunday rolled around. Maybe Jackson would stay out in the shed all night.

"Don't forget to send an email after you've talked to Amelia," Lucy reminded Lindy. "You might discover a clue. So far, Donovan is completely stumped. He hasn't made any progress on the case, and that means we've got as good a shot as he does in solving this mystery."

James bid his friends good night and quickly jogged out to his truck, getting unpleasantly wet beneath a curtain of chilly raindrops.

Bennett's brick ranch was on the opposite end of town from the Henry house, and no one followed James as he headed west. The trick-or-treaters had long since gone home, and there were no other cars on the road as James crossed over the Stony Creek Bridge.

Suddenly, a deer leapt out of the cover of trees at the far end of the bridge and James instinctively slammed on his brakes. The deer locked eyes with his car headlights, frozen in terror as James struggled to control his Bronco on the slick bridge. His tires couldn't seem to find purchase and the truck skidded sideways dangerously close to the rusted guardrail. James jerked on the wheel and pumped the brakes desperately while the Bronco careened wildly across the bridge. Passing within inches of the immobile deer, his truck came to an abrupt stop on the side of the road. The Bronco had stopped with the front right tire slightly dug into the ditch, causing the headlights to illuminate the shallow gulley.

Breathing heavily, James laid his forehead against the steering wheel and whispered a brief prayer of thanks. When he looked over his shoulder through the driver's-side window, the deer was gone. He sat still for a moment, calming himself and trying to cease the trembling of his limbs. Finally, he was composed enough to get out of his truck and survey his situation.

Dark black skid marks formed an erratic track across half of the bridge. The tires of his truck had bit deep into the muddy embankment, but James was confident that once he put the Bronco into four-wheel drive, he could back out of the mud using low gear. He couldn't help gazing down into the gulley, which was destined to fill with water if the rain continued at its current pace.

The rain was sharp on his skin as he bent to examine his front tire. Suddenly, a glint of metal was caught in the glare of his headlights. He peered into the darkness of the sloping hill, trying to discern what sort of object shone in the copse of trees. Torn between fear and curiosity, James stepped carefully, fighting to maintain his balance on the soggy ground. As he got closer, he realized that the wink of metal came from the twisted spike of an umbrella, and his mind tried to register the fact that an outstretched hand lay just a few feet away from the broken apparatus.

"Hold on! I'm coming!" James called, a sense of desperation surging through him as he rushed forward. The person didn't move or respond as James raced the rest of the way down the hill, repeating his cry, "Hold on! I'm coming!" His fright completely forgotten, James reached the inert form and knelt down next to a head obscured by a mat of dark, tangled hair. He reached for the hand. The thin fingers were cold and unresponsive. James gently pushed the mass of wet hair away from the face, noting that it was clotted not only with mud, but also with a thicker, stickier substance that could only be blood.

As the woman's features became visible, James gasped in horror. "No!" he cried, looking down at the full lips, smooth skin, and the delicate curve of the woman's cheek. It was a face he recognized. The face of someone who'd been falsely accused of murder.

James bent over the woman's body, praying with all his might that Whitney Livingstone was still alive.

Chapter Nine

Hazelnut Coffee

James drove his Bronco as fast as he could through the dark, slick roads of Quincy's Gap, heading for the Shenandoah Valley Memorial Hospital. At first he'd been hesitant to move Whitney. But after listening to what sounded like very shallow breaths, James checked her neck for any obvious breaks or injuries, and then loaded her cold, limp body into the Bronco. He reasoned that he could make it to the hospital in the same amount of time it would take the paramedics to arrive on scene.

Now, however, James was questioning the wisdom of his actions. He knew nothing about medicine and was filled with trepidation. Had he caused Whitney more harm than good? After wrapping her in a woolen blanket and laying her as gently as a wounded bird in the backseat, her shallow breathing developed a liquid sound that increased James's sense of urgency. His attention was torn between the road and the nearly inaudible sounds of life coming from the seat behind him.

Once the Bronco merged onto the highway, James was able to pick up speed. A luminescent moon broke through a collection of spidery clouds and illuminated the horizon. James took advantage of the eerie moonlight to dial 911 on his cell phone. He alerted the dispatcher that he would be arriving at Shenandoah Memorial with a seriously injured woman within ten minutes.

"Can you describe the extent of her injuries, sir?" the dispatcher asked calmly.

"No. There's blood on her head, and her breathing isn't normal. It sounds wet. Her color isn't good either. She's way too pale. I don't know if that's from blood loss, or if it's because she's been outside in the cold rain for too long."

"Does she respond when you speak to her?"

James shook his head and then remembered that he was on the phone. "No," he spoke so low that it was almost a whisper. "She's beyond that now. I don't even think she can hear me."

He was greatly relieved to see a team standing by as he came to a screeching halt in front of the red Emergency doors. Two male nurses whisked Whitney onto a gurney and rolled her into the inner sanctum of the hospital before James could even close the Bronco's back door.

"I'll park and come right in!" he called after one of the nurses and drove into the parking garage. He pulled into a space in the nearly empty facility and then exhaled. His hands were shaking violently. Staring at them as if they were foreign objects, he noticed traces of dried dirt and blood on his fingers. He knew he was reacting to the shock of finding Whitney and wanted nothing more than to talk to someone about what had happened. Without thinking about the time, James picked up his cell phone again and dialed the only number his distressed brain could recall.

"Hello?" a voice croaked.

"Lucy? It's James. I'm sorry to call so late. I'm . . . I just . . ."

James could hear Lucy sit up in bed. Next, he heard the switch of a lamp being turned on. "James? What is it?" Lucy's voice seeped into James's ear like a balm, and he immediately felt himself clinging to its sweet sound like a lifeline.

"Something awful has happened." He paused, letting his emotions take charge of his words. "Could you come to the hospital? I need a friend right now. I need you." James told her about finding Whitney.

When he was finished, Lucy said, "I'll be right there. Just sit tight."

Feeling much stronger knowing that Lucy was on the way, James headed into the hospital and repeated his story to the triage nurse.

"We'll contact her parents immediately." The nurse quickly located the Livingstones in the white pages, picked up a phone, and began dialing. James could feel the fist in his stomach tighten into a hard knot. What if the Livingstones were told that James had harmed their daughter by moving her?

Assailed by doubt and anxiety, he paced the hall like a caged tiger until he saw the welcome figure of Lucy Hanover hurrying down the hall.

Wordlessly, she enfolded James in a hug. He held Lucy tightly, and her warmth swept through him like a wave. "Thank you," he whispered into her hair. He could sense his strength returning. "Thank you for coming."

When she broke away, her eyes were glistening. "Anytime, James. I'm right here."

At that moment, the nurse arrived to tell James that Whitney's parents were en route. James sighed heavily and expressed his concerns to Lucy.

"You did the right thing, James. She was freezing cold and, from what it sounds like, in grave condition. If you'd left her out there another moment, who knows what would have become of her?" She tugged his damp sleeve. "Look! You're soaked to the bone yourself. I'm going to get us some coffee and rustle up a blanket for you." And before James could protest, she was gone.

Minutes later she returned, wrapped a blue blanket around his shoulders, and handed him a steaming cup of coffee with the most delicious aroma.

"It's hazelnut." Lucy took a tentative sip of the scalding coffee. "My favorite. I added a splash of half-and-half for you. I don't know if you take cream. And I've got some rat killer here for you, too."

James looked at the pink, blue, and yellow packets of artificial sweeteners displayed on her palm. "Rat killer, eh?" He smiled for what felt like the first time in ages. "I like that."

They sat and sipped their coffee in comfortable silence. James thought a better cup of coffee didn't exist anywhere in the world.

"Here come Beau and Caroline." Lucy pointed and then put her cup down. "I'll tell them what happened, James. It'll be easier for you that way."

James watched helplessly as the panicked couple entered the waiting area. Lucy met them at the door and gestured toward the cluster of seats where she and James were sitting and began to explain how James had found Whitney in the gulley. Caroline burst into tears at the thought of her daughter lying helpless and hurt in the rain. Beau gathered his wife in his arms as Lucy finished relaying the story.

"We haven't had word from the doctors yet, but they're sure to tell you everything they know, now that you're here." Lucy got the couple settled in the waiting room's uncomfortable plastic chairs and handed Caroline a tissue.

James leaned forward and said, "I am deeply sorry that your

daughter's been injured. I hope I did the right thing in moving her. I'd never forgive myself if I made things worse."

Beau reached across the empty space between the seats and clasped James's hand. "My friend, my little girl would still be lying there if it weren't for you. No matter what happens, we sure are grateful that you got spooked by that deer." For a moment, Beau's words stuck in his throat. "We're just thanking the good Lord that you were out when you were." He turned to Lucy. "And thanks to you too, for being here for our family."

Caroline nodded her head in tearful agreement, and then Lucy left to fetch two more coffees. While she was gone, James asked Whitney's parents what their daughter had been doing out on a rainy night.

"She worked the dinner shift tonight," Caroline said. "She usually rides her bike home afterward. We're only ten minutes away, and she's ridden into town since she was seven. If it's raining real hard, I'll go pick her up, or she'll get a ride home from Dolly or Clint. I guess the rain just caught her by surprise tonight."

James frowned. "I didn't see a bike."

The Livingstones exchanged startled looks.

"That's strange." Beau's expression was perplexed, then troubled. "I saw her ride off on it. Why would she come home on foot?"

Caroline's face filled with horror. "But does that mean that someone ran her off the road while she was walking home? How else would she end up in a ditch?" She cupped her hands together and pressed them against her mouth, as if to contain the anguish rising in her throat.

"Now, honey." Beau put an arm around his wife and stroked her arm. "We don't know anything yet. That nice nurse said the doc would be out soon. He'll tell us everything is going to be just fine. I know it."

Caroline gazed at her husband with renewed hope. Even James was comforted by Beau's confidence.

The minutes dragged by.

James and Lucy absently flipped through the random magazines spread around the waiting room. Beau sketched something on the back of a piece of paperwork given to him by the triage nurse. When James walked past Beau's chair in hopes of finding a magazine that wasn't about investing or fly-fishing, he noticed that the older man had drawn blueprints and the exterior of what looked like a Tudor-style doghouse.

"That's some house," James said with admiration. "Good enough for the president's dog."

Beau looked pleased. "Think so? I call them 'Pet Palaces.' I've been building a few cat and doghouses to sell at the big Veterans Day parade in Harrisonburg next month." Lucy put down her magazine and came over to look as Beau continued. "It all started with birdhouses. I began selling them right from the bed of my truck. Caroline will drive me to a shopping center and drop me off for a few hours with just a table and a chair. I set up my stuff and sit and wait. We've already hit most of the towns in the county, so I decided to try to expand my product line a bit."

"He's done very well," Caroline added proudly. "Sold every single birdhouse he's built."

"Were the birdhouses in different architectural styles? Like this Tudor doghouse?" James asked, pointing at Beau's sketch.

"Mostly red Amish barns or real colorful Victorians. Those two styles have sold the best." Beau's mouth curved into a wry grin. "Figures. All those tiny pieces of gingerbread take me forever to make."

"I'd like a Pet Palace for my dogs!" Lucy exclaimed. "You know what? Our friend Gillian owns the Yuppie Puppy, the grooming place in town. I bet she would love to see your products. Maybe you two could go into business together or something."

A spark lit in Beau's eye. "That sure would be great. I don't even want to think about the cost of . . ." He trailed off, embarrassed to express his anxiety about the expense of Whitney's medical care while his daughter's condition remained unknown. James sensed that Beau felt Whitney's accident was his fault because his inability to work as a roofer had forced his daughter to start working as a waitress in the first place. Luckily, Lucy must have come to the same conclusion, and she was quick to distract Beau by asking if she could take the sketch he'd made to Gillian. Once again, James was amazed by Lucy's ability to say the perfect thing during a difficult moment.

It was almost two in the morning when a doctor wearing royal blue scrubs walked down the corridor leading to the operating rooms and approached Whitney's parents.

Caroline jumped up. "How is she? How is my baby?" She clung to the doctor's arm.

The doctor gently removed her hand and held it lightly in his own. His bright blue eyes were filled with intelligence and compassion. He eased Caroline back into her chair and sat down beside her. "I'm Dr. Stauffer, the ER physician on call. Your daughter is alive. However, she's in a coma." Caroline's tense shoulders sagged in defeat and she uttered a painful moan. Dr. Stauffer squeezed her trembling fingers. "Whitney sustained swelling to her brain, which may be the cause of the coma. We see that in cases with head trauma. She must have hit the ground rather hard, I'm afraid."

"What does that mean?" Beau leaned forward, holding his hands out helplessly toward the doctor. "Will she wake up? Will she be herself when she does?"

Dr. Stauffer gave Beau a reassuring pat on the knee, and the anguished father sank back into his chair. "I have a few more things to tell you." The Livingstones steeled themselves. "Whitney suffered three broken ribs and a punctured lung. We had to put in a chest tube to reinflate the lung. She has also sustained a broken arm. I've got an orthopedic surgeon coming in to take a look at that arm—"

"Can we see her?" Caroline asked numbly, her eyes glazed in shock.

"Of course," Dr. Stauffer said sympathetically. "The good news is that your daughter is both young and strong. That will make a world of difference. We are really hoping for the best." The doctor readjusted his stethoscope. "I hate to use this phrase, as it seems like a cliché, but only time will tell what will happen next."

The Livingstones both responded with nearly imperceptible nods.

"I'll take you to see your daughter now," the doctor added softly, steering the stunned parents to Whitney's room in the intensive care unit.

James and Lucy stared after them.

"This sounds pretty bad," James said, feeling a twisting inside his stomach as he thought about Whitney's blood-encrusted hair and chilled limbs.

"She's a strong young woman. A fighter." Lucy sounded as

though she were talking more to herself than to James. "If anyone can pull through this, she can."

"But who would hit a girl walking home in the rain and then just drive away?" James asked, his voice tight with anger.

"No one would unless . . ." Lucy gazed into the middle distance. "Unless the hit and run has something to do with Brinkley's murder. If Whitney lied to us when she said she didn't invite a friend to her house over Labor Day weekend, then that person must see her as a threat. Someone stole that Coumadin, James, and that someone may have tried to kill Whitney tonight. I wish she would have told me the truth." She looked at him with frightened eyes. "If the driver was gunning for Whitney, that was no warning tap they gave her. That car ran her down! You heard the doctor. She's lucky to be alive." Lucy glanced around wildly. "Do you think she's even safe here?"

James longed to put his arm around Lucy's shoulders, to comfort her and show her how grateful he was for her presence. He was moving to close the distance between them when he heard the sound of a familiar voice. "Looks like they sent the cavalry." James jerked his head in the direction of the entrance doors.

Keith Donovan and Glenn Truett were marching double time in their direction.

"Should have known you had your nose stuck into this mess, Lucy Hanover," Keith said, smoothing his red hair.

James didn't care for his tone or the way he sneered at Lucy. He stepped forward so that he was partially shielding Lucy from Donovan's line of sight. Before she could speak, James said, "Actually, this is my mess. So you probably want to talk to me."

Keith blinked at James in surprise. But his stunned expression quickly turned hostile. "I didn't realize librarians kept such late hours." Behind Keith, Glenn smirked.

"Isn't there something more important you'd care to discuss other than my work hours?" James crossed his arms over his chest and waited.

Keith stared hard at James, clearly torn between continuing his bullying act and acquiring the necessary information. Flipping to an open page in a small spiral notebook, he uncapped a pen and gestured toward a group of chairs. "I'd like to hear your version of tonight's events, *Professor* Henry."

James ignored the deputy's churlishness. He recounted the scene in which he avoided the deer and how the wink of metal from Whitney's umbrella drew him to her side. He provided as much detail as possible, but was unable to provide any clues regarding the actual hit and run.

"So you saw no other cars near you? Just the deer?" Though Keith was obviously seeking clarification, he asked his question in such an accusing tone that James felt guilty over not having seen Whitney's attacker drive by.

"Sorry, but no."

Glenn had been silent during the interview, watching James intently. Finally, he let loose a sigh and said, "Hey, man. At least you found the girl. She probably owes you her life."

"If she's not brain-damaged." Keith abruptly shut his notebook. "I'm going to talk to her folks. After that, I'd like you to lead me to the exact spot where you found Whitney. Can you find it again?"

James struggled to ignore Keith's patronizing tone. "Of course, I can. I'd do anything in my power to find out who did this to Whitney." He watched the deputy swagger down the hall, his hand caressing his gun holster.

"Don't mind him," Glenn whispered to James so that Lucy couldn't hear. "He always acts like a big shot whenever a woman is around. He thinks they're all in love with him, including Lucy."

When Keith returned, Beau Livingstone was with him. Beau shook James's hand, thanked him again, and promised to call with any updates on Whitney's condition.

"Don't you focus on anything but your daughter," Lucy said, grasping the harried father's arm. "I'm going to talk to my friend Gillian, and we'll find some way to help your family out with all this." She gestured around the room. "Take care now."

James walked to the parking lot feeling like it was days, not hours, since he had pulled up in front of the emergency room doors. The rain had ceased, but the air was bitingly cold, and a sharp wind wrapped around his bare neck and sent chills down his arms.

"I'll follow you!" Lucy called to James, and he waved with an appreciative smile, relieved that she had decided to come along.

Driving back toward the Stony Creek Bridge, James began to feel the effects of lack of sleep. His head felt like a bowling ball, and he was positive that his neck couldn't possibly support its weight for another second. Desperate to be more alert, he rolled down his window and let the crisp air slap his face into wakefulness. He longed for another hazelnut coffee to give him the strength to make it through his next face-off with Donovan.

Keith pulled in behind James and got out of his patrol car carrying a flashlight the size of a baseball bat.

"*Someone's* compensating," Lucy mumbled, and James hid a laugh behind his hand.

"Say something, Professor?" Keith demanded.

"At least it's not raining," James replied quickly, thinking that at least "compensating" and "raining" sounded alike. Lucy shot him an impish grin.

"Whitney was this way." James retraced his steps down the gulley. Keith shone the powerful beam of his flashlight around the area.

"No bike," James said to himself.

"Why would there be?" Keith looked at him carefully.

"Mrs. Livingstone said that Whitney rode to town on her bike. I told her that I hadn't seen a bike when I found her. Just an umbrella." While Keith searched the nearby underbrush, James and Lucy trudged back up the slick hill. After a few moments, Keith joined them by the side of the road.

"Those your tire tracks?" He directed the beam of light at the erratic skid marks on the pavement.

"Yes. The deer was standing in the middle of the road about ten yards from this spot." James moved forward, pointing. "It stood just there. Never moved."

"Guess you city folk aren't used to wildlife." Keith spat his gum onto the road. "That's why it pays to drive with caution at night."

"I wasn't speeding. That deer came out of nowhere!" James snapped. His energy was too depleted to come up with a more demonstrative answer.

"Well, with your tracks crisscrossing the road from one side to the other, I doubt anyone else's will show up. Got anything, Glenn?"

Glenn had been sweeping the road and both shoulders with the beam of his flashlight, methodically covering the area where Whitney had most likely been hit.

"We'll have to come back when it's light out!" Glenn yelled. "I don't see anything here, Donovan."

James checked his watch. It was almost five in the morning. He glanced at Lucy. Her shoulders were drooping with weariness, and she was rubbing her tired eyes. It was time to call it a night.

"Guess I'll head home, then," James said, more to Lucy than to Keith.

Keith smirked. "I suppose *you'll* be calling in sick today, eh, Lucy?"

Lucy stopped on the way to her car and pivoted to face Keith. "Damn right I am. I spent the last few hours helping folks in our community." She lowered her voice so that only James could hear the rest of her sentence. "Too bad we can't say the same thing about *you*, Keith Donovan."

Chapter Ten

Poached Eggs

"What happened to my breakfast?" Jackson Henry demanded. He stood in the threshold between the hallway and James's bedroom, glowering at his son.

James opened half an eye and read the neon digits on his clock. Eleven o'clock. He groaned and covered his head with his pillow. This laborious maneuver was unsuccessful in blocking out his father's complaining.

"I had to eat that God-awful cereal you bought for your dumb diet. That crap tastes like twigs and bark. Next time you're gonna sleep this late, let me know, and I'll go outside and eat some pine mulch." Jackson paused, waiting for a reaction. When James didn't reply, he took a step into his son's bedroom. "What are you doin' in bed anyhow? Don't tell me you got fired from the easiest job in the world? Are you sick? Because if you are, you need to turn that damn phone off. Folks have been callin' for hours, invitin' you to breakfast. Don't they know it's almost lunchtime? Your friends half-wits or somethin'?"

James pushed the pillow away from his face. "Who called, Pop?"

"I'm not tellin'." Jackson was clearly pleased to be able to hold this piece of information ransom. "I think I erased the message from the answerin' machine, too. I can't figure out all them buttons." He tapped his forehead with his finger. "Not enough college degrees, I guess."

James sat up and sighed wearily. "Was it a woman named Lucy?"

Jackson pretended to think. "She your girlfriend? That why you're crawlin' home at an hour when most decent folks are just wakin' up?"

James threw back the covers and slipped his feet into a pair of tattered leather slippers. He stood and pulled on an equally ratty bathrobe and shivered, feeling goose bumps erupt along his arms and legs. He would need to make sure their oil tank was full for the coming winter. The experts were calling for record-breaking amounts of snow starting later in the month. James couldn't believe it was

November. He felt his new life in Quincy's Gap had actually begun years ago instead of months.

After getting dressed in his chilly room, James turned up the heater on the way downstairs and then grabbed the phone. He called the Fitzgerald brothers to explain his absence.

"We're just glad you're okay, Professor," Francis said, obviously relieved. "Scott and I were wondering what had happened when you weren't here this morning. I've got good news for you, though. The manager of Shenandoah Savings came over this morning with the real five-thousand-dollar check. We've got to figure out what to do with it!"

James perked up at the mention of the prize money. "Why don't you and Scott make a list of suggestions? You two won the money, so you should help decide where it goes. I'll be in after lunch, and we'll make some decisions then."

"Right-O, Professor," Francis said cheerily.

Next, James pressed the Play button on the answering machine and was informed that he had no new messages. His father had, in fact, deleted them. James pressed *69 and recognized Gillian's voice at the other end.

"Oh, James!" she cried. "Bennett called first thing this morning to tell me about poor Whitney. He heard all kinds of things on his police scanner while he was reading in bed last night. Come on down to the salon. I've made you and Lucy a late breakfast. You must be completely drained of energy after all you went through. You need food and company. It's the least I can do." A cacophony of barking erupted in the background, and Gillian excused herself and hurriedly hung up.

James didn't have the chance to thank her for the invitation, but his stomach growled in response to the idea of breakfast. Looking around for his car keys, James spied a wet paintbrush sitting next to the kitchen sink. Puzzled, he picked it up and examined it. It was a small artist's brush and appeared to be of high quality. James inspected the fine soft bristles for traces of color but found none. He was so intent on the mysterious brush that he didn't hear his father creep up behind him. In the blink of an eye, Jackson snatched the brush from his hand, stuffed it in the front pocket of his overalls, and marched out the back door in the direction of the shed.

James followed close behind, but by the time he reached the shed door, the dead bolt was already sliding into place. "We can't go on like this, Pop! You've got to rejoin society at some point!" he shouted, but the only sound he heard in return was Jackson's battery-operated television set being switched on. It was belting out the theme music to *Wheel of Fortune* as loud as its tiny speakers would allow.

Shaking his head, James returned to the house, shrugged into his coat, and drove to town.

A buxom brunette wearing skintight pink pants and a low-cut black sweater was carrying a newly perfumed and beribboned Pomeranian out the front door of the Yuppie Puppy as James arrived.

"You're a genius, Gillian! See you next week!" the customer called over her shoulder while receiving a series of doggie licks from her grateful pet. "Yes, yes, Sophia Loren. Mommy thinks you are so beautiful. Who's beautiful? You are! Yes, yes! Give Mommy kisses." James could barely squeeze past the affectionate duo, but he finally managed to enter the toasty interior of Gillian's grooming salon.

"James!" Gillian gushed, holding a hand over her heart. "I've got a pot of herbal tea waiting for you. It's made from peppermint, eucalyptus, and licorice root—the very things you need to calm your nerves and exorcise all of last night's negative feelings."

Lucy was already perched on a purple bar stool back in the Yuppie Puppy's kitchen area. While the storefront and grooming areas seemed rather clinical in their clean whites and chromes, the kitchen was an explosion of purple, yellow, and orange hues. James spied a handmade pottery platter containing an artistic display of bacon strips and what looked like poached eggs. A jar of Tabasco sauce and salt and pepper shakers sat next to the platter.

"Help yourself." Lucy smiled and beckoned at the food. "These eggs are delicious." She turned to Gillian. "I'm so sick of frying and scrambling eggs for breakfast. This is a nice treat. You told us that you couldn't cook, but I beg to differ."

"I *can* cook. I just got out of the habit. That's turkey bacon next to the eggs. I've heard that it tastes just like the real stuff, so don't worry." She eyed the bacon. "Poor little pigs." Gillian's face turned mournful as she poured tea from a porcelain kettle into a mud-colored pottery mug decorated with pink cherry blossoms. The mug's handle was so hot that James couldn't wrap his fingers around it.

"It's Japanese. They're the world's tea masters. The pottery is so thin that it retains the water's heat better." Gillian pointed at the scalding mug. "Now, Lucy, tell me more about these Pet Palaces. My next client doesn't come in until two. It would be nice to have something else to think about until then, especially a new business venture."

Lucy slid Beau's drawing across the marigold tabletop. Gillian examined it with keen interest. "This is really splendid!" Her eyes sparkled and she twirled a lock of hair around her finger. James thought Gillian's hair was an entirely different shade than it had been on Halloween night. In fact, it bore an uncanny resemblance to the Tabasco sauce he'd just splashed on his egg. "I could put these for sale on the Internet and make a killing. Do you know how many pet owners would treat their pets to something like this?"

"Beau uses indoor-outdoor carpeting. Do you see this?" Lucy pointed to a contraption inside the house. "That's an automatic feeding and watering system. This is a place for a raised bed, and this is a toy bin that the animal can access by pressing on this lever with its paw. And check this out! There's even a spot for a framed photo of the pet's family."

"So it looks like the cat houses get scratching posts on their front porches and the doghouses get chew ties on strings. I love it!" Gillian suddenly frowned. "Still, these can't be cheap to build, especially if Beau's using vinyl siding and other all-weather materials. We'd have to charge a bundle to have enough profit to split and cover shipping costs, marketing costs—"

"Whoa!" Lucy raised her hands. "I just thought you might like to talk things over with Beau. Maybe sell a few for him from here in exchange for a small commission. They'd look great in your front window." Her tone grew more somber. "This is the only way I can think of to help the Livingstones."

"We need to do more than sell a few houses for them." Gillian's eyes were lit with a fierce determination. "They have *really* suffered. Like you told us a few days ago, Beau is already swamped with medical bills. With Whitney's hospital stay, they're about to face a whole new stack of bills. But we live in Quincy's Gap, Shenandoah County, Virginia. This whole state is filled with good-hearted and generous people. If we could bring them together somehow . . ."

"You mean put on a benefit or something?" James asked.

Gillian thumped him on the back. "Exactly! A Help Your Neighbor Day!" Her face shone with fervor. "If we could get the local businesses to donate a few products and if Dolly and Clint would cook food at cost, then we could raise some serious money for the Livingstones."

"We'd need a huge turnout to make enough cash to help them with the kind of debt they're facing." Lucy looked thoughtful. "And tons of volunteers."

James piped up. "We should call Murphy Alistair. Maybe she'd like to take a break from murder headlines and use the media for good for once."

"Stellar idea, James," Lucy said. "You deal with Murphy, and I'll help Gillian solicit donations. What date should we shoot for?"

"This weekend!" Gillian exclaimed. "I know that's short notice, but if we wait any longer, people will forget. After all, one of their own has been injured and left for dead. People's hearts are overflowing with good intentions right now after reading about Whitney's injuries in the *Star*, and we need to take advantage of those warm feelings. We can use the field right behind this strip mall. There's plenty of parking out front."

"I knew you'd be able to help." Lucy beamed at her carrot-topped friend. "I'll make some calls from work. I'd like to ask the Shillings if they'd let us borrow some of their ponies for kid rides. We need baked goods, too. I'll see if Lindy can round up some parents, and we'll get students and teachers to organize other concession stands. James, do you have time to see Murphy before you go in to work? We need her to print an ad right away."

James glanced at his watch. He'd promised the twins that he'd be in after lunch, so technically, he could take a few minutes to visit the meddlesome reporter. Luckily for him, he didn't even need to drive to the *Star*'s offices. Murphy Alistair had been next door getting a manicure and practically slammed into James as she headed toward her car, flailing her hands about like a pair of startled birds.

"Professor Henry!" She offered James a phony professional smile. "I've been calling you all morning! Haven't you received my messages?"

"I slept in, actually. I had a rather late night."

"That's *exactly* what I want to speak to you about." Murphy's smile grew wider, giving her a maniacal appearance. "Can I follow you back to the library?"

James thought quickly. "I've had several calls from big-city reporters about last night, including Charlottesville's *Daily Progress* and Richmond's *Times-Dispatch*. I guess they see me as some kind of hero librarian," he lied, watching as Murphy's eyes grew round in alarm. "So far I haven't talked to anyone. And I'm willing to give you the exclusive on one condition."

Murphy's eyes narrowed in suspicion. "What's that?"

"I'd like you to write another story to be included in tomorrow's edition." James opened the passenger door to the Bronco and gestured for the reporter to get in. "One of them is about this weekend's, ah, Neighbor Aid Festival." Murphy gave him a blank look. "Trust me, it's breaking news. I'll explain on the way."

Murphy slid carefully into the car, her fingers wriggling like a pair of pale spiders weaving a web. She was uncharacteristically taciturn.

• • •

Jackson Henry threw the *Star* on the table with a snort of disgust. "That woman spreads poison faster than a nest of water moccasins." James looked up in surprise. He hadn't seen his father read the daily paper for ages. Reaching across the table, he took the crumpled pages from Jackson and examined the latest headline: PARENTS OF HIT AND RUN LIVE IN FEAR.

"Murphy," James muttered and shook his head.

"And what in the hell is this Neighbor Aid Festival?" Jackson grumbled, sinking his teeth into a piece of crisp raisin toast dripping with butter.

James continued scanning the front page, pleased to see that the entire bottom half had been devoted to the upcoming festival. Murphy's article on the Livingstones was touching and heartfelt. The enormous photo of a grade-school Whitney was perfect. Her hair was caught up in pigtails, and she stood in front of Goodbee's Drug Store with an enormous ice cream cone in hand. Her youth, innocence, and vulnerability shone through her eyes and served to remind people that she was a child of Quincy's Gap. She was one of theirs, and she and her family were in need of the community's help.

"The festival is meant to bring the townsfolk together in order to raise money for this young woman, Whitney Livingstone." James pointed at the more recent photo of Whitney taken at her high school graduation. "She's a part-time college student and a waitress at Dolly's. She's also the young woman I found lying in the ditch two nights ago."

Jackson squinted at the photo. "I know her. She's from good people. Her daddy used to work for me before he started his own roofin' business. Should have stayed with me, too. He could have gotten a job at . . ." Jackson couldn't speak the name of the new hardware store. "Well, he would have had insurance if he was with them when his heart gave out."

James was stunned. Not only was his father aware of Beau's troubles, but he'd also said something nice about the family in the same breath. "The Livingstones are good people," he agreed.

"What are you going to do to help out, set up a tutoring tent?" Jackson adopted his customary scowl.

So much for a change of disposition, James thought. "There's going to be a silent auction Saturday night. I'm donating all of my vintage Marvel comic books and a few signed first-edition books."

"Those books worth anything?" Jackson asked.

"Folks will pay good money for them. They're horror books by really famous authors." James wondered why his father was so curious about the subject.

"Maybe you should sell them and get our roof fixed," Jackson mumbled and left the table without clearing his plate. He walked to the door leading outside and put his hand on the knob. Without turning he said, "I'm gonna leave a box in your truck to sell at the auction. I don't want it opened until Saturday, you hear me?"

James stared at his father's lean back in bewilderment.

"Do you understand?" Jackson cast a fierce stare over his bony shoulder. It was a stare that allowed for no argument.

"Yes, sir," James said, suddenly reduced to a small child once again.

• • •

The Fitzgerald brothers were in a tizzy over the allotment of the float prize funds. Francis wanted to spend all the money on DVDs and audiobooks, Scott wanted to update the library's ancient matrix printer and buy a laser printer, as well as a new copier machine. James wanted to add another computer terminal to their single computer station. In the end, they decided to purchase more audiobooks and some large-print books for the bookmobile to take to the homebound. They also agreed to buy the laser printer and charge the patrons per printed page so that they'd make enough money to cover the costs of ink cartridges and paper.

"If I sell the old printer on eBay, can we use the funds along with the money from our donated book sales to buy some DVDs?" Francis asked.

"Absolutely," James said, feeling buoyant over the changes they were making. "I was also thinking that we might start a bit of a side business to benefit this branch."

The twins gazed at him with interest.

"You're both strong in the math and sciences. I'm not so bad at English and history. What do you think about us providing some tutoring? We can't charge a fee, but we could ask for donations to go toward that new computer. We can use the meeting room for our sessions." He turned to Scott. "If we do really well, a new copier will be next."

"I'm so in," Scott said. "I'd like to add computer classes to that roster once we get another terminal. Lots of people want to learn how to use email or surf the Internet but don't want to go to the community college and sit through their boring lectures."

"We could also help our patrons write their resumes or fine-tune college or work applications. I'll place an ad in the *Star* about our new tutoring services." Francis jumped up. "Meeting adjourned, Professor?"

"Yes, gentlemen." James smiled. "Good work. See you tomorrow."

James was just putting on his heavy barn jacket when the phone at the circulation desk rang. He waved to Mrs. Waxman, who was just walking in to begin her evening shift, and picked up the bleating phone.

"Professor Henry?" James recognized the voice of Caroline

Livingstone. "I thought you'd want to know that Whitney's awake. She'd like to see both you and Miss Hanover. Can you come to the hospital?"

"I'm on my way!" James said with elation and dashed out into the cold.

Lucy was already waiting outside of Whitney's room when James arrived. She held a plate of oatmeal cookies in her hands and greeted him with a warm smile.

"I only ate two spoonfuls of this cookie dough. Believe me, that's major."

"You're definitely looking thinner, Lucy." James glanced at her and then eyed the cookies hungrily.

"So are you, but let's not blow it by giving in to sugar cravings," Lucy said, noting the direction of James's longing stare. "And I bet Whitney's parents have hardly eaten since they got here." She knocked on the closed door.

Caroline opened it a crack and was clearly relieved to find James and Lucy on the other side. "Sorry to be so cagey," she said, "but reporters from all over Virginia have been trying to get in here. It seems like Murphy Alistair made a few calls, and now we're the 'big story.'"

"I think she's actually trying to help," James said in a muted voice. To him, hospitals were like churches or libraries, and he felt compelled to whisper within their walls.

"I suspect I know the folks behind this Neighbor Aid Festival." Caroline wagged a finger at them. "There aren't enough days in the year to thank you for all that you've done for us. Beau raced home to finish the Pet Palace he'd started before . . . the accident." Her smile wavered. "Well, come on in."

Whitney was propped up in her hospital bed, an IV tube in her left arm and a cast on her right. Her face was swollen and bruised, but she managed a crooked grin when they entered. Lucy pulled up a chair and took Whitney's hand.

"I'll wait outside," Caroline said, but Whitney shook her head.

"Mom," she croaked, her voice sounding scratchy and unused. "You need to hear this, too."

Warily, Caroline sat in a faded red recliner by the window. As there were no more chairs, James remained standing.

"First of all, thank you." She gazed at James and attempted another smile. "I hear I owe you my life."

James reached down and patted her arm lightly, just above the cast. "I'm just glad I was in the right place at the right time."

"And I owe you an apology," Whitney continued, turning to Lucy. "You've been so kind to me, and I lied to you."

Lucy nodded silently. "I know, sweetheart. We'll make it right, okay?"

Whitney nodded weakly. "Mom, when you and Dad went to that anniversary party, I had some friends over. Actually, they're not even friends. We just had something in common to talk about."

"Brinkley Myers?" Lucy guessed.

"Yes." Whitney released a deep sigh. "Brinkley asked me for money. He asked all of us for money."

Caroline's face crumpled. "What for, darling?"

"Because he knew secrets about all of us, Mom. I'm going to tell you mine. It's been eating me up inside for months anyway."

"Go ahead," Lucy prompted when Caroline didn't speak.

"I'm a horrible writer. When I had to write those three essays to apply to James Madison, I knew I would never get in, so I paid another girl to write them for me. Brinkley found out and threatened to call the dean of admissions and tell them what I'd done." A tear trickled down her cheek. "I'm not a liar. I'm really not. But if JMU ever saw my terrible grammar, they'd know I cheated, and I'd be kicked out. I've avoided that so far by not taking any English courses." She cast James an apologetic look. "The thing is, I had no money to give Brinkley. With JMU's tuition and helping out at home, I was flat broke."

"Honey, couldn't one of your teachers have helped you with those essays?" Caroline asked with surprising gentleness.

"Yeah, sure they would have. I took the easy route. That was before Dad's accident. I didn't see things like I do now. I was in a rush to move on, to get out of town and become a career woman. I was in a hurry to be on my way toward making the big bucks and living a life of shallow, stupid dreams. I'm real sorry, Mom. I know what's important now."

"So Brinkley was blackmailing all of you?" Lucy asked.

"I managed to pay him a few hundred dollars, but he kept at me.

I'd have to quit school to keep up with his demands, and then what would be the point? I was going to call his bluff the next time he bugged me about money, but then, well, he died."

Lucy locked eyes with her. "And you had nothing to do with that, right?"

Whitney shook her head. "No! I really didn't, Ms. Hanover. Swear to God!"

"I believe you," Lucy assured her.

The room fell silent.

"Do you remember what happened last night?" James finally asked, changing topics.

Whitney closed her eyes. "I was walking home from Dolly's. Some jerk stole my bike." She looked angry and then her face cleared again. "The rain came out of nowhere, so I walked on the road to keep my sneakers from getting soaked. Next thing I know, I woke up here."

"So you never saw the car?"

"I saw headlights, and so I moved off to the side. And I remember the car made an odd noise, and I think I turned around, but only for a second. I feel like I saw something too. Something weird, but I can't remember what."

James and Lucy exchanged perplexed glances.

"So who else was at your house the night your parents were away?" Lucy asked. "It's time to tell me their names now, honey."

Whitney didn't answer.

"Amelia Flowers was there," James said. "You might as well admit that."

"How did you know?" Whitney was obviously stunned.

"The day Brinkley died, he was probably going to ask Amelia for money, too. What did he have on her, Whitney?"

The young woman sighed. "It's not for me to spill her secrets, Professor. I'm sorry. I know I owe you more than that, but I just can't."

Even though James could see that Lucy was frustrated, he couldn't help but respect Whitney's sense of honor.

"The sheriff will ask you the same questions soon enough." Lucy's tone had taken on a hard edge. "He's not going to let you off this easily. Someone tried to kill you, Whitney! This isn't over, because there's a murderer running loose in our town."

Whitney began to cry, and Caroline hustled from her seat to stand protectively at her daughter's side. "That's enough for now. Please. I'll try talking to her later, but I think she's been through enough for one afternoon."

Lucy bowed her head in shame. "Of course. I apologize. I just want to make sure no one else gets hurt. I'm very concerned about Whitney's safety."

Caroline nodded and then turned to enfold her daughter tenderly in her arms. She began to hum softly in between pressing light kisses on Whitney's forehead. "Mama's here," they heard her croon as they closed the door. "No one is going to hurt my baby ever again."

Chapter Eleven

Chili Cheese Fries

The spectacle that had become Neighbor Aid was one James Henry would remember for the rest of his life. In just a few short days, the entire town had pitched together to set up a charity event the likes of which Quincy's Gap had never seen. It took place in the unused field behind the strip mall housing the Yuppie Puppy, and far outlasted its three-hour window. People gathered during the early-morning hours and stayed until dusk.

The work had begun at dawn on Wednesday. Several farmers had driven their industrial tractors into town at a laborious pace in order to mow the field. Next, the county's only party rental store, Party Like It's 1999, had erected their entire supply of large tents. Volunteers from the neighboring town of Elkton had helped the party store put up the tents. Next, they'd lined the interiors with long tables. Area merchants had plenty of space to display goods, and the largest tent had been reserved as a dining area for those who wanted to sit and have a meal.

Dolly and Clint had posted a sign on the diner door that they would be closed all day Saturday and patrons should visit the Dolly's Diner booth at Neighbor Aid. Il Pomodoro, the local Italian restaurant, had done the same. These eateries were joined by the Sweet Tooth, an ice cream parlor called Cups 'n' Cones from the town of Alma, and Adam's Ribs, a barbecue joint all the way from Keezietown.

On the day of the festival, the air was replete with the aroma of fried chicken, roasting corn, and sweet, tangy barbecue sauce.

"They have the world's best chili cheese fries!" James heard a woman exclaim to her husband as they quickly jumped at the end of the long line forming in front of the Adam's Ribs booth.

Farther down the row of tents, James spied Gillian and her assistant beneath a hand-painted banner reading "On the Spot." The two women were giving baths and nail clippings to a queue of dogs. Gillian and her mall neighbor, Mary Ann Pulasky of Shear Elegance, had bought extra-long hoses and extension cords in order to provide their customers with shampoos and rinses. They were offering a

"Parent and Pooch" special in which dogs and their owners could receive their beauty treatments at the same time. Luckily for Gillian, Mary Ann, and especially the Livingstones, the weather was cooperating by providing a rare sixty-degree day filled with sunshine and a cloudless November sky.

Men and women streamed across the mowed field. They ate with gusto, purchased all manner of goods donated from local businesses, and left bids at the silent auction tables. Children had their faces painted by a group of high school girls, and someone had rented a mammoth moon bounce for the younger kids. Pony rides, sponsored by Shilling's Stables, as well as a dressage and jumping demonstration conducted by the Shilling trainers, were also a big hit. James had just finished helping one of the stable's drivers back a horse trailer into a makeshift paddock when a woman called out his name.

"Professor!" James turned to see Murphy Alistair beaming at him. "Looks like my friend from the *Washington Post* came through for us. He put a short piece on Whitney and our festival in the Arts & Living section. He even sent a staff writer here to cover the event!"

James observed Murphy's triumphant expression and put a hand on her shoulder. "You did a good thing, Ms. Alistair. Look at the positive impact a newspaper can have on its community. I wish more reporters were like you."

Murphy's eyes shone. "I'm not *completely* bad, Professor. Not all reporters are scum any more than all librarians are prudes." She wriggled her eyebrows suggestively.

James felt his face growing warm. Was Murphy flirting with him? He paused for a moment, seeing her short, stylish brown hair and hazel eyes for what felt like the first time before he was distracted by the persistent blaring of a car horn. The driver of the horse trailer turned the truck off, and a woman with a puff of platinum hair wearing a pink skirt suit and beige leather pumps descended from the passenger seat.

"Who is that?" James asked Murphy, who was watching the woman with keen interest. Before she could answer, a silver Porsche convertible pulled alongside the trailer.

"Don't see many of those around here," James said as he admired the costly sports car.

"That must be Chase Radford, the senator's son." Murphy pointed at the tall youth as he leapt out of the car and raced around the hood to open the passenger door. "Rumor has it that he's been dating Allison Shilling. Looks like the ladies from Shear Elegance were right." Murphy made a few adjustments to her digital camera as she and James watched Chase help Allison out of the car and then plant a demure kiss on her cheek. "I'd better get some close-up shots." Without another word, Murphy hurried off.

James had no intention of following the intrepid reporter. He watched the trainer from Shilling's Stables unload a beautiful horse, and then spotted Lindy and a group of high school students manning a large table covered with pottery to the left of the horse paddock.

Trying to ignore the pungent combination of cooking meat and horse droppings, James headed over to Lindy's booth. Lindy was busily selling a variety of student artwork. Bowls and pitchers in glossy jewel-toned glazes were literally being grabbed right off the table while a pair of high school boys furiously unpacked more vases, plates, and mugs in bright glazes. At the neighboring table, three female students were selling watercolor paintings, charcoal drawings, and African masks.

"Hey, Lindy!" James sidled up to her table. One of the boys gazed at Lindy with interest.

"Yes, teachers actually have first names, Billy." Lindy shooed the boy away. "Can you wrap this bowl for Mrs. Samson?"

"Sure, Miss Perez," the boy said with a smirk.

"Looks like you're making a killing here," James said.

"I've never had people throw money at me like this before!" she exclaimed, her face flushed pink with exertion. "I think I could get used to it, too." She bestowed a prideful glance on the students in the booth. "My kids have really been the heroes though. They spent so many hours making these pieces, but the moment they heard about Whitney, they offered to sell them just like that." Lucy snapped her fingers and then lowered her voice to a whisper. "We've made nearly eight hundred dollars already."

"Excuse me," a snide voice interrupted. "My daughter and her fiancé would like to purchase that cobalt bowl. Do you think we could have some service?"

"Hello, Mrs. Shilling," Lindy said through gritted teeth. "And hello to you too, Allison," she greeted the young woman standing with her arms crossed and an expression of boredom on her pretty face. She gazed out over the crowd as if searching for something worthy of her attention. Finally, her icy blue eyes settled on the face of her former art teacher.

"Hey, Miss Perez," Allison muttered.

"Congratulations on your engagement." Lindy forced herself to sound enthusiastic. "I'd love to see your ring."

Allison held out her left hand, and James couldn't help but let loose a whistle when he saw the size of Allison's engagement diamond. He had seen smaller rocks at a limestone quarry. The stone was so large that it appeared to be weighing down the girl's thin finger. Allison's fingernails were painted a pale pink, and each nail bore a small rhinestone in the center. James wondered what kind of job a person could have and still manage to keep ten rhinestones intact.

"Wow! You could use that thing as a disco ball!" Lindy laughed good-naturedly. "And is this your husband-to-be?" She gave the young man at Allison's elbow a sincere smile.

"Chase Radford is the son of Virginia's own Senator Radford," Mrs. Shilling bragged when Allison didn't respond. "He just graduated from Georgetown University with a law degree. He plans to follow in his father's footsteps."

"Nice to meet you." Chase reached in front of his fiancée in order to shake Lindy's hand. His arm brushed Allison's, and she instantly recoiled from his touch.

Tugging at her mother's sleeve, Allison said, "Let's get going, Mother."

Oblivious to his fiancée's negative body language and the irritated curl of her lip, Chase slid an arm around Allison's waist. He gazed at her with such adoration that it was uncomfortable to witness.

James and Lindy exchanged befuddled glances.

Mrs. Shilling paid for her pottery and shot her daughter a warning look. "Come on, Chase." She hooked her arm through his. "Let's find out how we can donate our fine horse to the silent auction. We Shillings have always been devoted to helping our neighbors."

"Good luck today, ma'am." Chase gestured at the artwork as he was led away. "You must be an extraordinary teacher to have produced such gifted artists."

"Well!" Lindy exhaled. "What is that darling boy thinking getting himself involved with that pair of shrews?"

"They both look like they've been sucking on lemons," James said, watching Allison plod along next to her mother, her mouth fixed in a permanent sulk.

"Or sour milk," Lindy sniggered. "Allison spent most of her high school years at the Portsmouth School for Girls. Not to be catty, but I heard the Shilling princess left in disgrace at the end of her junior year. She now goes to Sweet Briar, where she's in the Equine Studies Program. I guess she's on her midterm break." Lindy ran her hand over the surface of a pottery soap dish. "Believe it or not, she and Whitney used to be friends."

James raised his eyebrows in surprise. "I can't picture that."

Lindy shrugged. "Whitney grew up and matured, while Allison didn't. Whitney has had to pitch in to help her parents make ends meet, and Allison just puts her hand out, receives a pile of cash, and then goes out shopping. Must be nice."

"She certainly doesn't look happy," James said.

"No joke. I've never seen such a miserable bride-to-be. Chase is clearly nuts about her too, but Allison acts like she'd rather have a cavity drilled than hang out with him." Lindy paused to hand a customer a coffee mug. "Have you seen any of the other Flab Fives?"

"Just Gillian. She's washing dogs like crazy. You?"

"I had a quick chat with Bennett earlier," Lindy said. "He and the other county postal workers put together a row of carnival games. Bennett is running the balloon toss booth—the ones where kids can pop balloons with a dart." She giggled. "He looked absolutely terrified watching those darts fly all over the place. I think kids might actually scare him more than Lucy's dogs!"

"Did I hear my name?" Lucy appeared from behind a pack of boys holding boxes of popcorn and sticks of pink and blue cotton candy. "Lindy! Your booth is wonderful! Hi, James. What are you up to?"

James smiled at her. "I'm heading over to the silent auction tent.

I've got some comic books and stuff to donate, and my pop gave me a mystery box for the auction as well."

"I'll walk you over. I've been given an unofficial job by Sheriff Huckabee to 'keep an eye on things.'" She held up a walkie-talkie. "Check it out. I even have one of the boys' toys."

"What? No gun?" Lindy teased. "Some kid might get high off too many caramel apples and turn Bennett into a pincushion."

Lucy laughed so hard she had to put a hand on the table to steady herself. "I saw him! He's standing in the far corner of his booth cowering like a little girl who's seen a really big spider."

"I'd better give my young artists a hand," Lindy said, noting the growing line in front of the table of paintings and masks. "Though I don't know how I'm going to get out of here today without a funnel cake. You guys bring any duct tape? You might need to restrain me when I walk by that booth."

James and Lucy were in high spirits as they headed to the silent auction tent. Lucy carried one of the boxes of comic books, while James struggled beneath the weight of a box of books and his father's box. It was big and long and firmly sealed with brown packaging tape.

The members of the Shenandoah County Historical Society had offered to run the silent auction booth, and James was amazed at the quality of goods they had managed to solicit within a few days. Jewelry, gift certificates, baskets of Virginia-made wine and gourmet foods, plane tickets, weekend getaways, and antique silver and glassware were tastefully arranged on maroon tablecloths. James was suddenly nervous about presenting them with his Marvel comics and signed horror novels, but one of the volunteers in the booth thanked him heartily for donating such valuable items.

"You've got quite a collection of items here. Very impressive," James praised the volunteer and left bids for the handyman service and for dinner-for-two at a steak restaurant in Harrisonburg.

"They are great," the woman agreed. "But Shilling's Stables has just donated our most amazing item yet. They've given us one of their thoroughbreds! And a writer from the *Washington Post* took a picture of me accepting the horse! My goodness, can you believe the generosity of Mrs. Shilling?" The woman was practically shrieking with excitement.

James shook his head. "Pretty hard to believe," he said under his breath as the woman turned away. He spied Lucy on the other side of the booth, scribbling bids on several clipboards, her face alight with enjoyment. James was finally able to turn his attention to the contents of his father's box. He tried to cut the tape using his car keys but was unsuccessful, and was just about to ask one of the volunteers if she had a pair of scissors when Lucy gripped him hard on the forearm.

"There's Amelia," she hissed. "Quick! We need to get some information out of that girl."

"But—" James started to protest, his hand still fastened to his father's box.

"Ladies! This box is yours, too!" Lucy pulled James along after her.

Lucy hustled to keep pace with Amelia. Her neon-orange top made her easy to spot in the crowd. James thought that most women would have looked like construction flagmen in such a shade, but Amelia wore the tight top like a runway model. In fact, she strutted across the uneven field as if she were on a catwalk in Milan.

"She's getting in line at the Adam's Ribs booth," Lucy said, withdrawing her hand from James's arm. She pumped her own arms and struck out on a furious, fast-paced walk. By the time she and James got in the same line as Amelia, they were both out of breath.

"Excuse me," Lucy said sweetly to the man in a cowboy hat standing directly behind Amelia. "I don't want to be rude and cut in front, but do you mind if I chat with my friend while we're waiting?"

"Sure thing, honey," the man said, tipping his hat. Lucy smiled, momentarily beguiled. James wished he possessed the man's natural charm as well as his flat stomach and chiseled pecs, which were clearly visible beneath the thin cotton of his white T-shirt.

"Hello, Amelia. Do you remember me from a few Saturdays ago?" Lucy asked.

Amelia nodded, and her large, golden brown eyes flickered with fear as she took a minute step away from Lucy.

James studied the young woman's face for the second time. When he'd gazed at her through the bakery window, he'd only seen a young woman with a plain face and a killer body, but as he looked at her more closely, he noticed that the hostile look in her eyes, along with her pinched and angry mouth, made her unattractive.

"Don't worry," Lucy said while James gave Amelia the once-over. "We're just here for the chili cheese fries. You know Professor Henry?"

Amelia shrugged. "I've seen him at the library." She turned to James and added, "I don't go much because you don't carry enough fashion magazines. Could you order a few more, like *W* and *Glamour*?" She leaned toward him so that he had a clear view of her cleavage.

"I'll look into it," James assured her, made uneasy by her abrupt change in manner.

"I'm glad to see you at the festival, Amelia," Lucy said. "Whitney's family needs all the help they can get."

Amelia shrugged again. "I'm working the Haunted Hayride down at Miller's farm tonight. He's extended it through the weekend just for the Livingstones." She glanced at the ground. "Have you seen Whitney?" she asked in a soft voice. To James, she suddenly sounded very young.

"Yes, I have," Lucy said. "She's banged up, but she's going to be okay." Amelia released a deep breath. She relaxed, and a smug smile crossed her face.

"So it wasn't that big a deal? Then why is everyone here today?"

James could see that Lucy was fighting to control her temper. He could see her compact hands balling themselves up into clenched fists. "It *was* a big deal. She got run over, Amelia. She's lucky to be alive." Lucy lowered her voice. "What I don't understand is why Whitney would want to protect you, when you don't even give a damn that she nearly died a few nights back!"

Amelia's eyes flew open wide. "Protect *me*? I don't need her protection," she practically snarled.

"No?" Lucy put her hands on her hips. "Let's start with the fact that you spent the night at Whitney's house over Labor Day weekend. That means *you* could have stolen the drug Brinkley was poisoned with."

The line moved forward, but Amelia stood rooted to the ground, her mouth hanging open as if she were sucking on a lollipop made of air.

"Did Whitney rat on me? I can't believe it!"

"Someone tried to kill her, Amelia. You can hardly blame her for coming clean. And speaking of her accident, where were *you* on Halloween night?"

"I was home with my mom," Amelia snapped, regaining her confidence. "You can ask her." She glanced ahead. Only two people stood between her and the server. "I'm not even hungry anymore, thanks to you!" she barked at Lucy and began to walk away.

"Whatever was on Brinkley's cell phone is still on there!" James surprised himself by shouting after her.

Amelia froze, and Lucy turned to James with a questioning look. Slowly, as if she were walking through knee-deep water, Amelia headed back to where they were standing.

"What do you mean?" she asked James, her face a mixture of petulance and fear. "That cell phone was smashed."

"But there was nothing wrong with its memory chip," James said, uncertain if that was the truth or not. "The sheriff can get it examined. That is, if someone points it out to him."

Without warning, Amelia sagged against his chest and began to sob dramatically. "Brinkley had pictures of me. Private pictures! No one can ever see them!"

At that crucial moment, the server asked for their order. Despite her confusion, Lucy asked for two plates of chili cheese fries, and James led Amelia over to a row of plastic folding chairs and pulled three chairs to the side of the rest of the feasting customers.

"Did he ask you for money?" Lucy asked gently.

Amelia nodded miserably. She pressed her face into a paper napkin and blew her nose. "I had a modeling job last year. It was my first one. Some guy put an ad in the Charlottesville paper, and I read it while I was getting a haircut at Shear Elegance. Five hundred dollars guaranteed. The photographer was looking for swimsuit models. I knew I had to get that gig. I've wanted to be a model my whole life." Amelia picked up a cheese-laden fry and twirled it around until it resembled a limp noodle. "Everything seemed fine at first. I was there with three other girls who were chosen out of, like, two hundred or something. We put on these string bikinis which were, like, skin-colored and almost see-through, but not totally." She paused. "Things got a little weird when we had to do poses with each other. We had to act, like, well, you know . . ." She blushed in embarrassment.

"Like you were attracted to the other girls?" Lucy guessed.

"Yeah." Amelia popped a fry into her mouth. "We had to sign a bunch of papers at the beginning. The print was so small that I didn't bother reading it. Besides, we got our money up front. And in cash! That was awesome, because I wanted to have a portfolio made, and my mom said we couldn't afford it." She grimaced. "We can never afford *anything*. It's no picnic having a drunk for a daddy. He took everything when he left that last time, and Mom and I have had to work like dogs ever since." She glared at James and Lucy fiercely. "I hope that bastard's rotting in a gutter someplace."

"So what happened to the pictures?" Lucy asked.

"They ended up on this Girls Loving Girls website. Brinkley found it, probably searching for nasty sites just like that one." Her eyes dropped to her plate of fries. "I never knew the pictures were for a site like that. We all look totally naked! My modeling career would be over if a real agent ever saw those. Once you do something like that, you get a reputation. And my mom would flip if she ever found out!"

Lucy bit into a fry. "She doesn't know?"

"No way!" Amelia yelped. "Brinkley came into the store to ask for more money the day after homecoming. He had the pictures on his phone and he threatened to show them to my mom."

"That made you angry, didn't it?" James asked and reached for a fry.

"Of course it did!" Amelia's eyes were blazing with fury. "Brinkley was a total scumbag!"

James thought this was an accurate assessment of Brinkley Myers's character. He remembered the rolled-up magazine Amelia had been holding so tightly at the crime scene. "So you hit him with a magazine," he said as the spicy chili, creamy cheese, and crisp, salty fries coated his mouth with an ambrosia-like flavor. His taste buds cried out in sheer bliss.

Lucy paused mid-chew and stared at James. "*That's* what started Brinkley's nosebleed."

Amelia began to cry again. "I didn't mean to kill him! I was just so mad! I already gave him the whole five hundred dollars from that horrible job, and he still asked for more!" Tears ran down her cheeks, and she suddenly looked very much younger than her twenty years. "I don't know anything about those drugs the paper talked about, though. I swear it!"

"I believe you," Lucy said and patted Amelia's elegant but work-worn hand. James could see tiny burns on the girl's knuckles, undoubtedly from the oven, and small cuts produced by nicks of a knife. He thought about how different Amelia's hands were from Allison's.

"Do you have to tell people about my pictures?" Amelia asked.

"Only if it's necessary," Lucy said. "As long as you've told me the truth about everything that happened between you and Brinkley Myers, I think we can keep your secret."

"Thank you. Look, I gotta go," the young woman said, glancing at her watch. "I'm one of the chain saw maniacs in the haunted field tonight, and I've got to learn the pathways and have my makeup done."

"Just one more question, honey, and then you can go." Lucy bit off the end of another fry. "Who else was with you guys that Labor Day weekend? Because if you didn't steal the drugs from Mr. Livingstone's bathroom, then someone else did."

"I don't know," Amelia said hurriedly and stood up. She wiped her cheeks, straightened her shoulders, and flicked a strand of long hair over her shoulder. Facing forward, she marched off, smiling alluringly at the man with the cowboy hat before disappearing into the milling crowd.

"Back to square one," Lucy muttered, gazing after Amelia. "Damn."

James didn't respond. His mouth was too crammed with chili cheese fries to utter so much as an intelligible syllable.

• • •

The afternoon shadows were lengthening as James and Lucy headed off to tell the others about their conversation with Amelia, and they all agreed to meet back at the podium for the festival's closing ceremony at five. The mayor planned to make a speech and then send the crowd down to Miller's farm to purchase tickets for the Haunted Hayride. Most of the locals had already been on the ride during the weeks leading up to Halloween, but Mr. Miller promised an even more fearful display for the benefit crowd.

James collected Gillian and then stopped to watch Bennett yank stray darts from the surface of several wooden tables and chairs.

Trying to suppress their laughter, they also saw him pull one out of his boot.

"Good thing they're steel-toed," Bennett grumbled as his friends helped him clean up his booth.

The Flab Five gathered to one side of the platform erected for the mayor's speech. As an assistant tested the acoustics of the sound system, Lucy quickly filled the rest of the supper club members in on what she and James had learned from Amelia.

"You're positive that this young woman is innocent of murder?" Gillian asked, her face looking drawn and tired. James noticed that her hands were wrinkled from having been submerged in soapy water all day long.

"Amelia admitted that she hit Brinkley in the face with her magazine, thus causing the nosebleed, but she swears that she doesn't know anything about the stolen Coumadin." Lucy looked at her friends in turn. "I'm inclined to believe her."

"She's already kept secrets from the law. How can you trust her?" Bennett muttered crossly and examined the hole in his shiny black boot.

"I can't see her planning a murder," Lindy said. "Whitney is smart, but—and I know from having taught her—Amelia isn't the sharpest tack in the drawer. She works hard, bless her heart, but she just doesn't have the brains to steal drugs, grind them up, feed them to someone, and then make sure he started to bleed."

"What's the story with her parents?" James asked Lindy.

"Megan's husband split years ago, when Amelia was a freshman in high school. Afterward, Megan moved here and opened the Sweet Tooth. I know they really struggled for a while. Even now, Megan probably couldn't make a go of it without her daughter's help."

"Brinkley must have made Amelia angry enough to want to take *some* kind of action," Bennett persisted.

"I'd most certainly want to see him punished after what he's done to these poor girls!" Gillian exclaimed. "Let's just pray he'll be reincarnated as a dung beetle."

The supper club members stared at her in amusement.

"Anyway," Lucy continued. "We didn't find out if there was another person at this sleepover. So far, we know that two girls have been the victims of blackmail. Was there a third? Or a fourth?"

"Maybe the two girls planned the murder together," Bennett suggested. "If not, why are they covering for one another?"

"I don't think that's it." Lucy frowned. "We're missing something—some clue as to the killer's identity. Whitney didn't run herself over, and Amelia doesn't even own a car. If she hit Whitney with the bakery's delivery van, I'd think someone would have noticed."

"Besides, Whitney said the car made a funny noise," James reminded his friends.

"I think we need to confront Amelia again," Lindy said. "I need to get her to tell us if anyone else was being blackmailed by that little punk. It would be fun to go to the Haunted Hayride anyway. Maybe Principal Chavez will be there. Maybe he'll need my protection." She pretended to hold an invisible man tightly to her chest.

At that moment, the mayor stepped up to the microphone accompanied by Beau and Caroline Livingstone. Beau was wearing a blue suit that looked a size too large for his frame, and Caroline had donned a long dress with black and white polka dots. They both looked slightly embarrassed and overwhelmed by the sheer immensity of the crowd.

"Welcome, friends," the mayor began. "I have never been so proud to be a Virginian as I am tonight." The crowd cheered. "You folks came from all across our beautiful state to help these good people beside me. I know that when we turn on our televisions, the news shows are filled with horrible stories about people hurting each other. Our books, magazines, newspapers—they all show how unkind or rude or thoughtless we can be. Well, I think that's only one side of our story. A small side. I believe that most people are good, and tonight, you've proved me right!" Roars erupted from around the podium. The mayor held up her arms to shush the audience. "I hold in my hand a piece of paper listing the total amount of money raised here today. Donations are still coming in, and I'm sure the fine men and women of our postal service will be delivering hundreds of letters to the Livingstones over the next week."

The mayor turned to Beau and Caroline, and she unfolded the piece of paper.

"Tonight, through the generosity of your fellow Virginians, neighbors reaching out from the Blue Ridge Mountains to the

Chesapeake Bay, I am pleased to present you with donations totaling a little over thirty-five thousand dollars!"

Caroline's hand flew to her mouth as Beau reeled in shock. Two reporters, Murphy Alistair and a suave-looking young man holding a mini recorder, began snapping pictures.

"We owe a special debt of gratitude to Shilling's Stables for the donation of their fine thoroughbred colt. It brought the highest bid at our silent auction at ten thousand dollars! Thank you all for your heartfelt contributions." The two reporters swung their cameras in the direction of Allison Shilling and her mother, but Mrs. Shilling hid behind Allison and Chase so that the couple appeared to be the generous donors. Allison produced a wide smile that never reached her eyes, and Chase put a proprietary arm around his fiancée's shoulders and waved benevolently at the crowd.

The mayor then offered the microphone to Beau, but he was too overcome with emotion to speak. Caroline, her eyes brimming with tears, profusely thanked the crowd and then sank down in a chair and started to sob. The crowd whooped and hollered for another five minutes and then began to disperse.

The supper club members waited to congratulate Beau and Caroline in person. After receiving bear hugs from both of them, James wriggled free and asked after Whitney's condition.

"She's finally at home," Caroline said, relieved to be discussing a subject other than the incredible amount of money raised on their behalf. "She begged me to get her out of the hospital. She said she couldn't take any more of their food."

Beau chuckled. "Can't say I blame her. I think that's what *really* caused my stroke."

"Anyway, it'll be quite a few weeks before she can go back to Dolly's since she's got that cast on her arm, so we told her to catch up on her schoolwork," Caroline added.

Beau smiled happily. "If my Pet Palaces sell as well in Harrisonburg as they did here, we should be able to let Whitney go back to school full-time next semester."

"I've got a few ideas for launching this product." Gillian gestured toward two chairs behind the podium. "Do you want to hear them?"

"Absolutely!" Beau looked like a new man. "Lead the way, ma'am."

"I'm off to the Haunted Hayride," Lindy said. "Someone has to come with me. Seriously, I am not going through that field at night by myself."

"Fine, fine. I'll go." Bennett jerked his thumb in the direction of the parking lot, where a pickup truck waited to lead the visitors to Miller's farm. "But don't expect me to act all scared when some teenager wielding a plastic axe jumps out from behind the cornstalks."

"Maybe they'll have an eight-year-old brandishing a dart instead." Lindy elbowed Bennett in the ribs and everyone laughed.

James and Lucy watched their friends walk away. "Well, I've got to go home and cook dinner for my pop," James said to Caroline and Lucy.

"How is he?" Caroline asked. "I never see him around town."

"He doesn't leave the yard anymore. He's pretty much a recluse these days."

Caroline pulled a face. "That's such a shame. I'd like to make some meals for him, if that's all right. You and your friends have done so much for us, and I'd like to show our gratitude somehow."

"Sure." James brightened at the thought of not having to cook separate meals for himself and his father all the time. Jackson never seemed to want what James was eating. He deliberately demanded pasta dishes, casseroles, potatoes, and sweets like brownies and chocolate cake, hoping to get his son to cheat. But so far, James hadn't succumbed to temptation. Until today. Remembering how he and Lucy had wolfed down the chili cheese fries, James flushed.

He was about to return to the silent auction booth in an attempt to finally discover what was inside the box his father had donated, when Caroline thrust an arm out to block his path.

"I almost forgot!" she said excitedly. "When Whitney first woke up this morning, she told me that she recalled something about the hit and run. Now that she's feeling better, a few details are coming back to her."

"What did she remember?" Lucy asked, her blue eyes sparkling with curiosity.

"She said that she thought the driver was wearing a mask. She only got a quick look, like a flash, but she swears she saw a mask."

James gave Caroline his full attention, his plans to visit the silent auction booth completely abandoned. "What kind of mask?"

Caroline paused in doubt for a moment, but then she lowered her voice to a whisper. "Whitney says it was a dog mask. It sounds crazy, but she thought the dog was a poodle."

Chapter Twelve

Bombay Catfish

On Sunday evening, Lucy was the first to arrive at the Henry residence. Instead of ringing the doorbell, she knocked timidly at the front door. When James opened it with a mighty creak, he noticed that Lucy's hands, which were holding a glass casserole dish, were shaking slightly.

"You okay?" he asked her.

She released her breath and smiled as she glanced down at her hands. "To tell you the truth, I was half expecting your daddy to come barreling out with a sawed-off shotgun, screaming at me to get off his land. I heard that he doesn't care for visitors much."

"No chance of him coming after you." James choked out a forced laugh. "He's still holed up in his shed. I told him this morning that I had friends coming over for supper and he pretended not to be listening, so who knows how he'll act when *his* dinnertime rolls around." He stepped back into the house. "Come on in."

James led Lucy into the kitchen and followed her glance as she took in the sad state of the space that had once been the heart of the Henry home. The floral wallpaper had yellowed with age and little cracks had sprung up around the edges, especially near the stove and refrigerator. The beige linoleum floor was stained and peeling in the corners, and though James had spent all morning cleaning, the overall impression was a tired and neglected room.

"You can tell men live here," Lucy teased, clearly searching for something to say.

James nodded and led her to the dining room.

Unused since his mother's death, this was the only space that time had treated gently. There was a warm patina to the dark pieces of antique furniture, the sage-green Oriental rug, and the framed botanical prints gracing the walls. James had dug out some green candles from the sideboard and placed them throughout the room. The chandelier had been turned to a low setting, and a cluster of deep red chrysanthemums set in a simple glass vase in the middle of the table created an intimate atmosphere.

Lucy seemed to grow a little nervous being alone in the candlelit space with James. Her eyes kept darting to and fro, as if Jackson Henry was in hiding, spying on the two of them from behind the sideboard or the potted palm. "So," she began. "I'd better preheat the oven. I'm serving fish tonight."

James grimaced involuntarily. "Ick."

"Don't worry." Lucy punched him playfully on the arm. "It's so well-disguised with spices you'll think you're eating chicken."

James raised his hand to give her a flirtatious poke in return, when the doorbell chimed.

All three of the other supper club members stood huddled on the front stoop, shivering in the November night air.

"Here we are!" Lindy exclaimed. "Oh, I can't wait to meet the mysterious father of our own Professor Henry. You know, I saw him on a regular basis when he owned the hardware store, but I don't remember talking to him much."

"That's because he's never been much for talking. Don't expect him to sit down and join us for dinner, either. He may never leave the shed while you guys are here." James draped their coats over one of the ladder-back chairs in the living room. "Come on into the kitchen. Does anyone need pans or pot holders or anything?"

Bennett held out a pie plate covered with aluminum foil. "I've created my own low-carb dessert, and it is really, really good. So good that I ate a whole one by myself last week."

"What kind of pie is it?" Gillian asked, a hungry gleam in her eyes. "May the Buddha provide that it is better than those awful tombstones I forced you all to eat last week."

"I'm not telling you until it's time to serve it," Bennett said stubbornly, placing the pie in the fridge.

Gillian held up her own baking dish. "Green beans with almond slices and Parmesan cheese. I can just nuke them for a few minutes when we're ready to eat."

"I've got spinach salad with homemade bacon dressing." Lindy put a heavy ceramic bowl on the dining room table. "James! You've made this room so pretty for us. What a warm and inviting space."

"Thanks." James felt himself relaxing. If his father stayed in the shed, there was a chance the supper club members could spend a pleasant evening together. Smiling optimistically, James began taking drink orders for diet soda or water.

"When can we start having wine or other adult beverages?" Lucy demanded. "I'm sick of all this caffeine-free, diet, chemical-filled crap."

"When you model your jeans for us, then we'll have a glass of wine to celebrate," Lindy said. "Deal?"

Lucy's cheeks flushed a deep pink, as if fresh raspberries had been rubbed all over them. "Deal. In fact, I think I'm not far away from fitting in them. When we're back at my house, I'll try them on when you're all there to see if I can get into them. Who'll bring the wine just in case I manage to zip them?"

James raised his hand high in the air like a kindergarten student anxious to share his show-and-tell item. "I have a great bottle of Merlot that I bought a few years ago. I set it aside for a special occasion, but it's been sitting in the back of my closet since. By now, it's perfectly aged and ready to be shared."

"What kind of special occasion? Like an anniversary or something?" Gillian asked, sipping a glass of water.

"Yeah. Jane wasn't much for celebrating our anniversary." James turned to Lucy, his warm brown eyes filled with hope and a hint of sadness. "But if you get in those jeans, Lucy, that's celebration enough for me."

Lucy returned his stare, her own eyes reflecting gratitude and affection. James thought he saw something else there too. A trace of longing, perhaps? But was she thinking of her desire to lose the weight and become a deputy or, dare James believe it, a desire for him?

The others sensed something charged in the nonverbal exchange between their friends and bustled off to prepare the dinner. James focused on setting the table, feeling like a teenager caught making out in the backseat of his parents' car. Lucy remained unfazed. Completely at ease in the Henry kitchen, she checked on her catfish and chatted away about the success of Neighbor Aid.

"Dinner is served," Lucy said, and they all took their places at the table. She placed a plate of fish in front of James with a flourish. "All right, James. Taste this. I dare you to tell me that you don't like fish afterward." She served everyone else and then sat down. "This is Bombay Catfish, my friends. It's a bit spicy, so get your drinks ready."

James took a hesitant bite. He loved Indian food, but was positive that the taste of fish would overpower the flavor of any of the other ingredients in the dish. Therefore, he was pleasantly surprised by the curry, paprika, and yogurt that Lucy had added to both sides of the tender fish filet. James still wasn't fond of the entrée's flaky texture, but he wasn't about to mention that to Lucy.

"Well?" She looked at him expectantly.

"It's good. Really. What's in it?" James said once his mouth was empty.

"Fat-free yogurt, curry powder, paprika, cardamom—and I had to drive twenty-five miles to find *that* one—cilantro, and salt and pepper."

"This is healthy? Honestly and truly?" Gillian stabbed at her fish with her fork.

Lucy nodded. "Yep. And it's easy to make too. I marinated the fish in the fridge for a few hours and then cooked it for ten minutes. Nothing to it."

Everyone ate in contented silence for a few minutes, passing dishes back and forth and enjoying the food and the company.

"So what's the next step in our investigation?" Bennett asked, putting down his fork and tenting his fingers over his empty plate. As usual, he was the first person to finish eating.

"We've got a new clue," Lucy said in a singsong voice.

Lindy swatted at Lucy with her napkin. "Don't hold out on us. Spill it!"

"Children, children." Gillian waved a warning finger at the other women. "Behave. Otherwise, I'll be forced to illustrate some of my fiercer jujitsu moves on you."

James laughed. Gillian had definitely loosened up since he had first met her a few weeks ago.

"Whitney remembered an odd detail about the driver who hit her," Lucy said, quickly growing serious. "She says he or she was wearing a dog mask. She's pretty sure it was a poodle."

"A poodle?" Lindy frowned. "How bizarre! And kind of silly."

Bennett cleared his throat. "Toy poodles are silly, perhaps, but did you know that the standard poodle is one of the oldest dog breeds in history? In fact, there are carvings on Roman tombs closely resembling the contemporary poodle. A noble and loyal dog."

Lindy scowled. "I just mean that it's a ridiculous mask for a killer to wear. Does Goodbee's Drug Store sell poodle masks?"

No one knew.

"Do you regularly groom anyone who owns a poodle?" James asked Gillian. "Maybe the killer chose the mask because he or she actually likes the breed."

Gillian considered the question. "That's not an unreasonable line of thinking, actually. People do often identify with their pets on a deep and spiritual level. I have several customers who own either toy poodles or standard poodles. I can't call up an image of anyone who seems particularly violent at this moment, but I'll flip through my customer list tomorrow and share the names with Lucy."

Lindy wiped her mouth with her napkin. "And I'll swing by Goodbee's after school tomorrow. Most of the masks are gone now since he put them on sale at seventy-five percent off, but I'm sure he's got a record somewhere of which ones he ordered."

"How will you justify asking him for an inventory list?" Lucy asked.

Lindy waved off the question with a flick of her wrist. "I'll just say that we need dog masks for an upcoming drama club production and I want to order from the same company."

Bennett chuckled. "Remind me never to play poker against you, Lindy."

"That's the only lead James and I were able to discover for now." Lucy turned to Lindy. "Did you get a chance to talk to Amelia last night?"

"Ha!" Bennett snorted. "That girl was too busy shoving her tongue down Darryl Jeffries's throat to even bother trying to scare us. Some haunted hayride. The only scary part was watching the two of them go at it."

Lucy leaned forward on her elbows. "Amelia was kissing Darryl Jeffries? Brinkley's friend?"

"The same." Bennett grimaced. "Doesn't say much about Amelia's taste in men."

"Wait a minute!" Lucy yelled, startling her companions. "What if Darryl killed Brinkley in a fit of revenge? If Amelia is Darryl's girlfriend, he must have been pretty ticked about Brinkley's blackmail attempts." She twisted a lock of caramel hair around her forefinger. "James, can you stop by the Amoco where Darryl works and try to get a read on him? Fill up your truck and have a nice chat? I'd better not, because I complained about the patch he put on my tire over the summer, and his boss reamed him out about it. I don't think I'm on his list of favorite customers."

"Sure," James said, though he had no earthly idea how he was supposed to initiate a conversation with the young man. "Anything to keep us in the game."

Just then, the group heard the slamming of the back door and the sound of shuffling footsteps in the kitchen. No one spoke. No one moved. James held his breath as his friends listened closely, their eyes round with anticipation. It was as if a ravenous grizzly bear was prowling around the next room instead of an irascible old man in a pair of worn overalls and slippers.

"What in the hell?" they heard Jackson holler on the other side of the door leading into the kitchen. "Where's the goddamn crust on this pie?"

"Um, who'd like coffee?" James asked, jumping out of his chair. "Decaf all around?"

His friends nodded mutely and James hustled into the kitchen. His father sat at the table, chewing on a pile of green beans and a slice of buttered bread. He was reading the paper with an air of complete absorption and didn't give his son the slightest glance as James collected the coffeepot and five dessert plates.

"Don't forget the Reddi-wip!" Bennett called from the dining room, and James could hear the sound of his friends' quiet laughter. Irritated, he made one trip with the coffee and plates, and then returned for forks, the mangled pie, and a can of Reddi-wip. Jackson never moved a muscle.

"Is that a pumpkin pie?" Lindy asked. "Or should I say, *was* that a pumpkin pie?"

"Aw, it's not that bad. The old guy just took a taste," Bennett said.

"Yeah, right from the center!" Lucy pointed out.

"So this is low-carb?" Gillian asked Bennett as James served the pie.

"Sure is. Made the recipe up all by myself. Trust me, it's good stuff. 'Course, it helps to have a nice, healthy dose of Reddi-wip on top. I always put a big 'B' on all my desserts." He sprayed the can of whipped cream on his pie slice to demonstrate.

"Bennett!" Gillian exclaimed, licking her fork. "I don't know how you're still single when you can come up with something as delicious as this. I'm going to march right down to the First Baptist Church and put a notice on their bulletin board announcing that there is a single, hardworking, trivia-loving postman who enjoys experimenting with food and is looking for love."

"Do that, and I will save everyone's junk mail for a month and deliver it to you over the next two years," Bennett retorted.

"Go ahead." Gillian shrugged. "If my bills can't fit into the mailbox then I won't have to pay them. Let's see the recipe for this pie, Chef Postman."

Bennett passed around copies of the recipe.

The Flab Five's Guiltless, Crustless Pumpkin Pie

2 eggs slightly beaten
1 can (16 ounces) Libby's solid pack pumpkin
1/2 cup (or less) Splenda or other sugar substitute made for baking
1/2 teaspoon salt
1/2 teaspoon nutmeg
1 teaspoon ground cinnamon
1 teaspoon ground ginger
1/4 teaspoon ground cloves
1 teaspoon pure vanilla extract
1 1/2 cups (12-ounce can) undiluted Carnation evaporated milk (or evaporated skim milk)

Preheat oven to 425 degrees. Combine the filling ingredients in the order given. Pour into a glass pie dish. Bake 15 minutes at 425 degrees. Reduce temperature to 350 degrees. Bake an additional 40–50 minutes or until a knife inserted near the center comes out clean. Cool.

After devouring their slices of pie, the supper club members filled coffee cups with decaf and planned their next meeting at Gillian's house. Gillian handed out directions printed on purple paper and James immediately recognized her street. The houses in Gillian's neighborhood were mostly historic homes.

"Are you in one of the houses on the National Register?" James asked.

"Not yet," Gillian said. "I'd like to be, but I need to finish a few more renovations to qualify. I think the business I am starting with Beau Livingstone might just provide the solution. I'd divide any extra cash between my favorite charities and making my home the beautiful piece of history it could be."

"That's great," Lindy said. "What are your plans to launch the Pet Palaces?"

"First, Beau and I need to hire someone who can build us a website. Beau has a bunch of photos of the pet palaces to put online—all stuff he built to take to the Veterans Day parade in Harrisonburg next week. After our website is up and running, I'm going to advertise in some of the smaller pet magazines. We can't afford to place ads in the big ones." She threw up her hand, her silver bangles tinkling merrily. "After that, we'll just sit back and let the orders pour in. I'm going to handle marketing, billing, and freight issues, and Beau is going to handle the building and design part."

"You know, I think the Fitzgerald brothers could make you a killer website," James said. "They'd certainly be cheaper than hiring one of those IT guys, and they'd love the experience. We're thinking about offering computer courses at the library, and they'll be teaching them."

"I will call them. First thing tomorrow, before the library gets too busy." She smiled. "I just adore those boys."

"And just like that, Pet Palaces, Inc., is born!" Lucy declared and held her coffee cup aloft in a salute.

As the group of friends toasted Gillian with their cups, the back door slammed once again.

"Out to the shed he goes," James mumbled.

"We should probably get going." Bennett shot James a worried glance. "It's hardly fair to keep your daddy out of his own house."

"It's by his own choice," James said with a hint of petulance.

Lindy rose. "I'm going to try to talk to him. When was the last time someone took the time to just listen to him?" She looked at James accusingly.

Gillian answered before James could even open his mouth. "That man is grieving. He might be acting like some kind of crazed hermit, but that's how he's coping with a major loss. It might seem like an odd way of showing grief, but people all over this world have different ways of dealing with death. For example, in China—"

"I like the way they turn funerals into a party in New Orleans," Bennett interrupted. "That's what I'd want. Jazz band, bright umbrellas, tons of food and booze. That's the way to go, yessir."

"See?" Gillian gave Bennett an approving nod. "Who are we to judge?"

"Well, I'm still going out there." Lindy headed for the back door.

"He probably won't unlock it for you!" James called after her. "And if he does, you'll be entering at your own risk!"

The remaining four friends brought their plates to the sink and began to wash up. They waited with baited breath for Lindy to be driven from the shed, but it soon became apparent that she'd been given permission to enter and had not yet been verbally eviscerated by Jackson Henry.

"I guess I'll head home," Gillian said as she dried off her bean dish.

"Me too." Bennett and Lucy also bid James goodbye.

A few minutes later, Lindy exited the shed and pranced into the kitchen to retrieve her salad bowl.

"Well?" James was dying to know how Lindy fared with his father.

"I'm sorry, James, but I promised your daddy that our conversation would remain confidential."

"What? Why?" James spluttered in annoyance.

"I can't say anything else. That's the nature of secrets." She winked at him. "Thanks for a great dinner!"

James watched Lindy drive off in bewilderment.

The lights in the shed were still on, but there wasn't the slightest indication that someone had entered the lion's den and had lived to tell the tale.

James had just blown out the candles in the dining room when there was a light tap on the front door.

"I forgot my casserole dish," Lucy said, avoiding James's eyes.

"Oh. Sure. Let me get it."

When he returned with the dish, Lucy was holding a framed

picture of a six-year-old James wearing a Batman costume. She'd taken it from the hall table and was studying it closely, a smile playing around the corners of her mouth.

"Do you remember this Halloween?"

James looked down at the photo. "I sure do. I loved that costume."

"You were really cute." Lucy returned the frame to the table and accepted her glass dish. She turned to go, hesitated, and then swung around to face James again. "Actually, I left it here on purpose."

James could feel his heart thumping against his rib cage. As if from a great distance, he saw himself reaching out to caress her hair, brushing it tenderly from her soft cheek. Lucy took a step toward him. He could smell her fruity perfume and the coconut scent of her shampoo. Sliding his arm behind her back, he gently brought her body close enough to his so that their lips could meet.

Lucy tasted of coffee. James kissed her once, cautiously, and then again, with more hunger. Just as he was about to tell her how much he cared about her, the unmistakable sounds of Jackson entering the house through the kitchen reverberated through the hall. James and Lucy jumped apart, wiping their lips and straightening their tousled hair.

"Good night," Lucy whispered and dashed out the front door.

James stared after her, wearing a goofy smile and waving goodbye until her Jeep's taillights grew smaller and smaller, like two red stars winking through the dense row of trees.

"Christ! Are they finally gone?" Jackson demanded, sneaking up behind James.

"Yes, Pop. We won't be meeting here again until December."

Jackson closed and locked the front door. "Guess I should say a prayer for small favors," he muttered sarcastically.

"So what did you talk about with Lindy?" James asked, his curiosity temporarily overcoming his desire to dwell on his romantic moment with Lucy.

Jackson raised his caterpillar eyebrows and smirked. "Lindy? Was that her name?"

"Come on, Pop," James prompted gently, thinking about what Gillian had said about Jackson still working through his grief. "It's okay to talk to people. Mom would have wanted you to."

For a second, James thought his father would erupt like a boiling teakettle, but Jackson seemed to be digesting the words without spitting out the first flippant reply that came to mind.

"The best parts of me, and I know there weren't many, died with your mother. I've got nothin' left to offer," Jackson said in a low voice and turned away.

James held him back by placing a hand on his shoulder. "No, Pop." He reached over from behind Jackson's back and tapped in the center of his father's chest, above his heart. "The best parts of Mom are living right here. She's in your heart, and she's in mine. She'll never leave us, Pop. Not ever."

Jackson pulled away, slowly. Halfway up the stairs, he pivoted to look at James. It was the first time he'd met his son's eyes for more than a few seconds since James had moved back home.

"Well, good night," he said hoarsely. And then, in a voice so soft that James nearly missed it, Jackson added, "Son."

Chapter Thirteen

Buttercream Frosting

The next day, James woke with a start. He'd tossed and turned the night before, wondering how to begin a casual conversation with a young man he had never laid eyes on before. Even thoughts of the kiss he'd shared with Lucy hadn't eased his anxiety over worming information out of Darryl Jeffries.

James didn't pass the Cabin Creek Amoco station during his short commute home, so he drove there during his lunch hour. Seeing how it had only taken him five minutes to gulp down the filling of two tacos and a beef and cheese burrito from the Quickie Mart, he had plenty of time left for investigative work. In fact, after he dumped the tortilla shells in the trash, he went back inside the convenience store to buy two hot dogs without buns. He then gulped down a bottle of water, frowned over the absurd cost of his lunch, and prepared to conduct his inaugural interview with a potential murder suspect.

Wishing for Lucy's guidance, James pulled next to one of the pumps and began to fill the Bronco with gas. He noticed that the gas prices were five cents lower than they were in town. No wonder the station was busy. The other three pumps were occupied, and there were two cars up on lifts inside the garage bays. James topped off his tank and entered the small checkout area. A short line of customers waited to pay for gas or to purchase sundries. It only took one glance for James to realize that the cashier wasn't Darryl, but a woman in her mid-fifties who had a lollipop stuffed into one cheek while she cheerfully nattered with customers and zipped credit cards through a machine.

James peered through the glass door connecting the Food Mart to the garage. He could see the shiny dome of a bald head sticking out from the undercarriage of a Honda Accord, but he couldn't tell who was working on the classic Camaro coming down from the lift in the far bay. James paid for his gas, walked around the front of the garage, and approached the man operating the lift. He had a broad back and was dressed in black jeans and a worn denim jacket.

"Excuse me," James said.

The man turned to face him, and James knew that he had found Darryl Jeffries. Though not as captivatingly handsome as Brinkley, Darryl was good-looking in his own right. He had almond-colored eyes, straight brown hair, and a boyish sprinkling of freckles across the bridge of his nose. His upper body was wide and muscular, and his hands were covered with smears of grease and oil. Like Brinkley, his midsection showed the beginnings of a beer belly. Darryl's cheek was filled like a squirrel's, and when he turned aside to spit into a cup, James realized the twentysomething was sucking on a wad of tobacco big enough to put a professional baseball player to shame.

"Can I help you, mister?" Darryl's tone reflected a mixture of impatience and the need to demonstrate courtesy to all customers.

"Uh, my Bronco has this strange habit. Sometimes, it keeps on running after I take the key out of the ignition," James said. No one in the car industry ever believed him when he mentioned the Bronco's odd quirk.

Darryl swung his head around to look to where the Bronco was parked at the gas pump. "That yours?" He pointed, a spark of interest lighting in his eyes.

"Yep. It's an 'eighty-five."

"An oldie but a goodie." Forgetting all about the car on the lift, Darryl walked to the Bronco and patted the white hood as if he was greeting an old friend. "I've got a classic like this at home. It's a 'sixty-eight that I'm fixin' up in my spare time. I've even got a bikini top for her."

James had a vague mental image of a Bronco from that era. It was a true outdoorsman's truck—exposed steel frames and giant wheels crying out to be driven through the mud. He decided to act supremely impressed. "That'll be a heck of a truck when you're done. You can tear all over these mountains with a powerful machine like that. What kind of work does she need?"

Darryl chortled. "Just a minor engine overhaul! Now, how long has your girl been makin' trouble for you?"

"Ever since I drove it off the lot." The irritating habit had existed since James owned the truck. It had happened to him several times, but never in the presence of any mechanic. Even after James explained the problem to the servicemen at the dealership, they'd examined the Bronco from top to bottom. Finding nothing amiss, they'd thrown up their hands in defeat. The problem only occurred when James was alone in his truck. He finally gave up trying to get the Bronco fixed and learned, by trial and error, that the engine would eventually cut off if he jiggled the keys frantically enough.

Darryl was staring at the hood thoughtfully. "Might be your battery leads. Do you want me to take a look?"

"If you've got the time, I'd really appreciate it," James said, pretending to be extremely grateful.

"Let me pull her into the bay. I just need to get that Camaro out of the way first. Be right back."

Watching Darryl hustle off, James tried to picture the young man as a killer, but failed. Darryl seemed like a helpful, good-natured, and hardworking kid. True, he hadn't become a nuclear physicist after graduating from Blue Ridge High, but he was obviously a competent mechanic. Judging from the cars parked alongside the garage, Darryl seemed to have plenty of work lined up for the day and, unlike many folks, he seemed to truly enjoy his job.

In the time it took Darryl to move the Camaro, a convertible Beetle zipped up to the pump next to James and a leggy brunette stepped out wearing jeans that appeared as though they'd been airbrushed to her gazelle-like legs, and a short leather jacket that cinched tightly around her waist. She shook out her long hair and then applied some ruby-red lipstick using the car's passenger mirror.

Here's my chance to talk about girls, James thought as Darryl walked over to the Bronco, overtly ogling the comely brunette.

"You get customers like that all the time?" James whispered, jerking his head toward the woman.

"Not as often as I wish!" Darryl exclaimed, eyeing the woman's legs. But his professionalism overcame his interest in the woman, and he got into the Bronco and drove it into the bay. As he popped the hood, he cast one more glance at the brunette as she sauntered from the Food Mart back to her car. "Man, I love a chick in cowboy boots."

"Who doesn't? I hope your girlfriend owns a pair," James joked.

"Tsss," Darryl made a sound through the mound of tobacco. "She doesn't wear boots, but she's pretty hot."

"Like model hot?" James prodded, feeling idiotically transparent.

"Yessir," Darryl said offhandedly, absorbed in his examination of the Bronco.

"Lucky man." James glanced around the garage. Behind him was a cluttered desk bearing a half-empty liter bottle of Mountain Dew and a soiled Atlanta Braves baseball cap. Above the desk was a bulletin board covered with phone numbers, parts diagrams, and a poster of a blonde in a bikini draped over the hood of a black Ferrari.

Darryl lifted his gaze from the Bronco's engine, noticed what had caught James's attention, and laughed. "*That's* not my girlfriend!" He gestured at the poster. "She did one modeling job, but decided it just wasn't her thing. You've probably seen her around. Her mama owns the Sweet Tooth and she works there. Works real hard." Darryl was clearly proud that his girlfriend held a steady job.

"I love that place," James said. It was nice to be honest for a chance. "I'm sure your girlfriend has helped me there before. She's a sweetheart. Her name's Amelia, right?"

"Yep, that's her." Darryl climbed inside the Bronco and began tinkering around inside the steering column.

"I bet Amelia's had a rough time lately, eh? What with that ex-football player dying in her shop and all. She doing okay?"

"Yeah, she's a tough nut." Darryl scowled at the steering wheel, and then turned the engine over. He removed the key, and to James's astonishment the engine kept running. Other than the frown he wore over the mechanical puzzle before him, Darryl seemed completely unperturbed by much, including the mention of Brinkley's death.

"You look like you might have played some ball yourself," James said admiringly.

"I was on defense. Not the same kind of glory as guys like Brinkley get." He paused and then added, "Got."

"Were you two friends?" James hoped he wasn't pushing it too hard.

"We hung out now and then after we graduated, but he started acting funny a few months ago, and I started spending more time with my girl. You know how it goes. Once a woman's got her hooks in you, look out! There goes your free time." Darryl sounded delighted to be able to complain about his relationship.

James was stumped. Not only was it evident that Darryl felt no animosity toward his onetime friend, but he gave no indication that he was aware of Brinkley's blackmail scheme.

"This truck has cost me so much money over the years," James said, changing tack. "But I have no regrets. It's got to be tough for you to come up with the extra dough you need to overhaul your Bronco," he continued. "All the long hours here, and then I'm sure you have to spend money on your girlfriend. I don't know how guys like you work so hard." James fidgeted as he prepared to lie. "Well, not *all* of you guys. Whenever I saw Brinkley he was eating at the diner or hanging around the video store, checking out three or four movies. Guess he didn't have a girlfriend to spend his hard-earned money on. Lucky man."

Darryl shrugged. "Brinkley always claimed to have more than one. Who knows? Girls thought he was some kind of god." He paused, adjusting something out of James's view behind the dashboard. "I don't know where he got his extra cash from, either, but he definitely had a pile. No way he mowed *that* many lawns." He grunted in exertion and then jumped out of the car and disappeared under the hood again. "I think I know what's going on here!" he shouted, pulling open a drawer near the desk and fishing out a tool.

James froze. His gig was up, and Darryl was calling his bluff. "You do?"

"I think so." The young man pointed excitedly at the Bronco. "Do you leave your car outside at night?"

James leaned into the driver's-side door. "Yes."

"Does it keep running like this in the summer or only in the colder months?"

James thought about the question and then his eyes flew open wide. "Only when it's cold! I never noticed that before."

"Then you've got a bad battery lead." Darryl smiled triumphantly, and James smiled right back. "It makes your battery drain in cold weather. I can fix that. I also think we should make a copy of your key. I think the original, the one that the dealer gave you, is messed up." He pointed at the ignition. "The tumblers connect to the ignition switch and my guess is that this key pushes the tumblers on its way out. It's only supposed to hit them on the way in. I can file your new key down a bit and then your problem should be solved. Can you leave it with me for the day?"

James stared at Darryl in amazement. "Man, you're a magician. I can't, because I've got to get back to work, but I can drop it off first thing in the morning and catch a ride from a friend."

"Sounds like a plan. I'll put you down for tomorrow. I didn't catch your name." James introduced himself and shook the young man's hand. Pleased to have solved a customer's riddle, Darryl jotted a note in his appointment book. While he was writing James's phone number, the sound of police sirens broke the midday stillness.

Two brown sheriff's department cruisers pulled in front of the garage and came to a grinding halt directly behind James's truck.

"What the hell?" Darryl dropped his pencil in shock.

Sheriff Huckabee and Deputy Donovan leapt from their cars and strode over to the young mechanic. Their faces were set in grim determination, and James felt himself grow tense.

"Darryl Jeffries?" Sheriff Huckabee asked. "We've got some questions to ask you. You want to answer them here or down at the station?"

James stood frozen in shock as Donovan turned a disdainful gaze on him. "Now just what are you — ?"

"What the hell is going on here?" the bald man who was working on the Honda suddenly demanded. "This boy committed a crime?"

"That's what we're trying to find out, Tom. We just need to ask him a few questions." Sheriff Huckabee stepped closer to Darryl.

"Well, damn it all! You don't need to drive in here like we're harboring terrorists! You're scaring all my customers. Turn off the blasted sirens, come inside, and sit down like civilized human beings. Does he need a lawyer?"

"No, no," Sheriff Huckabee replied in a placating tone, never taking his eyes off Darryl. "We've got a girl missing, and we need to know if your assistant has any information on her whereabouts."

The man named Tom, who James assumed was Darryl's boss, seemed satisfied with the sheriff's answer.

"What girl? What are you talking about?" Darryl asked angrily.

"Calm down, boy," Donovan said in his patronizing tone. "You sass me and I will drag you downtown."

James thought Donovan sounded like a complete hack, like some cheesy cop from a B movie reciting his lines in front of the mirror. Donovan was such an incredibly disagreeable person that James wished he could think of something to say to take him down a notch, but felt this was not the right time.

"When did you last see Amelia Flowers?" Huckabee asked.

Darryl was clearly startled by the question. "Saturday night. We worked Miller's Haunted Hayride. Why? What's going on? What's happening?" His voice turned shrill and echoed through the garage.

"Once again, I'm warning you to calm down, son. I won't stand for these outbursts," Donovan threatened. Tapping his gun holster, he continued. "Seems she's gone missing. You were the last person seen with her that night. You got anything to tell us?"

There was a long pause. Darryl shook his head, confused and worried. "Yeah, we hung out for a bit after the last group went through the ride, but then we split up. She said she was catching a ride with one of her friends, and that's it. I split and went home."

"What time was that?" Huckabee asked.

"Around eleven." Darryl shrugged helplessly. "I'm not sure exactly."

"How late do you usually stay out with Miss Flowers?" Donovan continued to grill the flustered young mechanic.

"Never past midnight. She's got to get up pretty early to go to work."

Donovan scribbled some notes in his pad. "Her mama's down at the station, and she's pretty upset. There anything you'd care to say that could make a frightened mother feel better?" Donovan barreled on without waiting for a reply. "What *exactly* were you two doing after the hayrides were over?"

Darryl fidgeted with the zipper on his jacket. "We were messing around a bit. She's my girlfriend."

A malicious gleam surfaced in Donovan's eyes. "Why don't you elaborate for us?"

"We were just kissing and stuff," Darryl said defensively. "We're both adults. It's not a crime!"

Donovan shrugged. "Maybe things got a little rough? Maybe Amelia didn't want to *mess around* anymore, but you did. Did you get mad at her over something like that, Darryl?"

Without warning, Darryl lunged at Donovan. The two men grappled with each other until Sheriff Huckabee intervened. He shoved Darryl into the back of his car and pulled Donovan aside to dress him down. James couldn't hear their conversation, but he could tell from Donovan's sagging shoulders that his superior wasn't complimenting him.

"Darryl was provoked!" Tom yelled. "I'm a witness! Where are you taking that boy?"

"Relax, Tom." Huckabee stroked his lush, walrus-like mustache. "I'm just going to carry him down to the station to get his statement. After he signs it, we'll bring him right back." The sheriff got in his car and drove off. Tom went inside the Food Mart, cursing under his breath.

Donovan ran a hand through his hair, which was fiery red beneath the November sunlight, and swung around. He practically spat at James, his voice a vehement hiss. "Don't you have some library cards to stamp, Professor?"

James waited until the second brown car had pulled out of the lot before carefully backing the Bronco out of the garage bay. He broke at least four traffic laws driving to the library, but he figured that every member of the sheriff's department was busy with something far more important. Namely, the disappearance of Amelia Flowers.

"You've got mail," James's computer announced as he raced to check his email upon returning from the most dramatic lunch break of his life. Lucy had written the supper club members about the morning's events at the sheriff's department.

> *Dear F. F.'s,*
>
> *I'm writing this at work because I can't call you guys right now, but I had to tell you what's going on.*
>
> *I feel terrible! I think that by questioning Amelia, James and I accidentally triggered a horrible event. Megan Flowers came to the station this morning to report that her daughter never came home after an overnight visit to a friend's lake house. When Megan called to speak to Amelia's friend Cyndi, she was told that Amelia was never expected at their house at all!*
>
> *Megan showed Sheriff Huckabee the note that Amelia had left under her van's windshield wiper. Amelia had written saying that she was heading up to Cyndi's lake house and would stay there Sunday night. Since the bakery is closed on Monday, Megan had no objection, though she thought it a bit odd that Amelia left a note on the van instead of inside the Sweet Tooth. Now that Megan's had*

time to really examine the note, she also believes the handwriting might not be Amelia's!

Do you realize what this means? Brinkley's killer and the person who ran Whitney down MUST have seen Amelia talking to James and me. Now, that person has taken her. What if he plans to kill her too? We need to call an emergency meeting to figure out how we can help. Lindy, I hope you tracked down that poodle mask — it's our only hope of finding out who's responsible for bringing all of this violence to Quincy's Gap.

I have to go. Murphy Alistair is here demanding to know what's happened to Amelia. Apparently, Darryl Jeffries has just been brought in for questioning.

James, can we come to the library after work? This is serious, and it's gone way beyond my playing at being a deputy. We've got to put our heads together and help this young woman.

Yours,
A Worried Lucy

James immediately wrote back to his four friends inviting them to meet at the library as soon as they were able. He also summarized his conversation with Darryl and shared how he didn't believe the young man capable of murder. James knew he would need to repeat the entire exchange so his friends could listen to Darryl's responses verbatim, but since he was the only person who'd been there to see the fear and shock on Darryl's face when he'd heard about Amelia's disappearance, it was up to James to convince the others that the young man was either a superb actor or had nothing to do with his girlfriend's kidnapping.

Around four o'clock, James told the twins to mind the fort and slipped out to the Quickie Mart to buy a snack for the meeting. Truth be told, he was too restless to spend another second in the hushed library. He desperately needed fresh air, a burst of music from the radio, and an errand to take his mind off Amelia Flowers.

As he pulled into a parking space, he noticed a beige Jeep a few spots over. It looked remarkably like Lucy's. Walking behind the row of cars, James could see that someone was sitting in the driver's seat, but he couldn't tell if it was Lucy or not. All he could really see was a fuzzy blue hat, a striped scarf, and a pair of shoulders covered by a black coat.

Slinking off to the side so that the driver wouldn't see him in the rearview mirror, James tried to get a closer look by pretending to squat down to tie his shoe. As he slowly straightened, he could see through the back passenger window that the person in the blue hat was Lucy. Even if he hadn't recognized her profile, James could have identified Lucy's car by the amount of trash covering the seats and floor mats. Just as he was about to rap on the window, James saw Lucy raise a spoon to her mouth, take a large bite of something white and creamy, and sink back into her seat as if relaxing for the first time in ages.

James craned his neck in order to catch a glimpse of the food that was giving Lucy such obvious pleasure. When her plastic spoon was licked clean, she dipped it back into a cylindrical plastic container. Reloading the spoon with the creamy substance, she popped it back into her mouth and moaned so loudly that James flushed and backed away from the Jeep as if he had just caught one of his former students doing lines of cocaine. He skulked to his Bronco, hopped inside his truck, and waited for Lucy to pull away.

Still flustered, James went into the Quickie Mart and chose a snack for his friends. On the way out, he walked down the aisle where the baking products were located in order to identify the container he'd seen in Lucy's hand. It was as he'd feared—Lucy had been pigging out on a can of vanilla buttercream frosting.

Chapter Fourteen

Low-Carb Ice Cream

"I'm guilty!" Gillian wailed before the other four supper club members had a chance to get settled in the library's meeting room. Gillian turned to Lindy with moist eyes, and, seeing her friend's expression of befuddlement, pulled an orange candy bar wrapper from her purse and slapped it on the table. "I have committed a food crime!"

"What is that?" Bennett peered at the wrapper.

"Evidence!" Gillian cried. "I had two peanut butter cups today. But I *really* needed them!" She shoved her hands into her hair and shook her head. "I called every single specialty shop in Virginia that might sell poodle masks. I finally got a hit from a place called Pampered Pooches in Richmond, but they wouldn't share their customer list, even after I told them this was a matter of life or death! We're going to have to tell the sheriff about the mask if we want to help Amelia. He can get those snooty groomers to talk." She reached out, grabbed the candy wrapper, and tossed it into the trash can. "No wonder I cheated! I'm a wreck right now!"

"About the mask," Lucy began, but Bennett interrupted before she had a chance to say another word.

"I'm a food loser, too!" Bennett gave his friends a sheepish glance. "Gillian called to ask me if I remembered delivering a box with a return label from Pampered Pooches. The crazy thing is, I do remember the label, because it had little paw prints all over it. I just don't remember *where* I delivered it. Gillian and I cross-referenced her clients with my mail route, and no one fits. I've been thinking about Amelia ever since I read Lucy's email on my phone. Man, the second I finished reading, I drove right to the store and bought myself some donut holes." He looked down at the table. "The empty box is still stuffed under the seat of my truck."

Lucy was about to speak again, but Lindy suddenly thrust her hands in front of her chest, wrists touching as if she were about to be handcuffed. "You got another cheater here. I ate the most scrumptious chocolate-caramel candy bar I've ever tasted today. *Delicioso!* Not only that, I had a lollipop on the way over here." She stuck out a bright purple tongue. "A grape Tootsie Pop."

"According to a study done by Purdue University, it takes an average of two hundred and fifty-two licks to get to the center," Bennett said.

"Thanks, but I bite mine. I don't have that kind of patience." Lindy rubbed her temples in dismay. "How can we expect to help Amelia? We can't even control our food addictions?"

"We *can* help!" Lucy half rose from her chair. "And our first step is to call Whitney and make her tell us who else was at her house that fateful Saturday besides Amelia." She turned an angry gaze upon Gillian. "And we can't tell the sheriff now. Do you know how much trouble we'd all be in for meddling and then not sharing our information? I'd probably get fired!"

"Let's think things over calmly." James's tone was quiet and authoritative. "Arguing won't get us, or Amelia, anywhere. It's been a stressful day for all of us." He pointed to the grains of orange dust gathered around the beds of his fingernails. "It took three snack bags to keep me from losing my mind, but we can worry about getting back on track with our diets once we've rescued Amelia. It seems that we're at a dead end with the mask for now, but I'll tell you about my conversation with Darryl, and then we'll form a new plan of action, okay?"

His friends nodded, fixing hopeful gazes on him. James quickly told them about his meeting with Darryl and did his best to remember every detail.

"He seems like a decent kid," Bennett said when James was done.

"It also sounds like he cares about Amelia and had no idea about Brinkley's blackmailing scheme," Lindy said.

"If he was sincere, Darryl had no motive for killing Brinkley." Gillian studied James. "Is it possible that he was playing you?"

"I can't be completely sure, because I don't know Darryl from Adam, but I believe he's a good kid," James said. "He was both surprised and upset when he heard about Amelia's disappearance. He didn't have time to put on an act. You could have knocked him off his feet with a feather when the sheriff told him that he was the last one to be seen with Amelia."

"He's still being questioned." Lucy sighed mournfully. "They've been at him for hours, and his story hasn't changed. I know Donovan wants Darryl to be guilty. After all, they mistakenly dragged Whitney in, and now they've got Darryl. If they've got the wrong man *again*, Donovan's going to be in hot water."

"Unless Darryl owns a poodle mask, then they certainly do have the wrong man." Gillian fidgeted with her silver bangles. "If that's true, we need to act quickly. Amelia's alone somewhere with the killer!"

"I tried to tell you about this earlier, but then I got distracted. Caroline Livingstone called the sheriff this morning and told him about the mask," Lucy said. "Glenn and another deputy are searching Darryl's house as we speak, but you're right, Gillian. I think that mask belongs to someone else."

"If I could just remember *where* I delivered that package, we'd have our answer." Bennett tugged roughly on his mustache. "How is it that I can recite the capital of every country in the world but I can't recall the shipping address on that box?"

Lindy grabbed Bennett's hand. "Don't be so rough on yourself. You deliver hundreds of pounds of mail every day and that package came through weeks ago." She looked around at her friends. "Let's all remember that there is an evil person out there doing these terrible things. We're not responsible for his actions, and we're trying to make things right. James, you saved Whitney's life. Now we have a chance to save Amelia's. We can't give up hope. That girl needs us to be strong and clearheaded."

"You're right, Lindy. I'll start by calling Whitney." Lucy jumped up. "Can I use the phone in your office, James?"

"Of course." When Lucy left the room, the others fell silent, lost in thought. "I don't suppose anyone would care for some low-carb ice cream?" James asked hesitantly. "I've got a few different flavors. A little food might help us think."

"Why not?" Gillian muttered. "My regular comfort food didn't work, so let's try something I'm supposed to be eating."

By the time James returned carrying disposable bowls, plastic spoons, and three pints of ice cream, Lucy was off the phone.

"Too late," she said. "The sheriff asked her to the station to make a statement about the mask and anything else she remembered about the hit and run. Beau told me that Caroline was going along to make sure that Whitney shared everything she knows."

"At least the sheriff will find out about the blackmail scheme," Lindy said. "And since he's bound to find out who else spent the night at Whitney's house over Labor Day weekend, I guess we're officially off the case."

Bennett twirled his spoon around in his ice cream. "I can't think of any other way for us to help."

"Me either," James said. He looked at Lucy. She was staring straight ahead, a glazed look on her face. James suddenly wondered why she hadn't shared her indiscretion with the can of frosting. Was she keeping other secrets as well?

Gillian stood. "Lucy, please let us know if anything new on Amelia comes in. I need to get home and pay the painters."

"And I have a bunch of short essays on postmodernist art to correct," Lindy said as she gathered her belongings.

One by one the supper club members slunk out of the library, looking tired and dejected. James watched them go. Lucy hadn't lingered. In fact, she'd barely glanced at James before walking off with Bennett. James felt hurt. He knew that Lucy felt responsible for Amelia's disappearance, but he didn't see why she had to ignore him because of it.

"Probably because I helped her question Amelia," James mumbled to a pile of books sitting on top of the circulation desk. "Lucy blames me as well as herself."

Mrs. Waxman arrived for her shift. She said hello and then headed over to the children's section, where a toddler was busy pulling all of the Dr. Seuss books off the shelf with great peals of laughter. James sighed and started to load the reshelving cart with the strays he had collected from the reading tables.

"Excuse me?" said a woman's voice.

James turned around to face Allison Shilling. The young woman looked as cheerless as she had at the festival. "Hello, Allison. Nice to see you again." James mustered a courteous smile.

Without returning the greeting, Allison removed a library card from her tiny pink suede purse. "I'm supposed to pick up some books for my mother." She said the last word as if she were chewing on her least favorite vegetable. "She said they'd be on hold."

"Sure thing." James grabbed a bundle of books marked "Shilling" from the back counter and took the card from Allison's limp hand.

He noticed that she was not wearing her engagement ring. He also noted that every book Mrs. Rachel Shilling had ordered from the neighboring branches was a wedding resource book.

"Someone is certainly excited about your wedding," James said, trying to lighten the mood.

"It's all my mother thinks about. You'd think *she* was the one getting hitched to —" Allison abruptly stopped talking. She accepted the books with a mumbled thanks and left the library.

To spare Mrs. Waxman the trouble, James decided to empty the book drop in front of the library before heading home. Brandishing the small key that opened the book bin, which was actually a full-sized blue mailbox painted green with the words "Books Only! No Trash or Mail" stenciled in white block letters, James opened the back of the box and paused.

Allison Shilling was backing out of her parking spot, and the noise coming from her car was slightly unusual. She drove an older model Mercedes, and, judging from the knocking sounds, the sedan had a diesel engine. James was struck by a sudden thought. What if the strange car noise Whitney heard came from a diesel engine?

As the car pulled out of the lot, James stood up and stared after it, his mind racing. Allison was the same age as Whitney and Amelia. And hadn't Lindy said that Allison and Whitney were good friends during their senior year of high school?

"It was you!" James pointed an accusing finger at the receding car. "*You* were the other person at Whitney's house. I'd bet a case of cheese puffs on it. You stole the Coumadin. But why?"

James dashed back into the library, grabbed his coat, and drove straight to Lucy's. He ran up the walkway leading to her front door, his stomach bouncing with every step, and had nearly reached the steps when Lucy's three German shepherds came racing around from the backyard. Three sets of teeth were bared, and they were barking wildly.

Terrified, James jerked open the screen door and used it as a shield as he pounded desperately on the front door. Lucy jerked it open, and he practically fell inside, the dogs nipping at his heels. Lucy pushed their noses back outside using the ball of her foot and told them to hush up. She held a phone up to her ear and winced as she tried to concentrate on what the person on the other end was saying above the braying of her dogs. Finally, she managed to close the door, and motioned for James to follow her into the kitchen. James positioned himself next to her kitchen table, which was covered with junk mail, plastic grocery store bags, and paper napkins.

"Just sit tight," Lucy said to the caller. "I'm going to tell James what you said. Call you right back."

Pressing the phone against her chest, Lucy blurted, "Bennett remembers where he delivered the package. He'd switched routes with a friend over a month ago, and that's why the address wasn't familiar."

"Because Shilling's Stables isn't on his regular route," James said.

Lucy's mouth fell open. "How did you know?"

"I don't have any hard evidence, but I think Allison's involved in Brinkley's death, and possibly Amelia's kidnapping too. She came to the library this afternoon, and I was outside when she was leaving. Her car's a diesel, and its engine makes a unique noise. If I could replay the noise for Whitney, she could tell us if that's the sound she heard before she was hit."

"Allison must be the killer!" Lucy cried, tossing the cordless phone onto the table.

"But what's her motive?" James asked.

Lucy flicked her wrist in impatience. "I'm sure Brinkley had some hold over Allison too. It must be something pretty serious, because not only did she commit murder, she was willing to do whatever needed to be done to silence Whitney. Which means Amelia is in grave danger. Come on!" Lucy headed for the door. "We'd better get out to the stables!"

"Hold on!" James grabbed her arm. "We can't just bust in and demand to see Amelia. We need a plan."

Lucy paused. "But we can't waste any time. James, Amelia's life is at stake!"

"We need to call the sheriff before we go." James sat down and gestured to the chair opposite him. "Take a minute to think this through, Lucy. Huckabee knows about the mask now, so just tell him where it was delivered. If you do that, you'll save him a lot of legwork. He can drive straight to the stables. Hopefully, with a warrant in hand."

Sighing with resignation, Lucy picked up the phone again. "Sheriff? This is Lucy. Listen, that poodle mask Whitney saw was delivered to Shilling's Stables. My friend is a mail carrier. I also think Allison Shilling might be responsible for Brinkley's death. Please call me back so I can explain. Thank you." Lucy left her home and cell numbers. "Voice mail. He must still be talking to Whitney."

"At least she's safe." James watched Lucy dial another number. "Now who are you calling?"

"I'm going to leave a message with the second shift assistant. She can tell Sheriff Huckabee that I have an urgent need to reach him."

As Lucy was dictating her message to the assistant, she hurriedly finished up by saying, "I need to go, Cheryl. I've got another call coming in." She pressed a button. "Lindy? Yes, I do have news, but I only have a second to talk." Lucy summarized the information she had received from both James and Bennett. She paused to listen to Lindy, and then said, "Call me as soon as you can," and hung up.

"Now what?" James asked, feeling very much on edge.

"Lindy has a teacher friend at the Portsmouth School for Girls. She's going to get in touch with her and find out why Allison was kicked out. Maybe that will give us her motive. If she's going to marry a senator's son, she needs a squeaky clean background."

James frowned. "That makes sense, especially since Chase has aspirations to hold political office in the future. But Allison doesn't even act like she wants to marry him, so why would she commit these crimes to protect that relationship?"

Lucy shrugged. "She's twenty years old. Who knows what a girl like her wants? Maybe she's marrying Chase for the money. Senator Radford comes from a family of real estate tycoons. I don't think Allison has much interest in pursuing her own career, do you?"

James thought back to the sight of Allison's rhinestone-encrusted nails and shook his head. "So are we waiting for Lindy to call us back?"

Lucy gave him a steely look. "I'm driving out to Shilling's Stables. Lindy will call me on my cell phone, and I've done my best to get through to the sheriff. I am not going to sit here when a young woman's life is at stake." And with that, she swiped her keys off the cluttered counter and headed for the door.

"I'm coming with you!" James shouted. Lucy had become so

unpredictable since Amelia's disappearance that he had no idea how to read her. Or how to talk to her. Without responding, Lucy called her dogs and hastily locked them in the backyard. She then turned to her Jeep.

"I'll drive!" James yelled, thinking of the trash littering the seats and floor. "That way you can answer the phone."

"Okay." Lucy climbed into the Bronco. Her lips were pinched and she'd balled her hands into fists.

"I'm as worried about Amelia as you are, you know. We're all worried." James started the engine and backed out of her driveway as quickly as possible.

Lucy was silent for a moment. "I'm sorry. I feel like I'm going crazy, like this is all my fault."

"I feel guilty, too," James said, softening his tone. "When we get to the stables, let's just park the truck nearby and check out the grounds. Maybe we can find Amelia without a confrontation."

Lucy didn't seem taken by the idea. "Maybe. Or we—" The phone in her hand began to chirp, and she raised it to her ear. "Lindy? Yes? Tell me!"

James drove through the shadowy forest leading toward the Shillings' large horse farm. It was almost six o'clock and night was already falling. As he listened to Lucy's side of the conversation, he felt chilled by the sight of the leafless trees, the colorless tufts of grass along the roadside, and the absence of traffic. Wishing he'd zipped his coat before getting in the car, James coaxed the Bronco's heater to a higher setting and accelerated toward the ridge of blue-black mountains. In the deepening twilight, they seemed to stretch and grow in size.

Finally, Lucy promised to be careful and then ended the call.

"It seems that Allison has a bad habit of stealing drugs," Lucy said. "During her junior year, her roommate at the Portsmouth School was prescribed codeine following a knee surgery. Apparently, Allison borrowed several pills and liked the affects of the painkiller. The roommate was continuously missing pills until she caught Allison taking them from her book bag. Allison had already been given a warning for marijuana possession, which she claimed wasn't hers, but the incident with the codeine was the last straw. She was kicked out of school."

"But Allison stole Beau Livingstone's Coumadin. That's a far cry from codeine," James pointed out.

"It just goes to show that the little lady knows her drugs. She deliberately took the Coumadin with the intention of killing Brinkley." Lucy pointed toward a dirt road off to the right. "Pull in here. We'll walk through the woods. For now, we'll focus on finding Amelia. I'm not leaving until we do."

James glanced forlornly into the copse of barren pine trees. Their bristly trunks were ragged, and the forest floor was blanketed with sharp pinecones and protruding sticks. Only a small line of pale light hovered above the horizon as James followed Lucy into the woods. He wished he shared her courage, but he was filled with dread over sneaking into the killer's territory.

By the time they reached a grassy slope leading to an enclosed pasture, the dying daylight could barely illuminate the shapes of three horses. In the near darkness, they loomed like strange beasts, silent and watchful.

"I don't trust horses," Lucy hissed. "You never know what they're going to do."

"The horses are the least of our worries." James led the way to the farthest corner of the field, his quick pace inspired by the sight of the sinking sun. "Night is falling," he said, pushing forward. "And it's coming fast."

Chapter Fifteen

Beef Jerky

James and Lucy tried to sneak through the field by walking carefully along the perimeter of the fence, but since neither one was light on their feet, they more or less plodded forward until they reached a wide gate. A cluster of horses was waiting there, and upon spying the two strangers, they whinnied, tossed their heads, and snapped their long tails in excitement.

"Maybe it's their dinnertime," James whispered.

Lucy eyed the horses nervously. "If it is, we might be seen by whoever feeds them. Let's hide inside the stable."

James saw no other choice. It was growing impossible to make out what lay beyond the large stable. During their march through the trees, the sprawling manor house had been visible, as had its kidney-shaped swimming pool and grass tennis court. And while outdoor lights chased shadows away from the house, the only illumination near the field was an inviting rectangle of yellow coming from the open stable door.

Lucy peeked inside while James tried to get his breathing and heart rate under control.

"Someone's in a stall at the far end of the building," Lucy whispered. "A woman."

Walking as softly as possible over strewn bits of hay, James and Lucy made their way toward the cooing coming from the stall closest to the stable's main entrance. The repetitive *whish* of a brush being run over the horse's coat and an occasional nicker were the only other sounds.

James motioned for Lucy to stop and, using the open stall door as cover, took a quick look within. Allison Shilling was grooming a roan-colored horse. Her back was to the door, and she was humming softly to herself. Lucy moved next to James so they were standing hip to hip, forming a human blockade.

"Hello, Allison," Lucy said quietly as James grabbed a pitchfork hanging from a nearby hook.

Allison jumped in surprise, startling the horse. Its ears twitched nervously, and it pawed at the ground.

"What the hell do you think you're doing?" Allison hissed at them. She seized the horse's bridle. "Easy, girl. Easy now," she soothed and picked up the brush again.

"I think that's a better question to put to you," Lucy said in an icy voice. "We know you stole the Coumadin from Whitney's house."

Ignoring Lucy, Allison continued to brush the mare. James watched her every move.

"The dirt Brinkley had on you must have been juicy," Lucy said nonchalantly.

Allison shrugged, acting just as casual as Lucy. "Brinkley Myers was a loser. I'm not too upset that he's dead. No one is."

"Maybe not, but nearly killing your friend Whitney upset lots of people." Lucy narrowed her eyes.

Allison set the brush aside and leaned against the horse's flank. "Is that why you're here? Because you're upset about Whitney?" She seemed genuinely confused. "What's the big deal? She's fine now."

Lucy let loose a humorless laugh. "She's fine until you take a second shot at her. Maybe you should drive one of the stable's trucks next time you run her off the road."

Allison's lip curled. "You're crazy. I didn't have anything to do with Whitney's accident. Why don't you go bother somebody else? There's a Golden Corral about fifteen miles from here. You and the professor could really make a dent in their All-You-Can-Eat buffet."

Lucy's fists curled into tight balls. "I work for the sheriff's department, Allison, and they're on their way to discuss the disappearance of Amelia Flowers with you. I believe they'll raise some other interesting topics as well, such as murder and attempted murder."

"Amelia's disappearance?" Allison's bravado wavered. James saw a flicker of anxiety enter her eyes. "What do you mean?"

"Like you don't know," Lucy said with a snort. She turned to James. "She'd make a good actress, don't you think? It would be a much better job for her. She's not really cut out to be a future senator's wife."

Allison put her hands on her hips. "I don't give a crap about being Chase's wife. As for Whitney and Amelia, I have no idea what you're talking about. And if you work for the sheriff's department, then where's your uniform? How about a badge?" She jerked her thumb angrily at James. "And who is this? Your K-9 unit? Get out of my way."

Lucy didn't budge. "Not until you come clean."

James shifted the pitchfork from one hand to the other.

Allison's eyes settled on the sharp tines of the pitchfork. She sighed in annoyance and said, "Fine. I stole Mr. Livingstone's drugs. I thought they were codeine pills, okay? I knew Whit's daddy had had some surgery so I figured he must have been given painkillers. I only had, like, a second to look in his medicine cabinet before Whitney called up the stairs to say that our pizza was ready. So I just grabbed the bottle." She shrugged again. "When I got home, I didn't recognize the name of the medicine, so I didn't take the pills. I was going to look the Coumadin stuff up on the Internet, but when I went to get the bottle from where I'd hidden it, it was gone. I didn't really care because I'd found something better by then."

"That's it?" Lucy asked incredulously.

"Yeah, that's it. You planning on arresting me?" She held out her hands. "Go right ahead. Or did you forget your handcuffs along with your uniform and your badge?"

Lucy frowned. "Why didn't you step forward when you heard that Brinkley's death had been triggered by Coumadin?"

Allison fell silent, seeming to process the information. "I didn't know about that until now." The girl's anxiety level was clearly growing. She toyed with the horse's mane, her eyes darting everywhere. "I don't read the newspaper. Anyway, I'm sure lots of people use that stuff. Lots of people around here have heart trouble. It's because most Americans are too fat."

"Unfortunately for you, Allison, the bottle you stole was the only current prescription in Quincy's Gap. That's how we know you gave them to Brinkley, hoping Whitney or Amelia would hasten his death by slapping him in the face. Or maybe he'd get cut by a branch, or at home, using his razor. Any blood flow would do, right?" Lucy's voice grew very quiet. "I know Brinkley hurt the three of you, but you can change how this story ends. Just tell me where Amelia is. It will go so much better for you if you help us. You're backed into a corner, Allison. It's time to do the right thing."

Averting her eyes, Allison chewed on a fingernail. Beads of sweat popped out on her forehead and she wiped them away with the back of her sleeve. "Brinkley knew about my drug problem," she finally said. "He threatened to tell Chase about it, but I told him he could take his threats and shove them where the sun don't shine. I had no reason to kill him. I called his bluff." She kicked at a bit of straw with her riding boot. "To tell the truth, I was disappointed that he died before he could narc on me."

"Because you don't want to marry Chase," James said gently. "You don't even love him, do you?"

"No, I don't!" Allison's anger flared. "But he's rich. He's from a powerful family. *Any* girl would consider herself lucky to be with him." Her tone was dry and cynical. "Isn't that right, Mama?"

"Yes, it is," came the flat, emotionless reply from behind James and Lucy.

Allison pushed past the stunned pair to confront her mother. Mrs. Shilling looked very different than she had a few days ago at the festival. Instead of a suit, high heels, and pearls, she wore faded jeans, a flannel shirt, and a down vest. Her white-blonde hair was tucked under a red baseball cap and she wore black leather driving gloves.

"Welcome to our home," she said to James and Lucy. Her smile was cold and reptilian.

"Mrs. Shilling—" James began.

"Oh, call me Rachel. We don't need to be so formal." She waved off the notion. "After all, you're our guests."

"What's going on?" Allison demanded.

Rachel glared at her daughter. "You've caused me enough trouble for a lifetime, young lady. Get me a roll of duct tape from the tool shed. And hurry."

Allison looked at her mother strangely. "But—"

"Now!" Rachel roared, and Allison leapt to obey.

"It was *you*," Lucy said breathlessly. "You found out about the blackmail. You got Brinkley to ingest the Coumadin."

"Well done, Sherlock." Rachel clapped her hands without making a sound. "Yes, I rid this town of a pest. Nothing is going to stop this wedding from taking place. Not some stupid, greedy boy. Not the two of you. None of Allison's nitwit friends. No one. My daughter is checking into a private rehab clinic this week, and her little problem will be taken care of for good." She took a revolver from the front pocket of her vest. "Now, I'd rather not have Allison see this, as she has no idea of the sacrifices I've made to ensure that she marries Chase Radford, but I will shoot you in front of her if necessary. Do we understand one another?"

James and Lucy nodded miserably.

Allison returned with the duct tape. Seeing the gun, she started pleading with her mother. Rachel dismissed her daughter's protests and pointed at the stable's back door.

"Go lock that!" she ordered, but Allison refused.

"We should have waited for Sheriff Huckabee," James muttered under his breath. "I don't think our plan has gone so well."

Lucy touched his arm. "I'm sorry, James. I was really foolish. I have no experience confronting suspects, and I had no business asking you to come with me."

"Your heart was in the right place," James said. "And you didn't force me. We both wanted to rescue Amelia."

During their exchange, Allison had closed and locked the back door and was now standing off to the side. "I am *not* going to tie them up," she told her mother.

Rachel grabbed her by the shoulders. "You *will*! These people have done terrible things, and I'm going to stop them."

"What things? I don't get it!" Allison started to cry.

Her mother gave her a quick hug. "Don't worry, honey. Mama knows how to fix things. Just do what I say, okay?"

Allison walked toward them holding a roll of duct tape, tears glistening on both cheeks, and James knew that he had to act now, before it was too late.

"You don't want to do this, Rachel." He sounded perfectly calm and reasonable. "You're putting your family's reputation in serious danger. The sheriff knows all that we know. We called him before coming here. This is your only chance to redeem yourself. Let Amelia go, and turn yourself in."

Rachel took a step closer to them and barked, "Put your chubby hands behind your chubby backs. I overheard everything you said to Allison. You were fumbling in the dark. For all we know, you're the killers." She moved even closer to them, her blue eyes burning with a feverish intensity. "I have to protect my daughter from people like you. And from blabbermouths like Amelia."

Lucy jerked away. "Is she still alive?"

"Hush up." Rachel walked around them as Allison bound their hands with duct tape. "Make it tighter," she commanded. "I don't want them climbing out of the trailer in the middle of Highway 33."

"What are you going to do with them?" Allison's voice was shrill.

"Nothing you need to worry about. Now, go into the house and tell your father that I've gone to the lake overnight. If he asks why, say that I'm stressed and in need of some alone time." Rachel removed one of her gloves and examined her manicured nails. "He won't bat an eyelash at that. And if anyone else comes snooping around here, call the police. We've got nothing to hide."

"Aren't you going to wear your poodle mask, Rachel?" Lucy asked derisively while tugging at her bound hands. James also tried to free himself, but Allison had bound his wrists quite efficiently.

Rachel took another step closer, rage flaring in her eyes. "I'd be quiet if I were you."

"Allison! Your mother is the killer!" Lucy quickly shouted as the girl reached to open the front door.

Allison hesitated, and Rachel immediately pressed the barrel of her gun into Lucy's back. "One more peep out of you and she'll see someone die right before her eyes."

"She'll figure out what you've done," James said to Rachel in a hushed tone.

"Maybe, but she'll be married soon, and that's all that matters. Go on, honey!" Rachel called to her daughter with false sweetness, and the girl reluctantly obeyed.

"She'll never forgive you," James said. "She'll never want to see you or talk to you again."

For the first time, Rachel seemed to consider the consequences of her actions. But she shook off the notion as if it were a fly buzzing around her head. Waving the gun in front of their faces, she grinned. "Mothers know what's best for their children." She jerked the weapon toward the back door. "Start walking. We're going on a little trip."

"Where?" Lucy asked. James didn't like the tremble in her voice. He longed to comfort her, but Rachel never gave him the chance.

She ripped off two more strips of duct tape and slapped one over

Lucy's mouth. "It's time for you to shut up." She then slapped the second piece over James's mouth and gestured at the back door with her gun.

Outside, she ordered them to walk to the horse trailer parked alongside the stable. She slid a key into the padlock, unwound a linked chain, and threw open the metal doors.

Inside, sitting on a pile of straw, was Amelia Flowers. She shifted in alarm at the sight of Rachel Shilling and whimpered. And then, she saw James and Lucy and dropped her head in resignation.

Rachel secured her new captives to the wall hooks using trailer ties. Thus restrained, they were unable to reach one another. Lucy and Amelia were tied to chest rails on opposite sides of the trailer and James was fastened to the padded butt bar in the back. The bars were made of sturdy aluminum, and James had no hope of breaking the metal.

In the darkness, the trailer began to move. The three passengers were roughly jostled as the pickup towing them accelerated. James looked through the narrow window, willing the sheriff's car to appear on the secluded road, but all he saw was a sickle moon. For the next twenty minutes he rubbed the end of the duct tape covering his mouth against his shoulder in an attempt to push it free. He'd made some headway, but each time he regained his balance and began working on the tape, the trailer lurched, and he'd be forced to his knees.

Finally, he felt the tape give way. He sucked in a deep breath and then turned to his fellow captives.

"Lucy! Amelia!" he said over the vehicle noise. "Rub the end of the tape on your shoulder. If we can talk, we can yell for help."

James heard his companions grunt in assent and begin working on the tape. While they did, he probed the floor with his feet, but found only bits of scattered hay. Kicking the back door in frustration, he then explored the sidewalls. Again, he found nothing that would help them escape.

"Got it!" Lucy suddenly cried. "Oh, when I get my hands on that psychotic—" She stopped abruptly.

"Are you okay?" James asked.

"I'm just out of breath. And really mad. You?"

James swallowed. "I'm fine. I've been trying to feel around with my feet, but there's nothing sharp near me. Can you try searching your spot? And Amelia, keep working at that tape."

"Ugh!" Amelia spat a minute later. "I've been trying to get that damned tape off for like three hours. I think half of my lip is stuck to that piece!"

"We are so glad to hear your voice," Lucy said as she swept her legs over the floor. "How are you doing, honey?"

"I'd be better if we weren't tied up inside a lunatic's horse trailer!" James heard Amelia fumbling around with her feet. "There's nothing here that can help us. We're screwed."

James waited for Lucy to say something positive, but she remained silent.

"Where do you think she's taking us?" Amelia asked.

"Lake Anna," James said. "I think she was telling Allison the truth when she mentioned going to the family's lake house."

"That's over an hour away," Lucy mumbled. "Even if Sheriff Huckabee realizes that Rachel's kidnapped us, he won't find out where we are until it's too late."

"What does that mean?" Amelia shrieked. "What's going to happen to us?"

"Nothing. We'll be fine." James desperately wanted to reassure the frightened girl. "There are three of us against one. Let's focus on getting untied so we stand a chance."

Lucy perked up. "You're right, James. We just have to keep our wits about us and wait for the right moment."

"We're going to get out of here, Amelia," James tried to soothe the girl across the darkened trailer. "Just hang in there. No one's giving up."

"Okay," Amelia said bravely. "Then I won't, either."

Forty-five minutes later, the trailer bumped to a stop, and they heard Rachel Shilling unlock the trailer door. She pointed the beam of a flashlight into their faces, momentarily blinding them.

Rachel climbed into the trailer and untied the trailer ties from the hooks on the wall. She then gathered the individual lengths of rope and tugged on the lines with one hand, while pointing her gun at them with the other.

"Move!" Rachel shouted, jerking on the ropes so roughly that Amelia almost lost her footing on the trailer ramp. "I'm tired of looking at you people."

"What are you going to do with us?" Amelia wailed.

Rachel frowned in annoyance. "It was too much to hope that you'd keep that damned tape over your mouths." She pulled them down a steep driveway that led to a narrow dock. "Luckily, I don't have many neighbors who visit their lake houses in November. Even if they did" — she wiggled the revolver — "the closest house is over a mile away, so scream all you want." Rachel paused next to a small boathouse and flicked a switch. A row of lights illuminated the boathouse and small dock, as well as a stack of lumber, two wheelbarrows, several shovels, bags of concrete mix, and a large Dumpster.

With only a few feet between dry land and the dock, James knew that they were running out of time. With their hands bound, their only chance of stopping Rachel was to ambush her while she was distracted.

Frantically, he searched for something to say that would shake the woman's frosty composure and give the three of them a chance to lunge at her. "What about Allison?" he said, breaking the pregnant silence. "She told us she won't marry Chase, no matter what. And what would be the point of all of this if she doesn't? You'll have murdered four people for nothing. Either you'll end up going to prison or alienating Allison. If you don't turn back now, you will lose your daughter forever."

"And don't forget about the press. If the media gets the slightest whiff of this, your family name will be tarnished forever," Lucy pressed the point. "Allison would be lucky to receive a marriage proposal from the garbage man."

"The press will never know. The police will never know." Rachel gestured at the wooden dock. "No one will find your bodies. There will be no proof. Do you think my daughter is going to turn against me? She won't say a word." She snorted. "I've *already* gotten away with it."

"Allison's in love with someone else," James blurted.

Rachel stopped. James had succeeded in getting her attention.

"Darryl Jeffries," Amelia said quickly. "He's a mechanic."

"A mechanic?" Rachel's eyes widened in horror. "Like, at a gas station?" Her gun hand dropped as she tried to digest this startling news.

"Like, at the Amoco station outside of town," Amelia said. "They've been seeing each other for months."

Rachel's hand lowered another foot. The revolver was now pointed at the ground.

"They're going to elope," Lucy said, her eyes never leaving the revolver.

While Rachel stared at the water in complete disbelief, James yelled "Now!" and the three prisoners launched themselves at their captor.

Rachel tried to raise the gun, but James was already barreling into her, knocking her off her feet. He heard a satisfying skid as the weapon slid over the wooden slats of the dock. As Rachel squirmed out from under James's torso, Lucy leapt forward. Unfortunately, Amelia did too, and the women managed to throw each other off balance. Unable to use their arms to steady themselves, they fell backward in a heap, and Rachel scrambled away and reclaimed her weapon.

She aimed the revolver at the center of James's chest. "Move and I shoot!" she yelled.

James froze and let loose a moan of anguish. They had failed.

"Nice try," Rachel said with genuine admiration. "I do admire your spunk, but I've had enough fun for one evening." She ordered them to walk to the end of the dock, where she tied their ropes to a pylon. "I'm so glad I decided to start our boathouse expansion project. It means that I have access to heavy materials, if you get my drift." She laughed, her voice echoing eerily across the black lake water. Muttering to herself, she walked back up the dock and disappeared around a corner of the boathouse.

When she returned, she was pushing a wheelbarrow filled with steel bars. "My daddy was in construction, so I figured a few of these would be hanging around. See, they're driven into the foundation for extra support. Tonight, however, they will be helping you three descend to the bottom of the lake."

As James watched in stupefied terror, Rachel gathered several steel bars and began taping them to Lucy's body using another roll of duct tape.

"You won't get away with this!" Lucy screamed in terror.

Amelia started screaming as well, and James was certain that someone had to be within hearing distance. He tugged at his arms again, but it was no use — he couldn't get them free.

Rachel finished with Lucy and started to attach the long rods to Amelia, who wriggled around as best she could until Rachel slapped her hard on the cheek.

"Stop it!" she commanded, and Amelia sagged like a limp rag. Her face crumpled, and tears dropped from her chin, but she didn't make another sound. To James, her silence was more agonizing than her screams.

"Almost done," Rachel said in a jaunty voice as she began to wrap four bars around his chest. Humming, she behaved as if she were casually pruning a rose bush, or frosting a cake, and not preparing to send three people to their deaths. "Just remember, you two brought this on yourselves." Rachel pointed at James and Lucy. "If you hadn't stuck your noses in my business, then you'd be home having dinner by now. At least the fish will dine well on the two of you."

Howling with laughter at her own joke, Rachel turned to Lucy. "Any last words?" she asked, untying their ropes and raising her leg in preparation to kick Lucy forward into the water.

"Wait!" James shouted. "Push me first!"

Lucy began to sob quietly, moved by James's plea and the hopelessness of their situation.

"How sweet." Rachel faced him. "Fine, Romeo. Here goes." She raised her leg.

James closed his eyes and prepared for impact, but the kick never came. Tentatively, he opened his eyes and saw Rachel staring back up the hill toward the house. Suddenly, a collection of flashing blue lights and blaring sirens broke through the hushed darkness.

"Damn." Rachel looked around her for an escape. She headed for a small motorboat housed beneath a tin awning. The boat was raised several feet above the waterline, but Rachel reached out and ripped its cover off and tossed it aside. Rapidly working the controls of the cradle-style lift, she lowered the boat into the water.

The tread of heavy footsteps echoed down the hill.

"Freeze!" a man's voice bellowed, but Rachel ignored it.

Two policemen sprinted onto the dock, their guns trained on Rachel. Without so much as glancing at them, she hopped in the boat and unfastened the stern line.

"Put your hands in the air!" one of the cops ordered. "We won't ask again!"

Rachel turned the key in the ignition with one hand and pointed her gun at James's torso with the other.

"Try to stop me and I'll shoot!" Rachel barked. "You know I will, so unless you want a dead civilian on your conscience, you need to lower your weapons."

The cops exchanged silent nods. Moving like lightning, the one closest to James leapt sideways and pushed him to the floor of the dock. The second cop jumped into the boat and wrestled Rachel for her gun.

A shot rang out. James heard the bullet tear a splintering hole in the side of the wooden pylon where he'd been standing seconds earlier.

Tossing Rachel's gun onto the dock, the officer cuffed her and shoved her facedown onto the wooden surface.

"Ow," Rachel whined. "There's a splinter in my cheek. Pick me up this instant!"

The other cop helped untie James, Lucy, and Amelia. James gathered both women in his arms, and they sank to their knees right there on the dock, weak with relief. Lucy's hands were shaking as her fingers clung to the fabric of his shirt.

A third set of footsteps came pounding up the dock. James looked up to see Lindy racing toward them, her flesh jiggling wildly as she ran. Sheriff Huckabee and Deputy Glenn Truett followed behind at a more leisurely pace. James also caught a glimpse of Bennett and Gillian lumbering down the hill.

"James! Lucy!" Lindy cried out. "Amelia!" She hugged all three of them. "Thank God you're all right!"

The little group held one another until Gillian and Bennett joined them. At that point, more embraces were exchanged.

"What are you doing here?" James finally asked, watching Gillian wipe tears from her face.

"After Lindy and Lucy talked on the phone, we decided that Lucy was likely to go after Allison, so we called the sheriff. He'd just finished questioning Whitney but had yet to listen to Lucy's voice mail." Bennett glanced over his shoulder at Huckabee, who was chatting with a member of the police force. "He was planning to go to Shilling's Stables, and we begged him not to delay another second. We also asked if we could go along. Surprisingly, he listened to everything we said. We filled him in on all we knew in the car."

"He didn't say a word when we were finished." Gillian's expression was pained. "I'm not sure how he's going to react when this all settles down."

Lucy smiled at Gillian. "Right now, I'm not concerned about what any of those guys think."

"Let's get out of here." Lindy gestured toward the cars parked along the crest of the hill.

"How did the cops find out about the lake house?" James asked Bennett as they walked off the dock onto firm, dry land.

"Allison told them." Bennett eyed Rachel Shilling as she was placed in the rear of one of the police cars. "She didn't want to talk at first, but I think she figured out that her mama was losing it. And Sheriff Huckabee was very persuasive. Never mess with a man with a mustache. That's my motto." Bennett grinned and smoothed his own toothbrush mustache. "We were only a few miles behind you guys. It's tough to go too fast when you're towing a horse trailer."

"Come on, folks, we'll give you a lift back to Quincy's Gap," Deputy Truett offered with a friendly wave toward his brown patrol car.

"Thank you," Lucy said wearily.

Amelia and James climbed in the back, and Glenn held open the passenger door for Lucy.

"Anyone hungry?" Glenn asked. "I have some beef jerky up here. I didn't get a chance to grab supper before we headed to the Shillings' place, so I've been snacking on this."

"I'll take a piece," James said, hoping some food would quiet the churning in his stomach. "Thanks a bunch."

Leaning against the supple leather seat, James took a bite of the jerky and tried to relax. He wasn't hungry, but the very act of chewing on the hickory-flavored meat settled him down.

"James," Lucy said, turning around in the front seat and looking tenderly at him. "What you did back there? The way you tried to give me a few extra seconds?" Her eyes grew moist. "That was the most amazing thing anyone has ever done for me. Thank you. You're my hero."

James couldn't think of anything to say, so he simply smiled in return.

Deputy Truett pulled the cruiser onto the highway, and before long the rhythm of the moving car soothed James. Looking out the window, he searched for the moon. It burst from behind a line of silvery clouds as if beckoned, carrying with it a sky filled with electric stars. The moon bathed his face and created a swath of soft, white light leading all the way to the mountains. It was like a path welcoming him home.

Chapter Sixteen

Pepperoni Pizza

The Flab Five spent the remainder of the week providing statements to the state police about Rachel Shilling, Brinkley's murder, and the kidnapping and attempted murder of Amelia, James, and Lucy. When they were done, they also had to give similar statements to the sheriff's department in Quincy's Gap.

"This jurisdiction stuff can get confusing," Lucy said one morning as James and Bennett waited outside Huckabee's office to complete their final round of paperwork. "The state police handled the incident at Lake Anna, but Brinkley's murder and Amelia's kidnapping fall under our jurisdiction." She smiled wanly. "That is, if I can still include myself as a member of this department once Sheriff Huckabee gets done with me."

"Have you already given him your statement?" Bennett asked, popping a handful of macadamia nuts into his mouth.

"I came in earlier this morning. Figured I'd get it over with," Lucy said.

James nodded. "And how did he seem?"

Lucy shook her head. "I couldn't read him. He was very businesslike. I think he's waiting until he has all his chickens in a row before he dresses me down."

Bennett stood and began slowly pacing the hallway. "You're taking the waiting part mighty well. I feel like a criminal just being here." He checked his watch. "I don't think I've missed my afternoon route since I started working for the USPS."

Lucy looked at James as she answered Bennett. "I do feel nervous about keeping this job, but there are more important things in this life than becoming a deputy." She stapled a stack of paperwork and laid it aside for filing. "Still, I'd miss it here. This desk is kind of the heart of this place. All of the information passes through me, and I've always felt useful, even if I've never been 'one of the guys.'"

At that moment, the door to Huckabee's office opened and Lindy came bustling out. She looked especially merry, and she embraced Bennett and James as if she hadn't seen them for weeks.

"Lord have mercy, Lindy!" Bennett choked in the midst of her fierce embrace. "It's only been two days since you squeezed my organs to pulp."

"I know!" Lindy cried. "But I can't stop thinking about how our little group almost shrunk in size. And I'm not saying that because we're losing so much weight."

She would have hugged James next, but Huckabee called his name.

"Into the lion's den," James muttered, drawing his hand across his throat in a mock slicing gesture.

"Oh, he's a big teddy bear," Lindy said. "You have nothing to worry about."

Lindy was right. Huckabee was the model of courtesy and decorum and James completed his lengthy statement within thirty minutes.

"May I ask you a question, Sheriff?" James said after signing several documents. "There are some loose ends about this whole thing, like how did Rachel Shilling find out about the blackmail, and why did she try to kill Whitney? That girl was no threat to her."

Huckabee examined a paperweight in the shape of a cowboy boot on his desk and seemed to be pondering whether or not to satisfy James's curiosity. Finally, he shrugged and said, "Rachel was searching Allison's room for drugs when she found a note from Brinkley. Once she read it, she knew that Brinkley would be at the diner that homecoming Saturday. Allison was supposed to give him a payment there. She never showed, but Rachel did. She slipped the crushed Coumadin into her soda, squeezed some lemon in, and switched her cup with Brinkley's." Huckabee shrugged. "I guess the boys were too busy talking football to notice."

Deputy Truett piped up. "And Rachel needed to get rid of Whitney because she didn't want Chase's family to find out that her precious daughter got kicked out of school. Allison told her mama that Whitney and Amelia were the only ones who knew what had happened. But Amelia had told Brinkley. According to Whitney, he and Amelia dated for a while during their senior year, and when Brinkley found out what happened and then noticed Allison hanging around with that senator's son, he decided to earn some easy cash."

"And that's why Rachel needed to kidnap Amelia." James

nodded his head as the pieces fell into place. "Amelia was the last person who could ruin Allison's future marriage. Thank you, gentlemen." He smiled. "I appreciate your sharing that information with me so candidly. Not knowing the details would have kept me up at night."

"Well, we can't have that," Huckabee said without a trace of sarcasm.

As James stood to leave, Huckabee turned to Deputy Truett and said, "Glenn, make a copy for Mr. Henry to sign. I'd like a moment alone with him."

James swallowed hard and sat back down.

"I hear you'll be offering computer courses at the library." Huckabee poured himself a cup of coffee from a thermos and then held it out to James. Even though his mouth was bone dry, James politely declined. He wanted to finish with Huckabee and get back to work.

"We are indeed," James said. "We'll cover the basic stuff like word processing, and using email and the Internet."

"A few of my deputies need computer training. They've been making a mess of our reports. Everything's online now, but these boys can't figure out how to access the shared files, and they need to learn." He stroked his mustache thoughtfully. "One of the things I learned from the Myers case is that our men need to see all of the important details as soon as they come in. Do you think they could benefit from your course?"

James stared at Huckabee's wide face and luxurious mustache and tried not to picture him basking on a rock while flapping a pair of flippers. "Absolutely. We're also planning a course on web page development. Miss Hanover expressed an interest in developing a page for the department."

Huckabee smiled. "That would be splendid." He rose and shook James's hand. "And might I suggest that the next time your group gets together, you stick to safer activities like reading. We know what we're doing here, so how about leaving the crime solving up to us?" Huckabee's eyes bored into James. He clearly expected no argument.

"Fair enough," James said. Relieved over receiving such a mild reprimand, he made a hasty exit.

• • •

On Sunday, it was Gillian's turn to host the supper club meeting. She sent her friends an email earlier in the week telling them not to bring any food, as she was planning a little celebration to commemorate the successful conclusion of Quincy's Gap's greatest mystery case.

On the afternoon before the meeting, James stopped by Dolly's Diner to pick up a chicken potpie for his father's dinner. The three Livingstones were sitting at the counter in the nearly empty diner, enjoying steaming cups of hot chocolate smothered by fluffy coils of whipped cream, and massive slices of apple crumb pie.

"Hello, Professor!" Dolly bellowed as she burst through the kitchen's swing doors. "Come in and take a load off. We've been worried sick about you and Miss Hanover and Whitney's little friend . . ."

"Amelia," Whitney said.

"Right. Megan's gal." Dolly grabbed a mug and the coffeepot and pointed to one of the counter stools. Her eyes glittered gleefully as James repeated every detail of his kidnapping ordeal. Even though he hadn't planned on staying, James just couldn't take his eyes off the apple crumb pie. He was also too fond of Dolly to deny her a firsthand account of the juiciest event in the history of Quincy's Gap. He knew she'd entertain her customers with a highly embellished version over the next few days, but that was just part of Dolly's charm.

"You should sue Shilling's Stables!" Dolly told the Livingstones when James finished his narrative. "I reckon you could make enough to pay for your medical bills and Whitney's tuition."

Beau shook his head. "We'd never sue anybody. Besides, that family has got enough trouble coming their way."

"Yeah, think of poor Allison," Whitney said. "She had problems before she found out her mother was a psycho."

"Are you referring to her drug problem?" James asked.

"She had issues with her mama, too." Caroline pushed a wedge of golden piecrust around on her plate.

Whitney nodded. "I think Rachel is the reason Allison got into drugs in the first place. Everything she did was wrong in her mom's eyes. She never studied hard enough, looked pretty enough, or said the right things. Rachel was always cutting her down." She put her good arm around her mother's shoulders. "I'm glad you love me for me, Mom."

Caroline beamed. "You make it pretty easy, sugar. Who could ask for a better daughter?"

James stirred his coffee, trying to quell the envy bubbling up inside. He could barely have a conversation with his father, and he couldn't even remember the last time they'd exchanged a handshake, let alone an embrace. How he wished he could close the distance between them.

"Here's your potpie." Dolly handed James a paper bag. "I threw in a free piece of banana cake too. Your pa used to love my banana cake." Dolly patted James on the cheek as if he were a little boy. "You're a good son, Professor. You just keep working on your pa. He'll come around. He loved your mama an awful lot, so it's gonna take him some time to get back into the swing of things."

James wondered if Dolly was a mind reader. "Thanks, Dolly. I needed to hear that just now." Her words were a balm, and the warmth of her smile was like a soft blanket around his shoulders.

As he turned to leave, Caroline enfolded him in a hug.

"We're mighty glad you came back to town, Professor," Beau said. "You've done nothing but make Quincy's Gap better with your presence."

The men shook hands, and James drove home with a full heart. Jackson was locked up in the shed, so James taped a note about the potpie to the fridge. Just as he was about to leave, he spied his father's toolbox on top of the kitchen counter. As far as James knew, Jackson hadn't touched a tool since he was forced to sell his hardware store. Opening the lid, it was clear that his father had meticulously cleaned every tool. The very sight of it filled James with hope. Perhaps his father was ready to reclaim a portion of his old life.

• • •

Gillian lived in a large pink Victorian house with a wraparound porch. The gingerbread trim had been painted in soft creams and sage greens. Dormant flower beds and neatly trimmed boxwoods surrounded the porch and two ancient magnolia trees flanked the front path. James passed through a wrought iron fence complete with a squeaky gate that allowed access, and knocked on a polished front door fitted with leaded glass panes.

Inside Gillian's periwinkle kitchen, a cluster of pink asters in a glass pitcher sat on the counter. James admired the cherry cabinets and the row of violet- and green-colored candles on the fireplace mantel.

"Your house is beautiful," he said. "Everything is so colorful."

"Thanks. You know, people always expect me to be a slob." Gillian gestured around the spotless kitchen. "I can be flaky, but when it comes to my home and my business, I'm as compulsive and order-obsessed as an accountant during tax season."

Bennett settled himself into one of the oak chairs at the breakfast table. "So where are you hiding supper in this paradise?"

Gillian grinned. "It's a surprise. First, I thought we'd have a toast over our first adventure together."

Lucy cheered as Gillian produced a bottle of champagne from the fridge. "Finally! Alcohol! I was tempted to buy a bottle the other night just to celebrate the look on Donovan's face when he found out he'd missed his chance to apprehend a killer."

"Was he off duty the night we were kidnapped?" James asked.

"No, but he switched with Glenn so he could bowl with the Rockingham Sheriff's Department in some league tournament."

"Man, he must be grumpy." Bennett laughed at the thought.

"He's been pouting all week." Lucy's eyes twinkled mischievously.

"So are we celebrating our weight-loss success or our sterling detecting abilities?" James said.

"Both," Gillian replied and distributed plastic champagne flutes. "Sorry about the glasses, but I don't normally drink. I prefer to take myself to other planes of existence through meditation." She filled the flutes with bubbly.

"To the Flab Five!" Lindy declared, and the friends knocked glasses together.

Lindy sipped her champagne and then raised her nose in the air. "I believe I can detect the tantalizing aroma of pizza."

As if on cue, the doorbell pealed.

"You're like a bloodhound, Lindy," Gillian said with a smile and opened the door to the town's only pizza deliveryman.

"Evenin', Miss O'Malley." The boyish deliveryman tipped his hat. "I thought you were mad at us or somethin'. You haven't placed an order in weeks!"

"I've been on a diet, Danny. Unfortunately, my meal plan didn't include pizza. Thanks so much." She handed him some cash.

Danny glanced at his tip and smiled gratefully. "I'm glad to see you again, ma'am. Enjoy!"

James heard his stomach gurgle with anticipation as the smell of hot pizza wafted through the spacious kitchen.

"I've got pepperoni, vegetarian, and four-cheese," Gillian said, tossing a stack of paper plates and napkins on the table. "Dig in!"

Everyone dove for a pizza box, grabbing the warm slices as if they were the last bits of food in the world. James bit off the end of a pepperoni slice and couldn't help grinning while he chewed.

"How did we live without this for so many weeks?" Lucy took a bite and moaned.

"And was it even worth it?" Lindy asked.

"Let's see," Bennett said. "Everyone write down the total amount of weight you've lost on this napkin. Without saying anything, pass it to the next person. I'll add up our total when we're done."

Gillian started. She wrote down a number and handed the napkin to James. He saw that she'd written the number eight. He'd lost nine pounds over the last five weeks, so he added his number below Gillian's and slid the napkin to Lindy. None of them stopped eating as they wrote. Finally, Bennett jotted down his own number and then added all of them.

"Shoot, we've lost the equivalent of a six-year-old child!" He looked at his friends' blank faces. "A six-year-old boy, to be exact. On average, they weigh forty-eight and a half pounds. That's what we've lost."

"That's amazing!" Gillian exclaimed. "Look," she said, racing over to her pantry. She pulled out two large bags of kitty litter and hefted them onto the table. "These weigh twelve pounds each. We've lost four of these bags. Pick one up and think about that. It will make you realize the *size* of our accomplishment."

"Wow." James was impressed. He put a bag under each arm and then passed them to Lucy.

"Who dropped twelve pounds?" Bennett asked, examining the

napkin bearing their weight-loss numbers.

"Me!" Lindy cried. "I've been walking to school instead of driving. I think the exercise helped me lose a few extra pounds."

"You were right when you said that we needed some cardio." Lucy swallowed a bite of cheese pizza. "We *do* need to start exercising."

"And watch a little less TV," Bennett grunted. "If we replaced two thirty-minute shows with some kind of activity, we'd lose weight faster."

"Then that will be our next adventure," Gillian said. "Not that I'm looking forward to sweating, but it's time to kick things up a notch. After all, the Flab Five can handle any challenge!"

"I'll drink to that," James said, refilling his plastic flute.

"Oh, James!" Lindy suddenly grabbed him by the arm. "I almost forgot. Lucy told me that with all the goings-on at the Neighbor Aid Festival that you never had a chance to see what your daddy donated to the silent auction."

James stared at her. "Do you know what it was? It would answer a question I've been asking myself for months, which is, what does that man do in our shed all day long?"

Lindy giggled. "Pretty soon, lots of people will know your daddy. Wait a sec. I'll show you."

Lindy left the room and quickly returned again with a moving box—the kind used to pack mirrors or paintings. She slid a canvas out of the box, showing only the backside to James.

"Wipe your hands first, please," Lindy said. "I don't want grease on this wonderful piece of art."

"Art?" While James hurriedly washed his hands, he thought back to the day he'd found the paintbrush next to the kitchen sink.

"Yes. See for yourself." Lindy gently placed the painting on the table. The painting wasn't large. It was only about twelve by fourteen inches and was unframed, but James held the edges of the canvas with trembling fingers, his mind a flurry of emotions.

Jackson had painted a male and female cardinal surrounded by dogwood blossoms. The birds and vegetation looked so lifelike that it was like looking out a window in the middle of spring. James examined the ruffled feathers of the male cardinal's bright plumage, the creaminess of the dogwood petals, and the brittle textures of the tree bark. He noticed how his father had expertly captured the glossy imperfection of the tree leaves, and how he painted dappled bits of foliage with a gentle light. He peered more closely, noting the delicate curl of the cardinals' feet and the spark of life in their eyes.

"He's as good as Audubon," Lindy said. "I sent a digital photo of this piece to my mom. She owns a gallery in DC. As soon as she saw the image, she called to say that she wants to set up an exhibit as soon as possible. If your daddy agrees, that is. I think he could earn decent money as an artist, James. People were bidding on the paintings he donated to Neighbor Aid like they were made of gold. You would have been so proud."

James could barely speak. "I had no idea. I never knew about this talent. I had no idea that he enjoyed art at all." He stared at the painting again. "I'm not sure that I've ever known him." His voice was tight with emotion.

Lucy squeezed his arm. "I guess it's a good thing you came home, then, isn't it? Okay, people." She drew out a plastic bag from beneath her chair. "I hope you've got that bottle of wine handy, Professor Henry, because I am putting on these jeans."

"Right now?" Bennett asked in alarm.

"Yeah, right now." Lucy shook out the wrinkled jeans and headed for the downstairs powder room. A minute later, she came back into the kitchen and asked Gillian if she could change in one of the upstairs bedrooms.

"I might need more room," Lucy said a little sheepishly.

"Take your pick." Gillian pointed at the stairs. "I have three bathrooms up there." When Lucy was out of earshot, she whispered, "I hope this works out. It seems a bit soon to try on clothes, even though we've been doing very well."

James heard a flapping sound from the back of the hall and gave Gillian a quizzical look. "What's that noise?"

"That's Dalai Lama, my tabby cat, coming through his cat door."

Hearing his name, Dalai trotted into the kitchen and began to meow. "He wants some pizza cheese. He's a shameless beggar." Gillian scooped the sleek feline off the floor and covered his pink nose with kisses.

James made a ball out of some of the cheese stuck to the pizza box and tossed it on the ground. Dalai gave the cheese a tentative lick, and then batted it with his paw until it rolled under the table, where he began to chew on it in earnest. Everyone laughed at the cat's overt delight.

At that moment, Lucy returned, her face red and slicked with sweat. She looked like she'd just run a marathon. She was wearing the jeans, but the seams were stretched to their limit. James was worried that the stitches would give way any second.

"You did it!" Lindy gave a dubious cheer.

Lucy frowned. "I'm not sure if it counts since I can barely move." She tugged at the bunched fabric between her legs. "If you can touch your toes, then it counts," Bennett declared.

"I couldn't touch my toes before I got big." Lucy scowled. "Let me tell you what it was like to even put these things on. First, I had to lie down on the bed. Then, I had to tug them up, one side at a time, to get them over my humongous hips. After that, I had to blow all of the air out of my lungs to slide the button through the buttonhole. That was a real challenge. Next, I had to fight with the zipper. It went up, like, two teeth at a time, so I had to draw in another quick breath, push out all my air again, and then yank on the zipper. It went halfway up. You see where I'm going with this."

"But you got them on," James pointed out.

Lucy raised her long shirt. A large roll of fat strained against the heavy material and it was clear to all of them that the zipper and button were barely holding together. "I can't sit down, people. I'm not even sure if I can make it back upstairs." Lowering her shirt, she sighed lugubriously. Dalai Lama approached her and gave her calves a thorough sniff.

"She smells your canine beasts," Bennett teased as the cat rubbed against Lucy, purring affectionately.

"What a sweet kitty!" Lucy immediately brightened at the sight of the cat. Forgetting about the precariousness of her pants situation, she bent over to pet Dalai. As her friends looked on in horror, the button from Lucy's jeans popped off and flew across the kitchen floor. Immediately following the button popping, the zipper burst apart, and the seam securing the fabric covering her backside gave way with a horrendous ripping sound. James couldn't help but notice that Lucy was wearing pink-and-blue-striped underwear.

Lucy screamed and dashed for the stairs, one hand covering her stomach and the other trying to hide her exposed rear. Her four friends sat in startled silence. They were afraid to say anything, lest someone break out into laughter.

When Lucy eventually returned, she snapped the waist of her black cotton pants and shrugged. "Apparently, I am not ready to end my long-term relationship with elastic."

Unable to control herself, Lindy started to smile, and then her shoulders shook as she attempted to stifle a giggle. Clamping a hand to her mouth, she avoided Lucy's glare, but when Bennett's shoulders also began to quiver, Lucy opened her mouth and laughed. The supper club members whooped so loudly that Dalai Lama tore out of the kitchen and dove through the cat door, fearing for all of his nine lives.

"I guess I was jumping the gun by trying to fit in those jeans," Lucy said once they'd all calmed down.

"Dieting *is* supposed to be a process," Gillian said, pulling at an orange curl. "You can go shopping for new jeans when the time is right."

Lindy picked up a cold pizza crust. "I'm really glad we had tonight off. There were so many times when I wondered if it was worth it, going on this diet. I know it was wonderful to meet all of you, but it's been a struggle to stick with our plan."

Everyone was quiet for a moment as they reflected on the ups and downs of the past few weeks.

"Come and look at my father's painting." James walked to where Lindy had propped Jackson's painting up on the window seat in the kitchen. The four friends gathered around the painting and glanced at James expectantly. "Your eye automatically goes to the male cardinal. His bright red feathers just call for your attention. But if you wait a bit, and you give yourself time, you really start to see the female cardinal, too. She might not be as colorful, but she is just as wonderful. She may even be more interesting due to her ability to blend in with her surroundings."

"So we're kind of like her." Bennett gestured at the group. "You don't see us at first, but when you really take a close look at us, we're kind of interesting."

"And kind of beautiful." Gillian stared at the brown bird.

Lucy leaned closer to the painting. "It looks like she's about to land on that branch."

James took her hand and gently moved it away from the glossy surface. "No, Lucy," he said softly. "She's not landing." He gazed at his friends, spending a few seconds to look each one of them in the eye in order to communicate how valuable they were to him. "She's like us in another way, too. Like this amazing little bird, we're all on the verge of taking flight."

About the Author

New York Times bestselling author Ellery Adams grew up on a beach near the Long Island Sound. Having spent her adult life in a series of landlocked towns, she cherishes her memories of open water, violent storms, and the smell of the sea. She now writes full-time from her home in North Carolina, which she shares with her husband, two trolls, and three keyboard-hogging felines. Adams loves coffee, champagne, kickboxing, 1,000-piece jigsaw puzzles, Pinterest, and black jelly beans.

Her traditionally published series include The Secret, Book, and Scone Society Mysteries; The Book Retreat Mysteries; The Books by the Bay Mysteries; and The Charmed Pie Shoppe Mysteries.

Her Indie series include The Supper Club Mysteries, The Hope Street Church Mysteries, and The Antiques & Collectibles Mysteries.